GW00640684

Frank Kippax wa
and went to Tas
had returned to
of twenty-one, working thereafter on ocean tugs
from Hull and Holland. Later he moved into road
transport, driving lorries in Europe, Scandinavia
and Ireland, where he lived for some years.

Underbelly, the BBC TV serial set in the British
prison system, was based on his first novel, *The
Scar*. His second, *The Butcher's Bill*, was a fictional
account of the Rudolf Hess Affair. A BBC TV serial
of *Other People's Blood*, his third novel, is planned for
1993. He has recently published his fourth novel,
Fear of Night and Darkness.

OTHER PEOPLE'S BLOOD
'What begins as a lark develops in this unusual
novel into tragedy, as healthy desire leads to a
coup de foudre. Though there is tension, political
plotting and murder, it is essentially a simple
but atmospheric and skilfully told story of four
young people trapped in a deadly situation. A
good, thought-provoking read.'

Hampstead & Highgate Express

THE BUTCHER'S BILL
'Twists like a devil's maze . . . calculated to leave
ageing colonels twitching and the rest of us open-
mouthed . . . seems unlikely to endear him to the
secret services.'　　　　　　　*Guardian*

THE SCAR
'A thundering great novel. What's really amazing is
how much he seems to know . . . what more could
you want from a thriller? A cracking good read.'

New Statesman & Society

FRANK KIPPAX

Other People's Blood

Fontana

An Imprint of HarperCollins*Publishers*

Fontana
An Imprint of HarperCollins*Publishers*,
77–85 Fulham Palace Road,
Hammersmith, London W6 8JB

Published by Fontana 1993
9 8 7 6 5 4 3 2 1

First published in Great Britain by
HarperCollins*Publishers* 1992

ISBN 0 00 647286 9

Set in Meridien

Printed in Great Britain by
HarperCollinsManufacturing Glasgow

For Hillary

And what's it to any man,
  Whether or no –
Whether I'm easy,
  Or whether I'm true.
And she lifted her petticoat
  Easy and slow –
As I hitched up my sleeve
  To unbuckle her shoe.

Irish song

ONE

The day was almost over before the young men made their move. Karen King – because she was English, Jessica insisted – had given over even thinking about them, let alone imagining what they might do with their hard, lean bodies and their tired, rope-burned hands, had given over bothering to deny she'd had such fantasies. When Jessica poked her in the ribs and swore they were coming for them, she hardly raised her head.

'Get off,' she mumbled. 'Don't wake me up just yet. Wait until you can see the whites of their eyes.'

'God, but they're tanned,' Jessica replied. 'They weren't here yesterday, or the day before. I wonder if they have a place at Fahan?'

Indeed, the men had first appeared from the Fahan Creek side, near the pier. They had been noticed by Jessica at half past ten that morning, searing the peaceful waters of Lough Swilly with a little sporty powerboat, bright red and snarling. They had waterskied, swooping round the northern end of Inch Island, making great arcs along the shore, as if looking for something. Women, said Jessica, languidly at first, but later with more interest. The day was hot – killingly hot, for Donegal – and the men did not wear wetsuits. She had definitely liked the look of them.

Later, they had returned on sailboards, taking advantage of the breeze that had sprung up around lunchtime. Jessica and Karen had by now brought a picnic from the cottage, and spread it on a blanket for a cloth. Karen, afraid of burning, had put on a yellow sun dress over her bikini, but had taken it off again when swarms of insects settled on her. Coincidentally, the two young men had come creaming close into the shore, as if attracted like the small, black flies.

'Rape,' said Jessica, laconically. She timed it well, and Karen raised her eyebrows. 'The insects. They think you're a field of rape, they've come to suck the goodness out of you.' She raised her head, stretched her neck, grinned. '*Honi soit qui mal y pense*,' she added, glancing at the sailboarders. And she stood, stretching her shoulders back, flexing her body in her scarlet bathing suit, dark hair blown across her eyes.

'You're completely shameless,' Karen said. 'Sit down and eat your cold pease porridge.'

It was, in fact, a classic picnic. There were crisp fresh rolls, smoked fish and swimming olives, two kinds of pâté and chilled Sancerre. Part of Jessica's upbringing, so she claimed, had been the satisfying of every appetite, high and low. Hence the blanket, she laughed – her own 'refinement' in case the men should make a landfall! But that time they did not. The boards turned and swooped away, their gaudy sails flashing across the lough until they dwindled and merged with others by Buncrana. Even Karen felt a tiny sense of loss, which amused her more than it upset her. She thought of Tony, back in Manchester, big, blond Tony working on the buses to get some cash together, looking after the bedsit and the cat, writing her long letters. She found herself looking down the length of her legs, squinting through the V-shape of her feet at the gaggle of sails across the water, to try and isolate 'their' two.

She giggled. 'You're meant to be respectable, you are,' she said. 'You're in Ireland now, what would your "daddy" say? You're a disgrace!' She tried to do the accent, but she could not even get the 'daddy' right. It fascinated her, the way that Jessica called her father 'daddy', in the Irish fashion. He was too big for it, by far.

'Oh God!' said Jessica, taking up the fun. 'Don't mention him, if he could only see us now! He thinks I'm sitting knitting, thinking of my one true love, as far as he's concerned I'm bloody well engaged! What can I do though, Karen, it's not my fault that I love it, surely? Oh I wish they'd come on shore, I wish they'd come.' She paused. She hooted. 'I want some bloody dick!'

Suddenly, they were screaming with laughter, Karen coughing tiny specks of olive across her biscuit-coloured stomach, spilling cold wine onto her arm. Jessica got to her knees, holding herself and snorting, then staggered to her feet and ran down to the water. She held her glass aloft in her left hand, waved hugely with her right.

'Come back, you bastards, come back!' she yelled. 'There's two young women here are dying for it!'

She put her glass down on a rock and walked into the waters of the lough, gasping as it rose up her thighs and touched her lower belly. It was icy cold by contrast, straight in from the Atlantic on the rising tide. God, she thought, those boys must be good on sailboards, or completely mental. If they fell in this without a wetsuit they'd be dead.

'They'd shrivel up like walnuts,' she said to Karen, who had joined her to wash off the debris of the laughing fit. 'I like them when they're like that, don't you? Lovely little walnuts. It makes me want to kiss them.'

Karen made a non-committal noise, and Jessica did not push her. She often laughed at her for her staidness, for her virtue, for her faithfulness to stodgy Tony – who was very sweet, for all that – but they rubbed along on it OK. They had been friends for two years, best friends Jessica might have said, with her formal, respectable private education in County Down, but some of their actions and their attitudes were miles apart, centuries, planets. Karen had watched, wide-eyed, as this woman like a chainsaw had cut a swathe through the young men of their department at the university, apparently unconcerned with looks, or wit, or age. She had a knack of breaking hearts and being mystified by the effect. She slept with boys (and men – some lecturers, too, fell by her wayside) as if it were the most natural thing in the world ('indeed it is, it is!'), then dropped them just as casually in the morning with a smile of disbelief that they should expect anything more of her, or any other woman. If they recovered and were friends she was delighted, and would flirt with them, and assume an easy physicality with them, and sleep with them again maybe, and break their hearts again if given half a chance. And all the time, it seemed, back home in Northern Ireland, she had a different life.

Karen sat down in the soft, dark sand and let the ripples of cold Atlantic water wash round her thighs. She still had her glass in hand, and sipped then passed it over. Jessica drank, then squatted, then lay, half-covered. Overhead a flock of seagulls passed, screaming.

'This bloke Parr, though,' said Karen, finally. 'You wouldn't really marry him, would you? I wish you'd tell me it's a joke, once and for all. Why don't you come to my auntie's with me? We could have a laugh. You could meet a millionaire or two.'

'Oh sure, and die of bloody boredom for my pain. I've had some of that, you know. The worst times I've ever endured were with a tax-dodger in Castletown. The bastard tried to pay me for it, the only way he could get excited was by the thought of buying me. That and sitting in casinos. You can stick your Isle of Man for me.'

'Port Erin's not like that,' Karen said, rather lamely. 'You can go for days without meeting a millionaire. We could walk, and so on. Do the beaches. Aunt Jane's OK.'

Jessica crowed.

'You're so transparent, Karen. You'll be out of your head with the tedium. Look – you've got your cross to bear, all right, I've got mine. You go and be nice to aged

12

aunties, I'll play the vestal virgin for my daddy and ma. In the meantime, let's go mad. Where are those bloody fellers? I've got something cool for them to slip into!'

Later, back up the shore beside their picnic blanket, beside Karen's sun dress that was now a mass of creeping black, the girls lay on their stomachs and talked again of Parr, desultorily. The name had been dropped into Karen's consciousness only days before, at Jessica's home near Belfast, and she could not rid herself of curiosity. Jessica had said, as they had dressed for dinner with her parents, that he would probably be mentioned, and Karen was not to corpse.

'Why should I? Parr, who's Parr?' Karen had replied. 'What, hasn't he got a Christian name, or anything?'

'He's not a Christian, not by our standards. He's one of your lot, a godless Englishman. I'm meant to marry him one of these days, that's all.'

She had disappeared, strategically, into the folds of her little black dress, leaving Karen gasping in her underslip. Jessica's face had emerged through the neckhole grinning.

'I thought that would bring you up. I bet you never saw me as the faithful little wife. Now listen – you mentioned boys at dinner on Monday. As if I even knew the meaning of the word! In future, watch your lip in front of mother and my da. Parr's the man for me!'

'But why? Jessica, what in heaven's name is going on? You can't get married!'

'Free, white, and over twenty-one. Why not, then? God, you're practically married to Tony, don't deny it.'

'But I've never heard of Parr! You've never mentioned him! I mean . . . well, do you love him?'

'Do you love Tony? There, then. Do my zip.'

Karen could never surely tell when Jessica was teasing her, and when Jessica found a good one she played it to the hilt. As Karen's lust for certainty increased, she threw in tantalising little snippets, altering some of the details from time to time. They had shopped round Belfast and she had teased her with the idea that this Parr was very rich, they had gone by train to Dublin and she had claimed he was 'hand in glove' with government circles there. Then driving to the house in Donegal in her pea-green Polo Fox ('I didn't choose the colour, it was a present from my daddy') she admitted, with amusement, she did not have a real idea what Parr did, and did not care a jot. She said once she might love him, she said once she might not. She said her parents liked him tremendously and surely that must count for something even in this day and age! She said why not, in any case, as there was no one else engaging her emotions.

'You're talking boys,' she said, when Karen mentioned names in Manchester. 'Don't you understand, I'm talking men.'

That afternoon, beside Lough Swilly, the game continued lazily, from time to time. Karen King read mystery stories, and in the gaps between the chapters of the latest P.D. James, asked subtle, Dalgleish-like questions that were fielded languorously. At last, the Sancerre finished, Jessica grew weary of the topic.

'Ach, I don't know,' she said. 'It's all a farce to some extent. Will I step up to the cottage for another bottle, or will you, or shall we go without? I don't know if I want to marry him, or if I will whenever it comes to the crunch. But I'll be back from Manchester in a year or so, and it's the thing to do in one way, over here. At least he's not a spotty adolescent or a man that smokes a pipe in bed or reads philosophy while you're making love. He's very good at it, Karen, he's an expert.'

'An expert?' Karen responded, primly. 'That sounds terrible.'

'Does it? You should borrow him one of these times. Be my guest.'

They slept for a while, they got the other bottle, they swam, they talked and sighed, Jessica scanned the Fahan shore for a friendly sail, they slept again. Karen had moved from P.D. James to a course book, and was nodding through the unhinged pastures of the higher criticism when Jessica brought her back to reality with the sharp bone of her eager knuckle.

'I want the curly one,' she said. 'God, but aren't they lovely, both of them? Look at the way he's lifting that great sailboard, like a toy.'

The young men turned to face them, panting slightly, their brown skin specked with goose pimples. One, with curling chestnut hair, was five foot ten, and thin, and wore long-legged swimming shorts that clung to him like skin in jagged gold and emerald. The other was shorter, big-chested, with black hair, black chin and deepset, glittering eyes. His bathing suit was brief and white, the front of it enormous, set in wild bushes of escaping hair. Before they set off up the beach, both bared white teeth in sudden, violent smiles.

'Oh God,' Karen King heard Jessica breathe. 'Oh God, Karen, but they're Catholics . . . '

TWO

'Hallo there, girls,' drawled the taller one. It was cod American. 'We are travellers from a far distant shore, and we wondered if you could see your way to giving us a drink. My name's Rory, and I've just sailed this darn thing from Tennessee.'

The girls, through some instinct that Karen resented in herself but could not isolate, had rolled onto their backs as the men had approached them up the beach. They lifted their heads from the stones and squinted, as if they'd only been half aware of interlopers. Jessica laughed.

'The Atlantic doesn't go as far as Tennessee,' she said. 'You're a liar.'

Rory turned gravely to his companion.

'The natives aren't friendly,' he said. 'That's the last time I let you plan an invasion. Now we'll have to give them beads. This is Mallachy,' he added. 'He's my navigator. We just popped out to get a beer and a burger, down-state a ways. That was twenty-seven years ago.'

Karen sat up. She shook the sun dress convulsively, dislodging many of the tiny insects. She bunched it up and placed it on her thighs. The shorter man seemed to understand.

'He's mad,' he told her. 'We'll just sit a minute, if you don't mind, and get our breath. There's no bars on this side, is there?'

Jessica was staring.

'Mallachy,' she said. 'That's a hell of a name for a Taig. If I offered you a glass of Sancerre would you bring the wrath of God down on me?'

The way she said it, the tone, the edge, shocked Karen. Mallachy coloured, but did not go red. It was more a darkening. His deep eyes regarded her for a moment, then he looked at Rory.

'You're right about the friendliness,' he said. 'But it's not the natives, is it?' To Jessica, he added: 'Where are you from? Holywood, is it? Slumming, are we? Popped across the border to patronise the underprivileged from the safety of daddy's cottage?'

Rory's face took on a regret that was almost comic. Lost opportunities.

'Hold on, hold on,' he murmured.

Karen, too, was hollowed. Jessica had turned an all-day fantasy into a full-scale row in seven seconds flat. Was she insane?

She certainly was not chastened. Her eyes held Mallachy's, full of bold contempt.

'Cultra, to be precise,' she said. 'Holywood's a little common, don't you think? And who are you trying to kid? If you come from round here, I'll eat your sailboard. Five more sentences and I could tell you which street you were born in. Where are *youse* slumming? The big hotel?'

'The big hotel!' said Rory, trying hard. 'We can only afford a caravan, God's honour. It's just a tiny forty-footer, hardly room enough to swing a champagne bottle. What with the speedboat and the boards, we had to park the BMW twenty feet away. A terrible long walk. We're just two humble lads.'

Everybody seemed to hold their breath. Mallachy turned away from Jessica, Karen studied Rory's face. It was hopeful, open, humorous. She could almost see him searching for another string of quips if Jessica would not thaw to the first attempt.

But she did. She made a noise with her mouth, of contrition maybe. She rolled onto a knee, then pushed herself upright and reached for the bottle of Sancerre in one complete, if clumsy, movement.

17

'OK,' she said. 'Have a drink, I'll go and get more glasses. I'm Jessica, by the way. This is my friend Karen, she's from England and is no doubt completely mystified by now. I wouldn't try and explain, though, they've never understood yet, have they? Do you want a jumper, Karen?'

The sun was due to leave them shortly. The shadows were already long. As Karen nodded, Rory failed to suppress a shiver.

'I'm much too hard to want a woolly for myself,' he said, 'but I wouldn't say no to an overcoat or two!'

'Mallachy?' Jessica's tone was neutral.

'I'll be all right,' he said. 'Thank you.'

When she returned, they rearranged themselves more decorously on rocks and set themselves to recover the mood that had been lost. Rory talked fast and funnily, told them of the rat they'd found in the caravan when they'd come to it, recounted the horrors of a little restaurant in Buncrana where they'd eaten the night before, and laughed at the way he and Mallachy had sailed past the beach a thousand times before deciding to boldly ask them for a drink. Jessica admitted freely that she was a cottage-dweller, one of the idle rich that cluttered up the streets and strands of Donegal from May to September, but at least she didn't drive a gas-guzzling BMW like some she could mention. Mallachy talked more quietly to Karen, asked her about Manchester, and what the girls did normally, and how long she'd known Jessica and Ireland. As the sun dipped behind the trees, and then below the western hill, the prospects of the night became a silent issue.

It was a dead one, though. Jessica and Mallachy had moved beyond armed politeness, but not significantly, and there was a palpable edge to many of their exchanges that Karen assumed meant they fancied each other, but could not climb down enough to acknowledge it. She did not fancy Rory, though, and she was glad. Earlier, for brief periods of the day, she had contemplated making up a foursome not unhappily, might have taken risks, might even have ended up in bed with someone, the classic holiday encounter. But Rory was not it, and Mallachy confused her, his powerful body and powerful dislike of something or somebody blurring in her mind. And there was Tony, her old man. It would not be fair to Tony.

Finally, the boys went. Rory made several suggestions, but no one seriously took them up. As the light began to fade, Mallachy – still dressed only in white trunks – gestured towards the sailboards.

'Come on, Rory. Time to cross before it gets too cold. I need a shower.'

Rory, who had been sitting next to Jessica on a large warm stone, stood reluctantly.

'Ah well,' he said. 'When you've got to go, et cetera. How long are you here for? We've got two days. I thought maybe . . . '

'Tomorrow morning,' said Jessica, levelly at Karen's face. 'So you've had us, I'm afraid. You should have kept your biting friend on a shorter leash.'

They both watched Mallachy, who was at the sailboards. The tide was receding, there was a fair way to shift them to the water.

'Ach, he's all right. It's just a minor chip he's got, not the whole damned plank. It's a pity, though. It could have been fun.'

'Do you go with him all the time?' asked Jessica. 'I'd have said he was a liability.'

'He's not my shadow,' said Rory, after a brief pause. 'Cultra, you said? Collins is my name, Rory Collins. What's your last name?'

She laughed.

'Jessica will do. Look, he's on his way. Don't forget the jumper, now, it would be terrible feeble as an excuse for coming back.'

He grinned, and dragged it quickly over his shoulders and head. He returned it with a little bow.

'Well, goodnight Jessica. So sorry we can't stay!' He turned, including Karen. 'Bye now, Karen. Early to bed, mind!'

The expression on his face was comical.

The girls did go early, as things turned out. They had a pleasant evening, but the vein of wildness that Jessica had lost on meeting Mallachy never returned. They drove down to Letterkenny and had a meal, then they walked along the lough shore in the darkness, looking at the lights across the water. They talked of nothing major, but they returned to some things several times. It almost seemed that Karen had a need to know what made Jessica tick, what drove her moods from hilarity to gloom and why. Jessica answered her questions, but not always with consistency.

'Are we really going home tomorrow,' said Karen. 'Or was that part of the scheme to turn them off?'

'Up to you. If the weather's nice, let's stay. Of course, we'll need an excuse if the boys show up again!'

'They wouldn't, would they? You made it pretty clear. Poor Rory looked like a whipped dog. Funny, wasn't it? Such a big strong bloke, and such a softie. Why were you so scratchy? Were you after Mallachy?'

'Mallachy? You're raving.'

'Oh, come on. All that sniping, all those nasty cracks. Methinks the lady doth protest, as old Bill put it.'

'I thought Mallachy was a nasty little bletherer. All that crap about the cottage and patronising the locals. A Belfast bigmouth. I'm just surprised he didn't claim to be one of the boyos.'

They were climbing slowly back towards the cottage from the water's edge. The surface of the lough was black and still now, mirroring the lights at Fahan and

20

Buncrana and between. There were boats on moorings, a rowing dinghy plashing quietly along.

'I don't believe you,' said Karen, at last. 'You fancied him, why not admit it?'

'Karen King, I worry about you. I hated him – well, I was indifferent. Now Mr Collins, say. Now there, I'd stretch a point. Maybe I was just annoyed that his friend tagged on and mucked it up. I couldn't exactly see you two clicking. He'll look me up, maybe. That would be fun.'

'But you wouldn't even give your name!'

'Cultra's small enough. If he's really got a BMW, maybe he has brains that he can apply. Anyway, even a Taig's allowed to make enquiries, isn't he? If he has a BMW.'

'You're terrible, you really are. This country's mad.'

'You're catching on. Look, I'm feeling better, I could get great again, I'm sorry if I wrecked the evening. Should we have another drink? There's lots of gin. Maybe we should drive round to Fahan and track them down.'

They did not. Jessica poured herself a gin, but only had two sips. Karen did not want one. Soon they were in bed. Stars lit the room, the occasional glow of headlights from the Buncrana road, across the lough. It was completely quiet.

'Did you really fancy him?' asked Karen, as they were drifting off. 'Rory Collins?'

Maybe Jessica was asleep, she thought. There was a long wait for an answer.

'I did,' Jessica finally replied. 'I didn't think he was soft, I put him down as shy.'

'A shy and sensitive type,' said Karen. 'That's just what you need, I don't think. You'd murder him.'

There was another pause.

'That's what I like, maybe,' said Jessica.

THREE

Next morning, whether or not Jessica had meant to change the plan, the weather did it for them. The girls awoke to the sound of rain rattling on the windows and the constant clattering of downspouts filling water-butts. The wind was north-westerly off the Atlantic, driving thick massed clouds and raising short white horses on the lough. It did not take them long to make their minds up: mobility, Jessica said, was the nicest thing she knew about being well-off. They pulled on jeans and jumpers, had a hasty breakfast, tipped their clothes into their cases, then scuttled through the dripping trees to the pea-green Polo. Lunch in Dublin, asked Jessica? Why not, why not.

Rory and Mallachy awoke with raging hangovers. They had tried a few in the Fahan Lodge Hotel after sailing back the night before, been seen off by two ugly English girls (Morally ugly, said Rory – they wouldn't screw) and had roared into Buncrana in the BMW and done the High Street bars. After that they had decided to get across the other side and 'maybe give the girls a fright', an entirely mad idea that could only end in tears, and all the better for it. By the time they reached Letterkenny they were thirsty, so had a drink, and by the time they reached the shore road between Ray and Drumhallagh could not have pin-pointed the cottage in the wood with any certainty to save their lives. They ended sitting high above the lough sipping from a bottle of John Powers, gazing at the lights of a house below them that could have been anybody's.

'I tell you what,' said Mallachy. 'Why shouldn't we try a pot-shot at it? That'd bring them from their beds.'

The thought sobered Rory slightly, but not enough to stop him going for the gun. It was in a concealed metal box underneath the dashboard, that he'd had one of the fitters weld in one evening for him, thirty quid and not a word to anyone, least of all Tom Holdfast. Only he and Mallachy knew about it, and sometimes he regretted that he'd told his friend. Mallachy could be too damn serious for fun.

It was a three-eight Webley revolver, which Mallachy derided as an infamously inefficient piece, issued for God knows how long to British Army officers, and policemen, and other types who knew no better than to accept it as their side-arm. It had, however, been the only one that Rory had been able to lay hold of, and at first he had been proud of it.

'English popgun,' said Mallachy, morosely. He held his hand out for it, but Rory hesitated. 'We could push it through the letter-hole and pull the trigger. No one would get hurt.'

Rory sat beside him and checked the chambers, which were full. The cold evening air washing in from off the water chilled his face, freshened him.

'You're pissed,' he said. 'We're not firing it here, and well you bloody know it. If the gardai got to us there'd be hell to pay. Goodbye driving licence, that would be the start of it.'

Mallachy belched. Raw Guinness fumes, and whisky.

'Gardai'll be pissed themselves. This is the civilised part of our country. You couldn't hurt a fly with that thing. Give.'

Rory handed it across. Mallachy spun the chambers and squinted down the barrel at the cottage lights.

'We could hold them up with it. Your fanny or your life. That hard-arsed Prod.'

'Aye, you'd need a pistol in your hand. She'd wither

23

you with a look. You'd be better off with the English one.'

'Anybody would. Jessica, eh? Nose in air and reeking of cash. Never done a hand's turn in her life. I'd bang some sense into her. Some humility. Nasty wee bitch.'

He lapsed into silence, coping with a rush of drink. Rory, whose head was clearer now, thought of Jessica, mainly with regret. A liability, she'd called Mallachy. Point taken.

'If money's what you're bitching about,' he said, half-aggressively, 'maybe I should let you walk to Fahan. I don't want you to betray your principles in the BMW. Listen, if you've finished waving it about, give me the pistol back. I want it in its place.'

Mallachy's eyes were swimming. He got ropily to his feet and raised the pistol in his right hand. His thumb felt surely for the safety catch and pushed it off.

'For Christ's sake, Mallachy!'

Mallachy levelled the Webley in the general direction of the lighted cottage. The barrel wavered in his grip. Rory side-stepped, getting well clear, his face clouded with anger.

'Mallachy!'

The smile became a grin. Mallachy moved the gun from horizontal to vertical, his hand directly above his elbow. Then, as Rory relaxed, he pulled the trigger. In the silence of the country evening, the report had a double impact, the crack and then a bang. It seemed to leap off the glossy surface of the black lough, it seemed to echo off the Inishowen shore, it rang in Rory's ears.

It was only a pistol shot. In the vast silence it was nothing.

'Bastard!' he spat. 'Stupid bastard!'

Mallachy handed him the Webley.

'Fucking toy. It wouldn't wake a mouse. God, Rory, sometimes you make me laugh.'

They drove back more carefully than they had come,

Rory well aware of every aching mile, all thirty-five and more of them. By the time they pulled down the steep road to the caravan on the loughside he had a headache and a mouth like death. In the morning, later than the girls across the lough, they awoke to lashing rain, and misted windows, and a drip onto the carpet. They did not breakfast, nor did they clear up. They'd paid for three days, so the rest could buy a cleaner, couldn't it? The hired boards and motorboat would surely be collected.

They drove home the Derry way, and as usual it set Mallachy off. They were waved through Customs on the Irish side without a pause, but they had to stop, like everybody else, at the Army checkpoint a few hundred yards further on. A soldier with a machine gun, bulky in his bullet-proof jacket, asked Rory for his licence, and where they'd been. Mallachy, dark-faced and obvious, grumbled obscenely just below his breath.

'Near Buncrana. Little break,' said Rory. He looked rich, a cream silk shirt and tailored dark casual trousers, the charcoal BMW also opulent. The soldier's eyes were piglike.

'Nice,' he said. He had a southern English accent. 'Yours, is it?'

'Fuck off,' muttered Mallachy. Both Rory and the soldier decided not to hear.

'I'm in a wee bit of a rush,' said Rory coldly, satisfying honours evenly. 'If you wouldn't mind?'

There was nothing to stop them for, and the brush-off had at least been done politely. The soldier waved them through. The barrel of his machine gun clacked against the glass as they pulled off. An accident. Eighty feet beyond the stopping point, still within the armoured barricades, wreaths were piled, straying flowers, heaps of roses on the roadside.

'Bastards,' said Mallachy, pulling himself upright in his seat to stare. 'That's new. That wasn't there before. The bastards shot somebody.'

Rory took the low-slung car cautiously over the traffic humps.

'They do,' he said. 'They'll shoot you one day, mate, the way you badmouth them. They're trigger-happy.'

'The way you crawl to them makes me sick,' said Mallachy. He mimicked: 'I'm in a wee bit of a hurry, officer. If you wouldn't mind.'

Anger stabbed up through the hangover, but the hangover won the fight. The stab was painful, the anger unsustained.

'I did not call him officer, you twat,' he said. 'Sometimes you push your luck, you do. I've got a gun down there, remember. If they decided on a search we'd be deep, deep in the shit. Both of us. They might get *really* trigger-happy.'

Mallachy was slumped again. He made a noise, half atonement, half contempt.

'English popgun,' he muttered. 'They'd know at least you were not serious.'

Rory drove. Taking the bypass, at least they missed out the Bogside, 'Free Derry', the streets that invariably aroused Mallachy's Republican ire. The bleak Shantallow estate was bad enough to pass through, with its tricolours and white-painted exhortations to 'ask about' the latest IRA martyrs to grace the concrete walls. He had not the stomach, literally, to wax serious about such things today.

Mallachy, indeed, was inclined to push his luck with Rory. They had been friends for long enough, they'd been to school together for a little while until geography had pushed them apart, then they'd met up again as older teenagers, both interested in bars and snooker, then in girls. Rory, having money, attracted loads of young fellers who would be friends, but Mallachy was better at it than most, more accomplished in apparent sincerity, and with more to offer, finally. Both his father and his uncle had been Stickies, while several younger relatives were reputed to have broken with the official wing and gone over to the Provies. Mallachy, when questioned, used the need for caution with great subtlety, with sliding eyes and tapping of the nose, and quickly became accepted by admirers as definitely in there somewhere, but too deep a man to make light comments on it. He was bold enough in his public demonstrations of hatred for the RUC and Brit soldiers, prepared to sneer and insult openly, and had certainly been 'beaten by the bastards' more than once. Quick wit and cleverness at school had shifted him quickly from his roots in the Belfast underclass, and his natural proclivities had led him to the theatre set, a wee bit of acting and extra-work from time to time, usually as a gunman or a thug and once, memorably, as a rather well-fed hungerstriker. He did well with the theatre and the media lot because he treated them contemptuously, co-opting Rory Collins as a fellow scourge of sloppy liberals, a man who for all his cash and flash was the real thing, the sort of guy you'd go into the jungle with, the sort of guy who was his father's son. Rory, sometimes against his better judgement, lapped it up. His father, now dead, had had a reputation, and the assumption of his mantle undoubtedly improved his standing in the eyes of the smarter people. And got him plenty sex.

Rory's true feelings about the matter were complex but red-blooded. After Derry, as they climbed into the rain-drenched Sperrins, Mallachy went to sleep, snoring lightly in the rhythm of the windscreen wipers. Rory was grateful not to get the lecture about the IRA men who had lived in foxholes in the soaking bog in the fifties, hunted out into the mountains by the B-men at the end of a long and terrible campaign, but he continued with the trains of thought. His father had been killed two years before, and Mallachy had been known to refer to him, with his grim-eyed smile, as some sort of hero, a victim of the UFF or someone like them. Rory, secretly, did not believe it, he held to his mother's bitter view that Michael had been a feckless drunk, another feckless Irish drunk, who had died at the wheel of his car while returning from a bout of cross-border carousing in Dundalk. Michael had had a farm across the border, a lonely ruin near a place called Hackballs Cross, where it was said that men with guns had been known to train, and where certainly only the barest minimum of farming ever happened, enough to get the EC grants and little more. The implication always was, the feeling, that Michael not only knew about the men in balaclavas, but was a part of them somehow, but Rory and his mother − although never discussing it − believed otherwise. Rory knew there was a woman in the question, a barmaid in Dundalk who was quite well off, considering, who had her own little place. This was his father's mistress, and he often wondered if his mother knew as well. Anyhow, he did not care much. He had the farm now, which had its uses, as well as the agricultural machinery business. If his father had been a hardnose Republican, he had been a very strange one, for the cash side of the firm, the accountancy, was run by a level-headed Protestant called Tom Holdfast, and a couple of the men were also Protestants. In fact, Michael had never talked to his son about politics, labelling him good-naturedly as an idle playboy. And Rory, throughout his teens, had thought about the struggle sometimes, and determined vaguely one day to be part of the broom that swept the Brits out of his country, and drank and screwed and spent and had terrific crack, and bought the three-eight Webley once, upon a whim. He knew he was a Republican, underneath it all, and Mallachy flattered that. His heart was solid, and if the time would ever come . . . At least he was not a drunken lecher, like his poor old man.

They were not far out of Belfast when Mallachy woke up, and all he wanted from the rest of the day, he said, was his own wee bed and no one in it. By evening, he would be recovered, and they could go out for a jar, maybe. What of Rosie, he asked Rory. Would there be something going on, or had she been superseded by the scrawny one from Holywood?

'Cultra, to be precise,' laughed Rory. 'No, it'll be a night out I would guess, although I'm for home myself first, to get some shuteye. She likes me fresh, does little Rosie.'

'Well at least you'll be able to tell her hand on heart you kept the faith,' said Mallachy. 'It'll save you the trouble of telling lies, and blackening your soul, and paving the way for your long sojourn in hell.'

Rory pulled the BMW over to the kerb. They were near the university, where the nice ones lived, the area which Mallachy had graduated to since embarking on the life theatrical. Far from all the troubles.

'Such a thing would never enter my head,' he said. 'Since Rosie came along I've been lily-white. The idea!'

'A whited sepulchre,' Mallachy grunted. 'Whatever one of them might be.'

He got out and jerked his bag out after him, from the back seat. His eyes, deep in pouched skin bruised from alcohol, still glittered.

'I'll await your call with barely contained impatience,' he said. 'As I recall it, it's your round. And keep that lanky rich-bitch from your thoughts. I can tell, you know.'

As he picked his way through the traffic, heading south, Rory wondered if it was as plain as that. It couldn't be, could it? Mallachy was firing in the dark.

But he had a vivid picture of her in his mind, lean and hungry in her scarlet bathing suit. He damn nearly took a left, made a huge detour to the east. Towards Holywood, in County Down.

Cultra, to be precise . . .

FOUR

In four days time, Karen King was due to go to her Aunt
Jane's on the Isle of Man, still hoping to persuade Jessica
to join her on the boat. In two days, Rory Collins tracked
them down.

The girls did not come back from Dublin after their
lunch. The weather was hateful, but Jessica had friends
at Trinity, and they spent the afternoon chatting and
drinking in people's flats. Being Ireland, they ended up
by eating three teas, then roared out to a singing pub
in Howth, then went for a major curry before returning
for a 'little party' in a student house. Karen crawled into
a sleeping bag at three o'clock, having last seen Jessica
deep in conversation with a blonde-haired willowy type
with beard and pipe who had pursued her earnestly for
several hours. On the journey back, she asked if they had
slept together – in fact, jocularly, if Jessica had notched
up another broken heart – but Jessica shook her head,
without the usual laugh.

'I have another on my mind,' she said, apparently not
joking. 'There's no point if you don't think you'll enjoy
it, is there?'

They reached the house in Cultra at four that afternoon, to find Jessica's mother alone and rather harassed.
She was a small, dumpy woman, nothing like her only
child in either looks or personality. Daddy, she said, had
had to spring some people on them for dinner, and she
was out of some basics.

On the last leg of the journey, the girls had planned
a little sleep, then a bath or shower and a night out in
Belfast. But Jessica put her arm around her mother and

gave her a great hug. OK, she said, give us the list and we'll shop for you. Is it formal, or can we attend in rags? Karen, who had been warned before she came to Ireland that some things in the household were extremely pukka, nevertheless marvelled at the ease with which Jessica changed her plans, and marvelled at her attitude. There was no hint of protest, no shadow of exasperation. The girls got their showers, a long time later, but not their sleep. And at seven thirty, Karen found herself sipping sherry in a borrowed frock and shaking fingers politely with a lawyer and his wife, whom she disliked quite intensely after fifty seconds. The call of duty . . .

Samuel Roberts – Jessica's 'daddy' – she found an impressive man. He was tall and broad with sleek dark hair, and a definite air of suppressed power, even violence, about him. He was in his fifties – the only child had been a late arrival – but he exuded physical well-being and self-confidence, reminding her somehow of a well-dressed bull. He was, however, quietly spoken, and also very humorous. Jessica adored him.

At dinner, he directed everything. He did not make it obvious, but he led the conversation, changed topics when he thought it needed it, enquired robustly of the lawyer certain things, and more gently of the females, as if to bring out gems of information they had stored in their pretty little heads. Karen, very tired and possibly a little drunk, realised slowly that she had seen him deploy this technique before, at an earlier dinner in the house, and that somehow it was probably quite offensive. She was too confused to pin the thoughts down, though, and Mr Roberts – catching her in introspection – threw her a question, cocking his big, handsome head on one side with complete attention to receive the answer. Which he did not want to hear, she realised; which meant nothing to him.

In the bedroom, afterwards, she tried to couch a question which would probe some of the doubts she had, without alerting Jessica to the fact she had them. A mug's game, because her mind was blurred and Jessica was far too intelligent, and caught her drift immediately. Half out of her dress, she hooted with amusement.

'He's killing, isn't he?' she said. 'He plays them like game fish. The poor saps come round here and act like they're his equals, and he plays with them. Otherwise, I suppose, we'd all go mad with boredom.'

But he plays us, too, thought Karen. Then she thought: Maybe he doesn't, though? Maybe it's just me, as another poor sap outside the family circle. To her annoyance, she could not remember the evening with sufficient clarity to be sure. She had been drinking far too long, too much. Twenty-four hours on tonic water. A vow. One day soon . . .

'You mustn't worry about him,' Jessica was saying. She was regarding her friend quizzically, her face concerned. 'You don't think that's the real man, do you? It's only a wee act, you know. He's a politician. He has to know these people, to socialise with them. He has to bow them to his opinions, that's the way we live.'

'A politician? I thought he was a businessman?'

Jessica's laugh was more muted. No more hoots.

'It's the same thing over here, isn't it? At a certain level? I don't mean he's involved in politics, he's not after anybody's vote or anything like that, but the whole place runs on politics. There's wild men out there, Karen, some of them more like wild animals, and not all of them are Catholics, believe you me. People like daddy have to hold the ring, they're a sort of bedrock, to make sure there's always some civilisation to fall back on. He has to keep an eye on his own kind as well as anybody else. He has to keep his finger on the pulse.'

Karen wondered if Mr Roberts dealt directly with the 'wild men', but she did not like to ask. Although they had not talked about the weird reality of Northern Ireland since her arrival, in Manchester Jessica occasionally had a little rant. The thing she found galling about the English was their idea that the place was violent, dangerous, like Chicago during Prohibition, or New York. It was a quiet, pleasant, law-abiding land in fact, with the lowest general crime rate in the British Isles. Only that a few madmen liked to kill each other, and the British Army and the RUC, and there was nothing anyone could do to stop it. It was to convince Karen, partly, that she'd wanted her to come and have a holiday, to see it for herself.

'I'll have an ally then,' she said. 'When all the bar-room experts bore my arse off with "The Trouble". It's only you lot that are obsessed with it, you and the Yanks. In the South of Ireland, people go to sleep if it's so much as mentioned, and in Belfast even the playwrights are growing out of it. We don't see it, we're not affected, it's the province of the great unwashed and unlamented, it's for the morons, it's a bore. The wild men are like loony aunties you kept in the attic in the old days, a bloody nuisance but you learn to live with it.'

To Karen, that had sounded like a lot of Jessica's most harsh and brittle statements, the harshness and the brittleness barely concealing something darker underneath. But in truth she'd found it difficult to sustain her patronising English mix of prurience and pity very long. Belfast seemed handsome and untroubled, Cultra opulent, the people generous and unafraid. The police stations were like forts, with enormous wire fences and armoured observation posts, but so what? Even Downing Street had tank-proof gates these days, and not many people lost sleep over that.

Jessica was naked now, about to shuffle her long legs into a pair of light pyjama bottoms. They had been given separate rooms, of course, but liked to gas late into the night, and dress together, and compare clothes and hair and notes. Karen, perplexed, was still in her petticoat.

'Your mother doesn't seem much like a politician,' she volunteered. 'I can see your father having his hard side, but your mum's too nice. In fact, I can't see how she survives with you two. It must be like living in a power station.'

'She has her moments,' said Jessica. 'She's not as soft as you might think. I'm not saying that she winds Daddy round her little finger, she does not. But she has a sticking point, even with him. I've seen him back down, many times.'

She was into the pyjamas. She slipped under her duvet, watching as Karen rather moodily undressed and got into her nightie.

'You look knackered, love,' she said. 'I bet you never thought you'd end up as a social accessory whenever you agreed to come here for a holiday! You'd better keep your mouth shut, by the way, after we've gone back to the department. A few tales here and there could wreck my cred completely!'

'Yes,' said Karen. 'The Irish fire-eater putting on a cocktail gown and tights to feed her mother's social aspirations. I know twenty men who just would not believe it.'

'Only twenty? Your memory's failing, so it is! That's the mother's steel I'm telling you about. She may give me six inches in my height, but what she tells me, goes.'

Karen sat down on the bed.

'Is it her that's telling you to marry Parr?' she asked. 'How did she get married, was that sort of arranged? I don't know, maybe it's the custom over here?'

'What, like polygamy?' laughed Jessica. 'That wouldn't be so bad, would it? Look, Karen, we're a hundred and twenty miles from Manchester in this spot, for God's sake – don't let your fantasies run away with you.'

'So why? Are you sure nobody's trying to make you?'

Jessica put on a grave expression.

'There are some traditions, I will admit. If I did marry Parr, and had two little children and made a lovely home, I'd be allowed to run off the rails a bit, so long

I was discreet. Once a woman's done the social bit, she's allowed to take a lover, as a right. A Protestant woman, naturally, I don't speak for the other sort.'

'You're teasing. Not fair, I want to . . . '

'To help?'

The tease had deepened. Jessica was smiling wickedly. Karen stood up, shrugging.

'Suit yourself. If you think I'm prying. Right, I'm off to bed. See you.'

Jessica touched her arm.

'Don't sulk, you fool, I can't help mocking you. Look, honestly, I don't think I'll make any utterly appalling mistakes. You don't know Parr. He's interesting. I can see all sorts of things in it, advantages. He hasn't asked me yet, not formally, he hasn't done the man-to-man bit with my father, I'm just expecting it to happen one day, maybe.'

'But you're mad about men!' said Karen, her voice alive with exasperation. 'All men, not just him. You're . . . '

'Go on. More compliments?'

'Just something Tony said. You know Tony. My little old Victorian.'

Jessica seemed cast down. She looked almost childlike in the big white bed, staring at the duvet.

'Let me guess,' she said. 'A tart? Dick happy?'

Karen went red.

'I'm not, you know,' said Jessica, seriously. 'You really shouldn't let him say things like that, should you? I've had a few blokes, a few more blokes than you. But if I was a feller, would Tony think I was immoral, then?'

Karen felt bad.

'Tony's got this thing; you know. About independent women. He's scared of promiscuity.'

'Sure. All men are, aren't they? I think deep down it's some kind of fear, a fear of comparisons. If a woman fucks a lot of men, each one fears he's up for a rating.' She laughed. 'They all think they're going to suffer by it too, that's what amazes me. They've not got a lot of confidence in the dick department, the ones I know.'

'Tony's young, in any case,' Karen said. 'God! What a feeble thing to say! It has a lot to do with it, though. I hope. He's afraid you'll lead me away from him.'

Both women were older than the people that they mixed with, in Manchester. Karen had dipped badly in her A-levels and had done two years in a commerce school before she'd been accepted for her degree course. Jessica was a year older still, at twenty-four. She had gone to Switzerland, then France. She was doing an M.Phil., on the works of Hélène Cixous.

'That could be one of his attractions, I suppose.' Jessica was musing. 'Parr, I mean. He's not jealous of my flings with other men because he doesn't have that fear. You'll have to meet him one day, Karen, seriously.'

'Seriously,' said Karen, 'you've already offered me his body, haven't you? You said he was an expert. I suppose he's so marvellous he's confident you'd come crawling back whatever happened? That's appalling, Jessica!'

She was half laughing, half genuinely appalled. Jessica grinned unrepentantly.

'You twist my words, you do. You twist my meanings, anyway. I said he's not afraid of comparisons, that's all. He's not a whining, namby-pamby little git like most men are. Look, Karen, he's got something, OK? He's not just good-looking, and rich, and *competent*, he's got something else, OK? He's got . . . oh, I dunno, he's *serious*. He's different, you know what I mean.'

Karen thought of Tony, and Jessica knew it from her face. Karen flushed slightly. They understood each other.

'OK,' she said, a shade defensively. 'But is it enough to marry him for? If you aren't in love?'

'Who says I'm not?' asked Jessica. Her eyes were bold, but she flushed in her turn.

'Well are you?'

'Oh I don't know! Don't ask, don't keep digging at me! It'd be a good match, wouldn't it? It would be excellent. He lets me have my freedom and he's everything the other boys can't be. And I'm smart, and hard, and self-contained, and capable of handling the social situations, and beautiful, and sexy, and modest too of course! And you're right, it sounds appalling! I won't do it!'

'But will you!' Karen yelled.

'But no one's asked me!' Jessica shouted back. The laughter had returned to her, it was her gift, her curse, to laugh things out of court. She didn't know, did she, what might happen in the next few days? The rest of her natural? She didn't have a clue what she really might do. She struggled to make her face straight, to present a thinking front to Karen. She loved Karen, so demure in her neat white nightdress, she loved her dearly.

'But I'm not a tart,' she said. 'I'm not just anybody's.'

'I know,' said Karen, carefully, guessing she was being set up. Whatever, she could not help responding. 'Look, Jessica—'

'Mind you,' interrupted Jessica. Her voice was cracking. 'I might have to stretch a point for Rory Collins.' She lost control. 'But only if he asks me nicely! Oh Karen, Karen! Oh!'

In her own bed, Karen calmed down slowly. It was a mixture of amusement and exasperation with her friend, with worry added. There was a wind outside, rushing in across Belfast Lough, soughing in the great, mature trees that surrounded the modern mansion at Cultra, buffeting the windows. She'd like to meet this Parr, to make her own assessment, although she mocked herself because of her presumption. Like an agony auntie in a newspaper, she thought. Jessica probably knew ten times more about these things than she did, she'd had a million times more experience, at any rate. But she'd like to see him, to try and set her mind at rest.

Fat chance of that, or of persuading Jessica to go with

her to Aunt Jane's in Port Erin. As much chance of Rory Collins tracking Jessica down, of even bothering.

When they left the house next morning, to a sunny, rain-washed world, the first thing they noticed as they stepped out of the drive was a charcoal BMW with two young men in it, parked twenty yards from the front gate.

'Maybe there's something in this religion after all,' said Jessica.

FIVE

Mallachy had taken some persuading, and as the two young women emerged, he gave a sour grunt. But as they swung along the road towards the BMW, his interest quickened. The rich-bitch hardly bothered him, he did not look at her, but the English one was better than he remembered. She was slightly taller than her dark companion, and had fair, fluffy hair that blew across her face. She was in a short, lightweight dress and her legs swung rather beautifully – there was a lot of them to swing. He also liked the way her breasts bounced. OK, he thought, I'll play the gentleman. If she's prepared to plead, I won't resist!

The clinching argument had worked along similar lines. He and Rory had had a drink the night before, and Rory confessed he'd driven up from Belleeks early to cruise around Cultra and reconnoitre. It was a small community, very snooty, of large detached houses set in lawns and trees. Of the infamous 'security' poor people might worry about, here was none, of course – no one bothered to go murdering the rich, they did not care enough about their beliefs. His own car was perfect camouflage, what's more. Another rich son come to sniff around the daughters of the ruling class and (ultimately) propagate the Protestant elite. Rory had been able to leave his car when he thought he was getting warm, and walk up people's drives until he found the pea-green Polo Fox. While Jessica and Karen had been helping with the salmon mousse, the dark-eyed alien had been lurking at the gate . . . He had been tempted, so amusing did he find the situation, to ring the doorbell and ask if he could borrow a jack to change a wheel, or something.

Having located the house, he had roared into Belfast and met Mallachy at the Wellington Park, where they'd had a pint of Guinness beneath the photos of the famous actors. Rory, having ducked out of meeting Rosie the night before, had said they'd pick her up later for a meal, but his talk was all of Jessica. Mallachy could tell he'd been ridiculous from his face, and Rory had confessed immediately. He'd found her, he said, and next day he'd either lay siege to the place, or boldly batter on the door and ask for her hand in marriage – or at least her something else in something else!

'You're bloody demented, so you are,' responded Mallachy. 'She'll set the dogs on you, or call the polis. Even worse, she might say yes, then you'll be lumbered. Count me out.'

'You're bloody in,' said Rory. 'You dog me and Rosie like a shadow whenever we want some peace to do bad things to one another, and this scam's a team affair to start with. What's wrong with the wee English? If I hadn't found the girl of my frigging dreams, I'd have screwed her just as happily. You're getting too much like a poofie actor, mate.'

'You're getting too much like a playboy,' said Mallachy. 'Just like your da used to call you. Forget it, Rory, for crying out loud forget it. She's trouble, she's of the other sort. Call it off.'

Rory banged his glass down.

'Oh for God's sake,' he said. 'Not religion, Mallachy. Spare me that old shite, for Jesus' sake. Spare me that.'

They called a pause. They both sat breathing through their noses, on the verge of anger. Mallachy had not liked the crack about actors, because it was a line that Rory had been peddling quite strongly recently, a rod he'd found at last with which to beat his friend. Even the fact that he, Mallachy, drank regularly in the Wellington Park was cause for comment.

'Ach, Jesus,' said Rory, after thirty seconds. 'Get off the puritanical high-horse, man. Look at it this way. If you refuse to come and help me out with this, you might miss getting your end away. Which of us can afford to forgo a chance like that in these troubled times?'

Mallachy capitulated. He took a drink.

'Powerful arguments, colonel,' he said. 'Powerful arguments. At least screwing the Brits is politically correct, whichever way you do it! They'll tell us to piss off, so what the hell?'

The girls put on a classy act. It was heads in air, studied indifference. It was meant to convey that they had no recognition of the young men in the car, and therefore no interest. This was Cultra, where an introduction was *de rigueur* before so much as a cocktail could be taken. But even Karen, rather to her amazement, swung her hips just that little extra.

'Morning, girls!' said Mallachy, whose window was nearest to the kerbside. 'Are youse walking to the lough to take the air?'

His smile was all sunshine. His mood had changed. The square, severe face had softened, although the ill-shaved chin still looked like granite. Once more to her surprise, Karen found she was attracted. Taking her cue from Jessica, she raised her nose a little higher.

Rory, seeing them moving past, abruptly opened the driver's door and hauled himself out. It was a fluid movement, elegant despite the low-slung seat. He had shed his Raybans and his smile was mixed with supplication.

'Don't just walk off!' he said. 'It's us! You wouldn't recognise us with our clothes on, maybe?'

There was a woman walking past. Jessica glanced into her face.

'I've told you before,' she said to Rory, frostily. 'Once

41

is all you're getting for a five pound note. Now away with you, before I call the law.'

Rory ducked his head below the roof to smother laughter. The woman, with supreme indifference, plodded on. Mallachy's grin at Jessica was genuine.

'You're mad,' he said. 'Welcome to the club.'

For a while they chatted, gathered round the bonnet in the sun. Rory hinted at a trip to Strangford, borrow a dinghy maybe, and wondered if they might be interested. Jessica glanced up at the sky.

'There's a lot of cloud,' she said. 'It could turn out a wet sail. Besides which, there's things we've got to do. Karen's going off soon, and we want to get some special linen up in town.'

Mallachy made a face.

'Going where? Just when I was about to sweep youse off your feet.'

'The Isle of Man,' Karen replied. 'Pretty boring, but I like it. My auntie lives there.' A grin flitted across her face. 'Jessica won't come with me because there's too many millionaires. She says they're—'

'Ach, you wee bitch!' said Jessica, putting her hand across Karen's mouth. 'That's the last time you hear my pillow talk!'

'God,' said Rory, ruefully. 'If you don't like millionaires, what chance have I got? I should've worn the jeans and jersey, like my posey mate. But we can't all be famous ack-tors, can we?'

Mallachy took a clout at him, and they regrouped.

'We could give you a lift, though?' asked Rory. 'Whenever you're ready to go up into town. You'll not want to take the little green job, the traffic's awful in the middle. We could go over to the Amsterdam and have a drink.'

'You're very bold,' said Jessica, 'but you've got the wrong types, we're not a pair of easy pick-ups, you know. Why would we be going for a drink with you?'

'Because we're handsome beasts,' said Mallachy. 'And

because poor Karen's got to go and hide her bushel in the Isle of Man. Christ,' he added, to Karen, 'that really is a downer, no mistake. For God's sake have some fun before your sentence. The crack's good in the Amsterdam, we can start off there, see what develops.'

'What comes up,' said Rory, and Jessica gave a dirty laugh.

'I'm game,' she said. 'But not till later, we've got things to see to, truly. Don't you ever work, then? Mallachy'll be resting, that's understood.'

Rory tapped the side of his nose.

'Flexi-hours. I'm the boss, and I pay a keen man with a brain and conscience to do the grafting.' A timed pause. 'One of your sort, naturally.'

'Naturally. The boss, though, or the boss's son? You're a little young to be the great tycoon.'

He bowed.

'Inherited wealth,' he said. 'None of youse Holywood fly-by-nights with your *nouveaux* riches. I'm the real thing.'

Later in the day, after their shopping expedition, Jessica and Karen drove down to the docks. The Amsterdam, lonely these days in a small street blocked by an enormous chained steel gate that had once guarded wharves teeming with commerce, had few cars parked outside, and no BMW. It was early yet – not even six o'clock – and they were high on spending money and trying lovely outfits on, so did not give a toss. They ordered gins, and sat on a wooden bench before a wooden table, while Karen admired the place. It was a relic from the great days of the docks, and had kept the feel of a sailors' and a stevedores' drinking hole, right down to the bare brick walls and flagstones.

'It's great in winter,' Jessica told her. 'They've great coal fires, and bands come in, and crowds and crowds of solid drinkers, you could stand a spoon up in the fug. See that fire over there, by the bar counter? See the black iron gate affair? It's to stop the punters getting thrust onto the coals and roasted. Terence is the only drawback. He comes in here a lot.'

Terence was Jessica's cousin, who had come sniffing at the Cultra house a couple of times early in Karen's visit. He was thin and keen and not unhandsome, but had found it hard to take her lack of interest seriously. Worse, he and Jessica did not like each other much. Karen had suspected he might be an early member of the Broken Hearts Club, but Jessica had denied it. She would not touch him with a bargepole, she said, and never would have done.

'Oh come on, Jessica,' Karen said, 'he's not that much of a problem, we saw him off OK last time. We can ignore him.'

'We did and we can,' Jessica agreed. 'He's a boring shite, though, and I don't like boring shites.' Her face brightened, she was looking at the door. 'See who's here,' she said. 'Eccentric millionaire and sidekick. Your round, Rory! Two gins, ice and lemon! And as you're late, make them big ones!'

The crack was good, as promised. Friends of Mallachy's came in, all fragile actor smiles and personalities, then friends of Jessica's. Various schemes were mooted for the night, various groups drifted in and out. At about eight, eating became the question, then that got overwhelmed in crisps and salted peanuts. Jessica announced she felt pissed and would have to go onto lemonade or leave the car outside the Amsterdam all night – which raised guffaws as to what she thought she'd find left of it the morrow – and Mallachy offered to drive it home for her for twenty quid plus his taxi back, although he didn't have a licence. Terence turned up at ten to ten with two friends nobody knew, although the threesome set Karen off, reminding her, she giggled, of the tormentors

44

of Fantastic Mister Fox, one fat, one short, one lean. Terence seemed thrown to find his cousin and her friend there, and approached with a cautious, questing smile. Jessica, in no mood for talking sense, told him it was a private party, which caused roars of laughter that were not directed maliciously at him, then told him to fuck off off her back, which raised a cheer that very probably was. Terence came close to being stroppy until Mallachy got to his feet and squared his iron jaw, but the incident was enveloped by a late surge to the bar. By now, the Amsterdam was heaving much as it might have been when the quays were lined with ships, although probably it was not half so fetid.

The girls got out alive, and were in their beds not long after midnight, little Cinderellas. Dancing had been suggested but it would have bust the spell, and moves by Mallachy and Rory to get them off alone were put down with spiteful glee, accepted with good humour. But both were kissed beside the black car then the green, and Karen felt a stirring of regret that she'd be off to Aunt Jane's and the lonely wind-blown beaches. The following night was agreed as a farewell binge, details to be arranged after they'd rendezvoused, but possibly with a meal and then some bopping afterwards. It had been a terrific evening.

'Did you see that slimy bastard of a cousin of mine?' said Jessica, as they went through their undressing routine back at the house. 'The gob on him whenever we left the Amsterdam!'

'Did you sleep with him?' said Karen, unexpectedly. 'You did, didn't you?'

'I was very young,' said Jessica, picking up her hairbrush. 'We all make mistakes, don't we?'

'Yeah,' said Karen. 'I wouldn't have minded making one myself tonight, with Mallachy.'

'You little slut!' said Jessica.

SIX

The girls were late at breakfast, but Mrs Roberts did not mind. They found her sitting at the table with the *Telegraph*, nibbling toast. Her husband had already left, but not for his office in the centre. Business in Coleraine, she said, he would be back in time for dinner.

There was an assumption in the way she said it that brought Jessica up. For the moment she busied herself making a fresh pot of tea, while Karen cleared the dirty plates and made room for their toast and marmalade. Mrs Roberts declined another cup.

'This dinner, Ma? You know we'll be out tonight, don't you? I never forgot to mention it?'

Mrs Roberts raised clear grey eyes to her daughter's. Jessica, of course, was lying.

'I doubt if you forgot anything,' she said. 'But Daddy is expecting it to be a sort of little God-speed thing. Karen's leaving, isn't she? Oh, by the way, I forgot something: Martin rang last night. I told him you were at the theatre.'

Jessica flushed.

'Why did you tell him lies?' she said. 'Parr doesn't think I stay home knitting waiting for his calls!'

'It was a joke,' said Mrs Roberts, mildly. 'Martin knows your attitude to culture. He'll ring back later.'

'We won't be in.'

'He'll ring back till he finds you. It's not important. Except he's coming over very soon. In the next few days.'

There was a tiny silence, a catch in time. Karen King smiled cautiously. So Parr did have a Christian name.

'I'm really sorry about tonight,' she said. 'I hope it won't upset anybody.'

She said this with conscious boldness, a pre-emptive strike. One could not argue with the honoured guest, could one? Mrs Roberts gave in gracefully.

'I expect I can make him understand,' she replied. 'I'll try to reach him in Coleraine. Sam does still look on Jessica as his little girl sometimes. I sometimes think he must walk around in blinkers.'

Jessica treated her to a tight, satirical smile. She said: 'Try and persuade him to come home for a special tea. High tea. We could open a wee bottle or two, sit out on the grass. We're only meeting friends, they'll not expect us to be sober.'

'I expect you to be sober, if you're driving.'

'Ach, mother! Stop pretending to be a dry old biscuit. Anyway, we'll take a cab, it'll be a long night I expect. We can't send Karen to the boring Isle of Man with anything less than a nineteen-carat hangover, can we?'

'Well all right, I'll try. Will you run into the shops for me, get some deli? I've got some nice salami in the fridge. Get a piece of Brie and some Vignottes, that'll put him in the forgiving mood.'

'Good idea,' said Jessica. 'I'll get some Greek stuff, too. Some retsina. Daddy loves that, God knows why. I wouldn't wash my smalls in it.'

'Jessica, you're disgusting.'

At about ten thirty, while the girls were drying their hair after showers, the phone rang. Jessica switched off the drier and lifted the receiver beside her bed, expecting Parr. It was Terence.

'Hi,' she said, then: 'Oh, you. What brings you out from underneath your stone in daylight?'

She laughed across at Karen, hardly bothering to cover the mouthpiece: 'It's the wee shite cousin Terence.'

'Listen, Jessica,' said Terence. 'You're very funny but

I'm giving you a warning. As a relative. You're playing in the wrong league with those Taigs.'

Jessica's mouth actually dropped open slightly, she was quite astonished.

'What?' she gasped.

'You heard.' There was a note of malicious pleasure in the voice. 'I'm telling you, you picked the wrong—'

Jessica drowned out the rest with a shout of pure anger.

'You little shit! You cheeky bastard!'

She banged the receiver down so hard the telephone skidded off the bedside table and clattered to the floor. She bent down and picked the whole thing up and slammed it back.

'God, Jesus, hell,' she spluttered. 'I'll kill the sod! I'll tear his nasty sneaky eyes out, so I will! The brass neck of the guy!'

Karen took the hair drier. Drips were running down her neck.

'What did he say?'

Jessica stood up and strode about.

'He's warning me,' she said. 'I can't believe it! I really can't believe it!'

'Warning you about what?'

'Being seen with Catholics, what do you think? He was threatening.'

'But you weren't with Catholics. Not only Catholics. How could he tell? You can't really tell by looking, can you? That's a joke?'

'Wish it bloody was,' said Jessica. Her rage had run down. She sat on the bed, ran fingers through her damply tangled hair. 'Oh, you can sometimes tell. You *know*, in any case. I don't know. He was damn right, wasn't he?'

'Mm,' went Karen. She burnt her ear, and yelped. 'Does it matter?'

'Of course it doesn't matter,' replied Jessica. 'Terence

the Province is part of it, he spends half his time
tinental businessmen, Krauts and Dutchmen
He speaks more languages than a penteco
opened a tin of beans, was flopping th
at the stove. 'Anyway, I've a horribl
to talk to him just at the mome
the atmosphere that I don't li
Karen, putting bread int

got fed up.
'Go on? A premon
Jessica dropped
turned.
'Yes: Oh
one. I sa
'Yo
ab

...is. Give us

Dressed, they went into Holywood to get the high tea specialities, then extended into Belfast because retsina was not in stock locally. They met some girlfriends of Jessica's, and ended up having cakes and coffee and a laugh. When they got back late for lunch Mrs Roberts had gone out, leaving a note. Martin Parr had rung again, there was a number.

'He's persistent,' Karen said. 'Why don't you get it over with?'

'It's too much fag,' Jessica replied. 'If I did ring he'd have moved on, anyway, he's more elusive than my daddy. He'll get me if he really wants me.'

'What does he do? Honestly, none of that "don't know" bullshit.'

Jessica waved a hand. 'Honestly, I don't. He's something in the government, I guess. Bringing commerce to

with con-
and Italians.
stalist.' She had
m into a saucepan
e feeling I don't want
t. There's something in
ke. I've got a premonition.'
the toaster, waited. Until she

ition of what? Oh . . . '
the bean-tin into the flip-top bin. She

she said. 'I think it could just be the formal
d it had to come one day, didn't I?'
amaze me, Jessica,' said Karen. 'You're so offhand
ut it, so bleeding calm. You don't even know what he
does for a living properly!'

'Calm,' said Jessica. 'Hah! Calm!' She picked a saucepan off the cooker and raised it high, as if she might
fling it across the kitchen like a hatchet. Then she put
it down. 'Well, what do you expect me to do?' she said.
'Go bananas? Cut my throat? It's what I wanted, isn't it?
It's what I decided was the best idea all round. And let's
have none of your crap about arranged marriages, OK?
I probably love him, in my own sweet way. It's what I
bloody *wanted*.'

The toaster popped. Noisy in the sudden silence. Karen
watched her friend's face and saw it closed, hurting. She
thought she understood.

'So what about Rory?'

But Jessica had caught herself again. She ran the tip of
her tongue across her upper lip, red and pointed.

'A little bit of healthy lust,' she said. 'What else d'you
think? If I end up in bed with Rory I'll have a lovely time
and then I'll quit. Or maybe I won't! What's wrong with
married women with a little on the side? You ought to
try it, sometime!'

That sounded like the end of it. Jessica had slammed a drawer open, was sorting knives and forks out, brittle, self-absorbed. Then, unexpectedly, she said: 'You mustn't worry, Karen, it won't come to anything, all this crap. I'm only edgy because there *might* be something being planned, but I'm probably completely wrong. Parr's probably coming for a business deal with my daddy and feels the need to have a grip of me, the usual thing, that's all. If they have got something cooking, and if I found I didn't like it when it came, I'd tell them to get stuffed. It's simple really, isn't it?'

Karen buttered toast, and put more bread in the machine. She had a mental picture of Samuel Roberts' fine, hard face.

Simple.

That evening, they met the men at eight o'clock, all parties quite well oiled from the off. Jessica and Karen, under the eyes of Mrs Roberts, had booked a taxi, and had had to take a farewell brandy with Mr Roberts while it waited, in case he should have gone to work before they rose next morning. Rory had been down home in the country all day long, working on some bad debt accounts with Tom Holdfast, so he and Mallachy had taken a couple in the Wellington Park to wash away the nasty taste of commerce. Rory, crazed as ever, had his car.

They drank some spirits in the Amsterdam, then repaired to a French restaurant on the Malone Road, where seats were booked. The evening was quite riotous, with Mallachy and Rory misbehaving badly enough (in Karen's English opinion) to be thrown out. But Rory said his 'insult credit with the Frogs' was high, and so it appeared. They shrugged at his noises and Mallachy's, and winced gallically at their jokes, some of them translated for their benefit. Being Belfast, none of the other customers appeared to mind the row at all. Afterwards they went to a nightclub and danced and smooched in the smoky blackness, cleaning their throats from time to time with champagne.

In the car, on their way to Holywood at past two in the morning, Karen rested in the crook of Mallachy's arm and shoulder and tried to sort out what she felt. Drunk certainly, thank God – too drunk to suffer anything but minor guilt pangs, extremely muted and infrequent. Excited, perhaps, but more contented, happy to let his hand range soft across her breasts or rest on the inside of her thigh, protected by the trousers she had deliberately worn. She liked the taste of his mouth, the feel of his tongue caressing hers, but she did not feel threatened by the thought that she might be expected to 'go all the way' like some poor teenager on a heavy date. She wouldn't have minded screwing him – she thought she would have liked to – but it would not be an issue. She looked at the back of Jessica's head, tucked sideways onto Rory's shoulder as he drove, and she smiled. It was rather like a mid-West movie, as pleasant as that. She turned her mouth again to Mallachy's.

They stopped on the promenade at Cultra and looked out over the blackness of Belfast Lough, alive with twinkling lights. A ship was moving slowly down the main channel, its engines throbbing in the stillness.

'That'll be you tomorrow,' said Mallachy. 'Hey, that's a pity, isn't it?'

'This morning, not tomorrow,' said Jessica. 'That's a bigger pity still. Why don't you give it up, Karen? Go sick!'

'Why doesn't Mallachy go too?' said Rory. 'What would your auntie say if you brought a Thespian?'

'I'm not a Thespian, you cheeky bitch!' trilled Mallachy. 'I wear trousers because they're comfortable!'

'Karen wears trousers because they keep out ack-tors' hands,' said Jessica. 'Me, I wear a skirt.'

There was a car moving along the promenade towards them, on dipped headlights. As it got closer, its lights went up to full beam.

'Aye-aye,' said Rory. 'Holywood Moral Majority Patrol, is it?'

But his humour was uncertain. They all fell silent as the harsh glare played on them. At about a hundred yards, the car came to a halt. They heard the engine being gunned, like a racer at the grid.

'Shit,' said Jessica. 'What's going on?'

The engine noise changed abruptly as the car leapt forward. It came at them like a bullet from a gun, faster, faster, the tortured motor on a rising scream. Karen screamed as well, and dug her fingers into Mallachy's hard neck. Their white faces glared more whitely, stricken, lurid, paralysed as they all moved sideways, pushed by the sound and light, crushed across the car. Their world became a blinding wall of white, howling towards them, too fast for thought or action. Jessica felt her eyes close but could see the light, two hot white searchlights, hot red spots.

It was over in an instant. There was a metallic crescendo of machinery, a squeal of rubber, a buffeting of wind that rocked the BMW on its springs. Then anti-climax, as they watched its tail-lights in the pitchy dark, lights that seemed to throb and waver in their seared sight before they blazed redly when the brakes went on for the corner by the sailing club slipway.

'Go on!' said Mallachy. His voice was slightly strangled. 'What are you waiting for?'

There was a moment's pause.

'No!' said Karen. Rory hissed, a sound denoting amusement, possibly. Another tiny gap.

'Come on,' he said. 'Let's not play silly games. I can't see straight, I'm blinded.'

'Toyota,' said Mallachy. 'I'd put my life on it.'

'Your own life,' said Jessica, dryly. 'I grew out of joy-riding ten years ago.'

'Christ,' said Karen, shakily. 'Is this considered normal, this sort of thing?'

Jessica turned in her seat and touched her on the arm.

'Just lads out for a thrill,' she said. 'Off-duty soldiers from the barracks, maybe.'

A snort from Mallachy: those lousy fucking Brits, it meant.

'No harm done,' said Rory. 'Jasus, but it's upset the *ambience*, however. And no mistake.'

Shortly afterwards, he drove them back to the house, a half a mile away. They kissed, briefly, and made a date for about eleven the same morning, to see Karen onto the ferry. Exhausted, the young women did not talk much as they prepared for bed. Karen felt herself in turmoil, felt the horrible excitement of the car attack would never let her sleep. Within seconds, she was gone.

But Jessica, lying in the soft warm darkness, pondered on the car. She had her suspicions, and she hated them. She hated them.

SEVEN

Tearful farewells, after a night on the toot, were not really on the cards. Karen and Jessica both had puffy eyes, and were well aware of it. Jessica, more for the crack than anything, wore big dark glasses, like a thirties film star. They were not feeling too bad, considering, although Karen, as soon as she had awoken, had been flooded with guilty thoughts – the pangs unmodified, this morning, by champagne or brandy. She tried to clear them from her mind, but was broody over breakfast. Jessica picked up on it, but did not tease. Sometimes she felt sorry for her uptight, upright friend.

They hardly expected to see the BMW waiting for them at the dockside, but after they had parked the car and got the ticket, they began to look at their watches, and each other. It was a fine, bright morning, so they wandered about the quay, watching the activity at Harlands and the dinghy sails farther down the lough. The tannoy on the Isle of Man boat gave occasional coughs, and tinny, inaudible announcements, but they did not begin to panic for a while.

'Well,' said Karen, 'it's a damn good job I didn't drink enough to go overboard with Mallachy, isn't it? Is this the Irish way? The famous unreliability? Where are they?'

Jessica lifted her sunglasses and scratched her nose.

'The Irish way is to go back to some shebeen and carry on with the whisky all night long,' she replied. 'If that's what happened, Rory can whistle for it, the backsliding little Taig.'

'They couldn't have had an accident, could they?' asked Karen. 'It's terrible the way Rory drinks and drives.'

Even behind the glasses she could see Jessica roll her eyes.

'For God's sake, Karen!'

'But they were so keen to be here.'

She was aware of how pathetic she was sounding, so she forced herself to stop. But she was hurt. She thought of Tony, wincing. The taste in her mouth was slightly sour, despite toothpaste, despite hot coffee.

'Look,' said Jessica, sympathetically. 'Look, it's not the end of the world, love. They may have been delayed. They may have been held up. Rory's got a long drive in, and Mallachy hasn't got a car. It doesn't mean anything.'

'No,' said Karen. 'I know.'

'You couldn't blame Mallachy, anyway. Could you? I mean – suppose he's fallen wildly in love with you? Perhaps he just can't face the parting!'

The sympathy had not been long-lived. Karen tried to laugh. She did not know, now, if she regretted leaving Belfast, or was glad.

'Oh Christ,' said Jessica, her voice completely changed. 'Look over there.'

A car had pulled up by the gate. Three young men had got out and were looking at them. One raised a languid hand. The car was white.

'The slug,' said Jessica. 'Looking for a juicy lettuce.'

'Bunce, Boggis and Bean,' said Karen, flatly. 'One short, one fat, one lean.'

'I wish you wouldn't say that,' said Jessica. 'I don't know what you're talking about. This could be nasty, you know. It was them, last night. This morning.'

Terence Rigby and his two friends were sauntering towards them. All three glanced about the dockside, as if looking for somebody else.

'What?' said Karen. Then she knew. 'What, in the car? Oh. Are you sure?'

Terence was tall, quite thin. One of his friends was, indeed, heavy around the hips and bottom, almost bell-shaped, the third was small and foxy. Somehow, the comical aspect had gone. They were smartly dressed, they did not look like thugs, but their faces were stamped with unpleasantness.

'Look what the tide washed up,' said Jessica, when they were ten feet away. 'The cheap thrill brigade. First they come to peep, then they play at racing cars. How many red lights did you jump, going home?'

The men stopped.

'I don't know what you're talking about,' said Terence.

'You're a liar. You were ever poor at it. Now go away, we've got a boat to catch. We want to say goodbye without an audience of perverts.'

Water off a duck's back.

'Suit yourself,' said Terence. 'Better we should see you off than those bastards you expected, isn't it?'

'Now what?' demanded Jessica, irritably. 'The only bastards here are youse bastards. Go home Terence, you're getting in my space. I'll tell my mother off for this.'

Terence showed a glimmer of discomfiture.

'Your mother's nothing to do with it.'

'Away!' said Jessica. 'She'll have told you we were coming for the boat. The rest you dreamed up for yourself, you obvious wee shite. Now go to hell.'

The tannoy on the ferry crackled and buzzed. The level of activity on the decks had increased. Karen did not want to miss it, any more.

'Come on,' said Jessica, 'you'd best go on. Sorry about the third-rate cabaret. Pity me. I have to stay here.'

Terence said: 'You're so fucking clever, Jessica. You know fuck all, that's your trouble. These lovely friends of yours, who've let you down. They'll be off killing someone, have you not caught on yet? Do you not know the sort you're running with?'

Jessica removed her sunglasses, staring at him. He held her stare.

'You may not like it, but it's true,' he said. 'The wee one, Mallachy O'Rourke. Pretends to be an actor, doesn't he? He's known. He's on the list. We've come to see you as a friendly warning. All the thanks we get.'

'On what list?' blurted Karen, but Jessica pulled her roughly by the arm, towards the knot of people gathered at the square steel entrance to the boat.

'Come away!' she snapped. 'Terence, you disgust me. Get out of here before I lose my rag.'

'The fingers that mould the Semtex,' said the fat one. He was laughing, confident, everything had changed. 'Supple little fingers, would you say?'

Jessica drove Karen before her like an angry shepherdess. She was furious.

'Is it true?' asked Karen. 'Do they mean terrorists? Jessica?'

Jessica made a noise to silence her. People in the crowd were watching, curiously. At the barrier she was not allowed on board with Karen, the officer told her it was too late. Flustered, they kissed each other and Karen blundered into the noisy stomach of the ship. It took her some time to orientate. She lugged her case up the wrong stairway, came out facing the open lough, had to find her way around the superstructure. By the time she overlooked the quayside, the decks were vibrating and black diesel smoke was pouring from the funnel.

Below her, she picked out Jessica on the concrete, scanning the upper deck, shielding her eyes. The three young men had moved back some twenty or thirty feet, but were still watching Jessica. Karen waved until her arm ached, but Jessica did not see. As they moved out onto the lough, the wind began to bite through her light dress, but she still stood, still waved. Soon Jessica was lost among the jumbled people on the quay.

Karen went below and found a table in the cafeteria. She stared out through the thick, salt-streaked glass as roads and fields and houses moved slowly by. Already Northern Ireland was becoming just a pretty landscape, a backdrop to the pain behind her eyes. She looked at Carrickfergus, across to Holywood, back to Belfast, interested by the dullness of her reactions. Truly, it was a dump, a land of weirdos. Someone had once called it the biggest open mental institution in the world, one of the twin armpits of the British Isles, presumably with Glasgow as the other, Glasgow before the tartan yuppies got to it. Indubitably it was full of madmen, and women too, much as she found them fun to be with. What was Mallachy? Some bloke she'd snogged with, pissed, and no harm done as long as Tony never got to hear of it. In the cold light of the morning after, she did not think she even fancied him, could hardly bring what he looked like into focus, she had gone briefly crazy that was all, gone native.

Was he a terrorist? It seemed highly unlikely. Did she care? Karen sighed. It was a land of fantasists. She did not imagine that they would ever meet again. Ah well — roll on Port Erin and Aunt Jane.

Back at Cultra, Jessica Roberts was also cast down. She had watched the ferry until it was tiny in the water, upset at having failed to locate her friend. Terence had tried to talk to her as she had gone to her car, then the fat one had cat-called like a teenage oaf. At the gateway to the dock a black sports saloon had passed across a junction, unnerving her, but she doubted it had been Rory's. Despite her bold words to Karen, she found his failure to turn up gnawing at her, nagging, worrying. Unlike Karen, she could recall every feature of the face she'd kissed, lingered over his eyebrows and his hands almost obsessively. She remembered what the fat one had said about Mallachy's hands. Semtex. Her stomach chilled. The trouble was, you never knew. How could you?

Mrs Roberts was not home, and Jessica thought about going back to bed for an hour or two. She kept looking at the telephone beside her bed, willing it to ring, dithering. Although she had had a shower before going to the boat, she decided to take a long bath. She filled it with sweet oils and bubbles, shrugged her clothes off, and got in. Remembering the phone, she went to fetch it, leaving a soaking trail across her carpet. As she touched it it rang, and she jumped a foot. She snatched up the receiver and sat wetly on the bed. Her heart, she noted wryly, was thumping.

'Hallo, yes, it's . . . '

It was Parr.

'Jessica? You sound flustered.'

Jessica felt more than flustered, she felt devastated.

'Oh. Do I? I suppose I do. I'm all wet. I was in the bath.'

'It's gone midday. All right for some.'

Parr's voice was pleasant, humorous, controlled. She could imagine him, sitting in an office somewhere, no doubt in a sharkskin suit and Gucci slip-ons. She could see his smile in perfect detail, ironic, thin-lipped, in command. She felt gloom descending on her shoulders.

'I'm tired,' she said. 'Is that a crime?'

Parr, as usual, appeared to understand. Oh God, that understanding! How it irked her. His voice softened perceptibly. A saint.

'Look, I've got you at a bad moment, sorry. I've been trying for days, though, I'm coming over tomorrow. I'll be at Aldergrove about four, do you want to pick me up?'

Jessica did not reply. She was fighting hard not to be

60

unpleasant. What had he *done*, for God's sake? She could see his smile, his sympathy, but her perception of the picture had drastically changed. She could see another smile, overlaid on his, a looser, browner smile.

'Jessica?'

The voice was not impatient. Parr knew her moods, her snappiness. In a way he revelled in it, it amused him. He waited.

'I'm here. I'm thinking.'

'Look, I'll have to go. If it's any trouble, I'll get a car. I'll ring McCauslands.'

She laughed. She could have predicted it.

'Now what?'

'Nothing.' She had a sudden change of mood, a swoop of the old affection. He was very sweet, really. 'Don't get a hire car, I'll be there.' She would be. She cleared her head of Rory, all that nonsense. Good God, was she a teenager? 'If I'm a wee bit late,' she added, 'you won't have to mind, will you?'

'I'd be astonished if you weren't. You'll be pleased to see me, then? Just a little bit? I'll be bringing my DJ.'

There was something in it, something that frightened her. The mood swoop went the other way.

'You always do,' she said. 'What is it this time?'

To her suspicious ears, Parr sounded furtive.

'Nothing too terrible. A little family do, it was Sam's idea. Just the four of us.'

Jessica's voice was hard.

'Tell me, Parr. You know I don't like mysteries.'

'No mystery, honestly. Well, maybe a little one. Look, I've got to go. I promise you you'll be pleased, I promise you. Four o'clock, right? I love you, Jessica.'

He hung up, and she listened to the empty line. There was panic in her, not far beneath the surface. This was her lover, the man who made comparisons ridiculous. But she was hollow, not with dislike for him but with indifference, a faint and empty sickness,

61

something that had gone away. It was not Rory, surely? She was attracted, but so what? She had not had as many men as Karen gave her credit for, there was an element of blarney in all that, but there'd been quite a number, hadn't there? Rory was just another one, he'd not stand the comparison either, Parr was the real thing. In any case, she thought, I'll not give him the opportunity to try. I will not.

She put the phone down and it rang again, immediately. Her stomach dropped. It had to be. It was.

'You shit,' she said. 'You lousy bastard.'

'Listen,' said Rory Collins, cheerfully, 'enough of that old crap. I'm off to Galway City. Business. Urgent. Now. Will I bring you with me?'

Despite herself, she let out a yell of laughter.

'What sort of business? For the IRA?'

'You what? What kind of talk is that?'

'Terence says you're a Provie gunman. That's why you missed the boat.'

'Whoever Terence is, Terence is a toe-rag. Provie gunman, my arse! I can sing God Save the Queen in several languages, including Irish! I missed the boat because—' He stopped, laughing in his turn. 'Well, come to think of it, I *was* detained on urgent business with a Catholic. A wee green patriot, indeed. Are you coming?'

'Tell me more.'

'If you come.'

'Is Mallachy—'

An explosion down the phone.

'The hell he is! The two of us!'

'OK. Where shall I come to meet you?'

'The roundabout at Moira. Do you know it? You can leave the pea-green there.'

She did know it, everybody did. They fixed a time.

When the phone was in its cradle, Jessica reached for the clothes she had discarded. Then she changed her

62

mind, and went back to the brimming bath. She was exhilarated.

Oh God, she told herself, as she sank into it. I'm going to get myself shot for this.

EIGHT

They crossed the border at Blacklion, by which time they already felt like lovers. Indeed, when Jessica had locked her car with all the others at the Moira roundabout – travel-sharing, she assumed, hardheaded Ulstermen saving on the petrol – Rory had walked up to her and kissed her lightly on the mouth as if they owned each other. He was in black trousers and black shirt, dark glasses, handmade shoes, and was smiling easily. Jessica had deliberately gone the other way – she wore old jeans and a denim shirt and scuffed brown flatties. If it was a business trip in fact, she was not about to be mistaken for the personal assistant/mistress.

'I like the outfit,' said Rory. 'They'll be hard put to it to think I'm sleeping with a scruff like that!'

She grinned, delighted at this mind-reading.

'Yeah, yeah,' she said, dismissively. 'Although I must say you look every inch the boss yourself. What is this trip?'

Rory opened the passenger door of his charcoal car for her, just like a gentleman. There was a black briefcase on the rear seat, but nothing else. The radio was tuned to the BBC, to her surprise, but Rory switched it off as he got in.

'Bloody news,' he said. 'It's enough to make you cut your throat. I thought a bit of lunch in Sligo on the way? I know a place. All right?'

He had put the car in gear and was waiting to pull out. Jessica studied the angle of his chin, his ear. She found him lovely.

'Sligo? Jesus, that's a funny way to get to Galway City. What time is the business?'

Rory took the car round the roundabout and slipped left onto the M1. He accelerated hard, the engine humming throatily.

'Tomorrow morning,' he said. 'I thought I wouldn't mention that until we'd left the pea-green incorruptible behind. We could spin round at the Lurgan turn-off if you're furious, I could take you back to Moira?'

He glanced across. He put on a soppy-dog look that she'd seen before. She shook her head.

'You're a cheeky bastard, Mister. First you stand me up, then you kidnap me. If the business is tomorrow, and we're off to Sligo now, presumably I don't get home tonight?'

'You could catch a train. It would only take three days or so. I know a good wee hotel in Galway.'

'Don't tell me, you've booked us in. Mr and Mrs Smith.'

His lips curved.

'Oh God, I made a bad mistake there. I forgot you were a Prod. I called us Murphy. There's more of them in Galway City than there's ever Smiths. Are you wild?'

'Religion means nothing to me, Mr Collins. Smith, Murphy, it's all one. I was a believer until about my fourteenth birthday, when I heard an Easter service on the radio. The Reverend Canon Something-or-the-other was rounding it off. I can quote the fool exactly. "In this service so far," he says, "we've concentrated on the *ordinariness* of the Resurrection." That was it for me. Although I'd had me doubts before, I will admit. Are you religious, Rory?'

A van passed them on the other carriageway. It was white, emblazoned on the sides in red. The Saviour's Army, it proclaimed. Ulster Still Needs Jesus. Rory pointed.

'Everywhere you look,' he said. 'Do you know, something like eighty per cent of the mad bastards in this Province are members of a church? Ulster needs a fucking

65

break, more like it. Me, I'm meant to be a Catholic. I meant about the booking of the room, though.'

She brought a window down by pressing on a button. Wind whipped through her hair.

'I sometimes think I might convert, you know,' she said. 'There seems a lot more fun with your lot. God, how I used to envy the Catholic girls going to the schools in Belfast when I was waiting at the bus stop like a fresh dog's dinner to be carried off to Dothegirls Academy in me big grey interlocks with double gusset for the hockey stains. The names they have! Conceptua, and Carmel, and Dolors, can you imagine calling someone Dolors, it means misery, doesn't it?'

'I've an Auntie Dolors. She's a misery. Still, she's married to me Uncle Dennis.'

'Do you know,' said Jessica, 'I was standing at the bus stop once, and two little Catholic girls came along so sweet you would have thought that they were angels. There was a wee wasp buzzing round behind the neck of one of them, and the other one was waggling her school bag at it, at arm's length. Then she says to her, in this lovely, trilling little voice: "For fuck's sake, Immaculata, will you *run*!" Oh, save us, I nearly died. Immaculata! For fuck's sake, Immaculata. I wanted a name like that. I cried myself to sleep for days.'

'Your daddy shouldn't have left you at a bus stop in an area where a girl would hear language like that,' Rory told her, sternly. 'What was your daddy doing not giving you a lift to school? Were you in Holywood, still?'

'Cultra, to be precise,' said Jessica. 'No, we moved there later, when he got the riches. At this time he only ran about half the companies in Belfast. Small-time stuff.'

Rory jumped on it.

'Now come on then,' he said. 'Why "Cultra, to be precise"? You always say that. Why?'

She had a friend, Jessica explained, who lived in England, on the south coast at Brighton, which he

66

knew, of course? Only she lived in the posh part, called Hove, and whenever people said 'You live in Brighton, don't you?' it was normal to reply 'Hove, actually' until it almost had become the name, Hove-Actually. Cultra, to be precise, was her adaptation.

'There,' she said. 'Aren't you glad I told you that? Aren't you just bowled over with my brilliance? Do you have a girlfriend, Rory?'

'Well I suppose I do,' he said, unthrown completely.

'And you a feller? Is he in England, at the university, or do you have one here, as well? I shouldn't be surprised if you have both. Lots. You deserve it, with thighs like yours.'

They were coming to the end of the motorway – which went nowhere, after the fashion of the country, having been built to please a politician it was said – and both of them knew a bar. They stopped for drinks and crisps, and sat out on a low stone wall, looking at the cattle and the traffic and green fields. Rory told Jessica about his girlfriend Rosie, not a great deal but nothing too disloyal, while she for her part realised after some moments that she was not listening with more than half an ear, but wondering what she should tell him about Parr. Rosie worked in a chemist's shop, she heard, and was a nice wee thing, if rather young, and it was not serious. No hearts were going to be broken, he told her with the frankest face, if he were to run off with a Protestant and have a dozen kids.

It was not true, although he damnwell wished it were. He had spent the morning in bed with Rosie, which was why he'd missed his date down at the docks, she had rung him at ten to eight. A morning off, she took them occasionally when she felt put upon, but this time her ire and suspicion were aimed at him. She had a little flat in the Falls, a house she shared with girlfriends, her family home being in a village outside Derry, and she told him in blunt terms that she hadn't seen enough of him at it for too damn long, at it or anywhere else. Rory had driven up and slipped into her bed like lightning, because he had already cooked up the plan to try and entice Jessica Roberts to go with him to Galway, and needed to sweeten Rosie for another evening's absence. She had gone back to sleep when he'd agreed to come, and she'd woken warm and fuzzy, naked in her narrow bed. She was only nineteen, and short and plump and cuddly, and they loved to fuck each other. By the time he told her he must go, and was off to the Republic for a day or two, she was placated.

They moved on after that, with Jessica dropping in bits about Parr as they occurred to her – although not that she was due to meet him the next day. He was an Englishman, she said, an associate of her father, who'd come across for years on whatever business it was he did. She'd thought at one time that it might be serious, be love or something weird like that, she'd even thought they could get married.

'Who knows,' she added, eyes out of the open window, unable to look at Rory for a moment, 'it could still come to that.'

'No,' said Rory Collins. 'That would be a waste. God, if you're not crazy about someone, if you're not completely mad for them, where's the point in marrying? Jesus, you're a Protestant, and your daddy's loaded, you can suit yourself in everything. Why chuck away your freedom?'

'Are you saying if I was a Catholic I couldn't suit myself? Next you'll be telling me this Rosie girl's a virgin!'

'The hell she is. She got rid of that nonsense somewhere down the way before she came to me. I just meant the old wedding bit, the tradition, the custom and practice. I've always thought we had it stronger on us than you other lot, forgive me if I'm wrong.'

'So if she had her claws in you, you'd be hard pressed not to marry her? Is that the truth of it?'

Rory did not answer that immediately. The subject had not arisen, but he did have qualms about Rosie, occasionally. She had said she loved him, once, and it had chilled him, so clearly that she'd never mentioned it again. They'd been together for eighteen months or more, and she had no one else. She suffered so much when he did casuals that he'd lied about it for a long time.

'Ach, no,' he said. 'You've got a nasty way of expressing yourself, d'you know that? There's no question of claws in anyone. We're just . . . '

'Good friends? Heavens, Rory!'

He shook his head, exasperated, but did not respond. They talked of other things as they approached Blacklion, parts of Ireland they both knew, the parts they liked the best. In the Republic, slowed down by the roads, they took a detour, turned left at Manorhamilton, followed the Bonet river, peeped at the old great mansions in the trees, dreamed up a whole world of the madly rich lurking in this lovely countryside, their children educated at the Convent of the Little Daughters of the Wealthy which they placed on Inisfree, serenely sited on the gleaming waters of Lough Gill.

'Nine bean rows shall I have there, and a hive for the honey bee,' chanted Rory. 'The honey is to keep the beans on the knife, of course. Those old poets thought of everything.'

After lobster in Sligo, eaten late and washed down with Macon Villages, they took the southward route to Charlestown, on the landward side of Slieve Gamph, then on to Claremorris and Tuam, because Rory said he didn't trust himself to take the coastal roads, to get too near the sea. They would linger, he insisted, he could never tear himself away, they'd miss the business in the morning, and the hotel.

'Mark you,' he said, 'I did have a fantasy of doing it with you on some lonely western strand, in time to the roaring of the Atlantic. What would you have said if I'd suggested that?'

She mocked him.

'You didn't, so you'll never know, will you? I never even consented to the hotel, did I? It could be money wasted, still. Have you legislated for that contingency?'

'Ah well,' said Rory, slowing to avoid a pair of sheep that had come dribbling across the road. 'Easy come, easy go. I'll tell you what. Next time we'll go the coast way. Westport and Leenane and Letterfrack. We used to take our holidays on Inishbofin, it's where I learned to sail. I love it, all this area. We'll go and stay in Roundstone, there's a wonderful pub there, you'd fall in love with me as soon as step inside.'

All too easy, thought Jessica, suddenly. She shivered slightly. A ghost across her grave. Christ, where was she going?

She asked about his father, then his money. She did not want him to think, she said, that she was really rich, that was only a kind of joke. They had the cottage in Donegal – but who didn't, these days? – they lived in Cultra, but they were only ordinary, not millionaires or anything.

She reddened as she explained, but Rory understood. He felt the embarrassment himself sometimes, as all his friends were stony broke, and his came from his father, also.

'It's agricultural machinery, tractors and such stuff – John Deere, naturally, they're green! He started up twenty years ago, he could not have picked a better time. Mind you, I only got it because he died intestate and me mother doesn't care. He never thought I was fit to run a shoe shop. Damn right, too! Bad thing to say for the old feller, but I was lucky.'

'How did he die? He couldn't have been that old, could he?'

Rory pondered. He was tempted to come out with the stuff about Michael and the IRA. The men in berets at the

70

house at Hackballs Cross, the possibility he might once have been a gunman in his wild and woolly youth. He did not want to, but on the other hand . . . it might be taken for romantic, it might impress. He did not want to talk about the woman in Dundalk, though, the double life, the scenes and drunken violence.

'You're such a high-born lady,' he said, 'I don't know what to say. There is a possibility he was murdered by the Proddie roaring boys, the UVA or UFF or somesuch, but I don't know. Officially, he died in a car smash on the border. He was coming from Dundalk, he spent a lot of time there. You know Dundalk, they say the bars are stiff with wanted men.'

'Oh,' said Jessica. She gave it all some thought. She laughed. 'If only my daddy would see me now!' She paused. 'But you're not . . . you know – connected, are you?'

He waggled his eyebrows.

'God, would you fancy me if I said I was? If I told you I'd a revolver hidden in my glove compartment? No, of course I'm not. I agree with Tom Holdfast, he's the man who runs the company. He says all the trouble in this land is caused by two per cent of bastards who should have been drowned at birth. When he's in a jolly mood he blames it on their potty training. And he's one of your sort, too. My employee.'

'And Mallachy?'

'He's all talk. A spoofer. The only one I know that's—' He stopped, kicking himself. The only one he knew that well was Rosie, who had cousins in it, brothers maybe, although she never talked of it except in the most general terms. She had emigrated with half her family to England when a baby, but they had all come back the night an auntie's house in Derry had been seen on TV news, with the sofa flying from an upstairs window and loyalist thugs pouring petrol on the geraniums. He and Mallachy, between themselves, called her the Wee

71

Green Patriot, but steered clear of all argument on the subject.

'Go on?'

'Just a thought,' said Rory. 'You haven't answered me. If you would fancy me if I was one.'

'I fancy you already,' Jessica replied. 'Stop fishing. "The only one you know . . . "?'

'Who's Terence? You said Terence said I was a Provie gunman. That's an awful dangerous claim to make. I could sue for slander.'

Jessica gave up on her question. There would be another time.

'He's my Mallachy equivalent,' she said. 'The skinny one in the Amsterdam with the rat-trap mouth. He's my cousin. He turned up with his pals at the Isle of Man boat this morning, looking for a spot of trouble. That car on Cultra promenade, earlier. That was them as well.'

'Christ, is that a fact?' He did not seem concerned. 'How did they know we'd be there?'

'Well, if I'm right,' said Jessica. 'No, I'm sure I'm right, it's just his style. He worked it out, I guess. Cruised down on the off-chance and struck gold.'

'The dirty shite. And he says I'm . . . ?'

'Mallachy, to be honest; he didn't mention you. A known terrorist, or somesuch. He's a bletherer. He was lifted once. He had a gun. Even the madmen wouldn't have him in real life, I'd put money on it. It's nasty, though.' She slipped another probe in. 'This business that kept you away this morning. You said a Catholic. You said a wee green patriot. You said you'd tell me.'

Rory Collins pulled the car over to the left, putting two wheels up on the pale grass verge. Into neutral, handbrake on. He turned his head and looked into her face.

'Look,' he said. 'That was a little joke. I'm not involved in anything like that, anything at all. I said it for the crack, to wind you up. I had some business I couldn't wriggle out of. Even playboys have got to earn the crust, OK?'

'OK,' she said. 'And you haven't got a gun?'

'I haven't got a gun.'

'Good,' said Jessica. She glanced at her watch, yawned suddenly.

'How far is it to Galway City? Is it far?'

'An hour, maybe. If you want a sleep, wind the seat back.'

'No, I don't want to sleep, I only yawned. Is it a good hotel?'

'It is. It's very good. Why?'

She yawned again, and licked her lips.

'I think I have to have you soon,' she said.

NINE

How soon is soon? Rory realised quickly that Jessica was playing with him, and enjoyed the game immensely. When they had negotiated the outskirts of the city, she demanded to be driven instantly to the hotel. But on a bridge across the Corrib, she saw an itinerant girl, barefoot, selling flowers, and said she needed some. They parked nearby, and bought a huge selection. The girl, thin-faced and undernourished, watched with complete indifference as Jessica then took them to the parapet and scattered them onto the turbulent black surface of the river, where they swirled beautifully, made changing patterns as they swept between the steep stone walls.

'I was here last Christmas,' Jessica told Rory. 'There were itinerants on this same bridge then, I think the same girl, in a pale cotton dress. She had a young boy with her, about thirteen, and he had no shoes on either. Jeans and a tee-shirt. It was raining, sleety rain, and so cold you could have frozen milk. I did my shopping, had some lunch, and they were still here when we crossed over, going home. They were selling Christmas trees. It was dark by then.'

After she had scattered the last few blooms, she went and gave the girl a five pound note, Ulster Bank pounds, not punts. The girl said . thank you, possibly, it was something not quite audible, but her face did not change. Rory mocked Jessica.

'The ould habits do die hard,' he almost sang. 'Whyever don't you take her home with you to be a lady's maid!'

'Who'd want undressing by a maid,' said Jessica, 'if

they had you to do it for them? Will you bring me to the hotel now, or are you frightened?'

But the smell of fresh ground coffee took her nostrils, and they went and had almond buns and Vintage Colombian, roasted on the premises. It was her opinion, she told Rory, that there was something awful funny going on, that this western city in the poorest part of a poor country should have such places, and such shops as they could see all round them, and such terrific *style*.

'It makes Belfast look like a dump,' she added. 'And look at all the people in their designer clothes, and all. Someone's kidding someone, so they are.'

They drove down to the harbour and watched the cargo boat for the Aran Islands loading up, the crew of black-haired ruddy men chatting easily to them, amused – delighted – by their northern accents and their contrasting styles. Jessica dropped in a reference to the Playboy of the Western World, her eye on Rory, but it passed as far over him as it did the seamen. They moved on to see some fellows working on a lovely Galway hooker raised on sleepers at the waterside, then crossed to a quiet little bar and had some Beamishes. It was getting early evening now, it was getting time to eat.

'For a woman who's dying for it, you're holding up extremely well,' said Rory. 'Now I don't know if you know it, but there's one of the finest restaurants between Paris and New Orleans just down the road. I've seen strong men crying at the salmon mayonnaise, and the wine cellar would turn a camel off the water. Shall we try a bite, or are you still screaming out for intercourse?'

Jessica settled for the food, over which they lingered, rounding it all off with cognac, armagnac and calvados just for the hell of it. Back at the hotel, instead of heading for the bedroom, she led him to the bar, where they took a couple of glasses of malt and fell to chatting with some locals who'd 'just dropped by to have a nightcap' despite the fact it was gone midnight and they all had work to go to in the morning. When the bedroom door finally closed behind them, Rory was fit to burst with laughter, and told her so.

'My God, you're such a spoofer, Jessica. You're such a bloody teaser!'

Jessica stood facing him, her face gone serious. She undid her denim shirt, exposing her pale breasts. She kicked off her slip-on shoes, unbuckled and unzipped her jeans, and pushed them and her pants rapidly to the floor, where she stepped out of them.

'I fucking amn't,' she said. 'I'm serious.'

'God,' said Rory Collins, as if mesmerised. 'You're so very . . . God.'

Jessica, still in her shirt, moved to him and undid the buttons down his chest. She pulled the black cloth back over his shoulders, then breathed deeply at the catch of sweat, mixed with deodorant, that rose from his armpit. She put her mouth, wide open and wet, onto his chest, among the dark curly hair beneath his neck. She took his belt, unbuckled it, undid the top stud and his zip, and pulled the dark trousers down. His penis, thrusting from the displaced briefs, she licked in one fast movement, root to tip, tasting the tang of its confinement, the elasticity of the drop of fluid she had generated. Then, as she pulled the briefs down, she enclosed its head in her warm mouth, just for an instant, then moved backwards away from him, on her knees, his clothes bunched at his feet.

'Lift,' she said. He lifted one foot, then the other, stepped out of his leather casuals then the clothes and socks. Jessica stood, jerked his black shirt further down his back and off his arms, stepped back again, looked at him. His prick was throbbing, his hair was tousled, his face wonderfully bemused.

Until she had seen him without his clothes on – so she had told herself – Jessica had not been sure. She had undressed many men, she had read somewhere that nakedness was safest, because with the mystery gone humans were just humans, not that exciting, nothing special, and she believed it, for some times and for some human beings. But here she stared at something she found heart-rending, and beautiful, and horrifyingly dear, already.

'Oh Christ, Rory,' she said. 'Your dick is bent.'

He looked down, his rueful dog-look on his mug.

'It is,' he said. 'I jammed it in a mangle as a child. Does it matter?'

'You never did!' She raised a hand, as if to strike him. 'You bastard! Why is it bent?'

She moved forward, and took the length of it in her right hand. Lying in her palm, strained, weeping with desire, it had a definite bias to one side, a kink almost. It was trembling, and so was she.

'Don't you like it, Jessica?' he said. 'It's the only one I have.'

She did like it. She could not even say so.

'At least the bias is to the left,' he said. 'It's politically correct. Unless you're a – Holy Mary, you will be, I suppose! Cultra, to be precise! Unionists to a soul!'

'But inside me, the bias will go right,' she said. 'Unless I'm on my face. Oh Christ, you've got to get it in me, Rory. Now.'

She let go his penis, wet and sleek now, and grabbed both his shoulders with her hands. She walked two paces backwards to the bed, only in her shirt, and tried to pull him on her as she fell. He resisted, kept them almost upright.

'I'll be no good,' he said. 'I'm half coming already. You've got to give me time. I'm just not used to this. You Proddie girls.'

'You're wonderful,' she said. 'Your dick is wonderful. It's everything I've ever dreamed of in a cock. Just don't be too expert. Come in me, come now. I couldn't stand it if you go for expertise.'

77

She had begun to pant, and Rory Collins had begun to come. She fell onto the bed, he fell on her, spilling hot gushing sperm onto her belly and thighs. Jessica grabbed his bursting penis and almost pulled it into her, then threw her legs around him and her arms and crushed him until he gasped, still coming, and then she let out a mighty hoot, a hoot to wake hotel guests two corridors away, she had come as well, once, hard, like a violent convulsion. In the aftermath, as they instantly relaxed, Rory slipped off the bed and out of her and banged his shin against a chair and shrieked in agony.

Jessica threw herself onto the floor on top of him, and put her tongue into his open mouth and kissed him till he smothered, rubbing her wet vagina hard onto his knee and thigh. As he seized her ears to get some breath she came once more, panting like a dog, licking at his face. They rolled slightly apart.

'Fuck me,' said Rory. 'Who said drinking dulls the senses? I'm sorry if I—'

Jessica smacked his face, quite hard.

'I'll kill you if you say another word. I'm sick to death of men who want to prove something. I shouldn't say this, because you'll just get swollen headed. That was the best fuck of my life. Bar none.'

Rory lay down on his back, the carpet pricking him rather pleasantly, content not to reply, not believing her, not caring. They lay entangled, breath slowing down, slippy limbs entwined. In a minute, they climbed into the big bed, Jessica having discarded her blue shirt, and cuddled to each other. They turned the light out.

There was something, somewhere, in both their heads, something they had to think about, something strange.

'It was for me as well,' said Rory. 'I think.'

They were drugged with sex. They slept.

* * *

In the morning, Jessica wanted toast and coffee, not more love-making. They rang room service, then she had to push him off like a young puppy.

'I want to do it properly,' he yelled. 'I want to take control, be masterful!'

'Bollocks,' she replied, and slipped out, brown and naked, and whipped into the shower. The bathroom, she noted with relief, had a very noisy extractor fan, it damn near vibrated the outer wall off. Which was good, because she needed the lavatory, and did not know him that well yet. Which was crazy, she reflected as she sat there, after all the things they'd done to each other with their bodies, and the things yet to be done.

She got back in the bed wet through, and sat up brazenly as the young girl brought the tray in. She crunched through toast and marmalade while Rory had a shower, then said they had to hurry down to breakfast, she'd need the bulk to make sure a hangover did not develop from the great variety of booze they'd sunk the night before. In the breakfast room, wet ringletty hair dripping on the tablecloth, she read out headlines from the Galway papers that caught her fancy, and earned some dirty looks. The locals thought she was a stuck-up bitch from Belfast, which she played up to the hilt, and the other guests – foreigners, mostly Dutch and Germans by their collar sizes – were taken by her vivacity, and the calm indulgence of the quiet, handsome man opposite her, who said little, smiled a lot, and ordered a second full fried breakfast in a way that had the waitress fit to melt into his arms. As they walked to the hotel car park across the road, two young art student types, thin girls with long black hair and western eyes, stopped and asked him if he could help them work their camera, they were out on an assignment and it wouldn't go at all, and Rory fiddled something on the side and gave it back and said: 'That should be it now, the poor ould thing should be in a museum', and as they went away looked back at him, and back again. 'They love you,' said Jessica, with delight. 'Rory, they *adore* you, you should stay here forever and pack me off back home!' And they put their arms around each other, and they hugged.

For the moment, though, he had to pack her off alone, to do the business that he'd come for. Galway City is quite small, but your man lived just outside, so he took the BMW. He dropped Jessica off at the harbour, because it was so beautiful and there was that little bar if she should get fractious.

'I'll only be an hour or so,' he said. 'I bet you thought I was lying about the work to do, and all? I'm not entirely a playboy, and I'm better than Tom Holdfast at some of the things we have to do. They wouldn't like him too well down here, he's too damn dry for them.'

'From what you tell me of the EC grants, he's too damned honest,' Jessica laughed. 'I suppose it's more Catholic wheels and deals, more wee green patriot doings?'

'Ach, you're a racist just like all your sort,' Rory replied. 'Just that you've got such lovely thighs and things! It's impossible to do business in this land completely straight, that's one thing the Brit government and the IRA have achieved between them. The criminal economy. You ask your daddy, he'll be a part of it as well, he'll be in the Brotherhood.'

'What Brotherhood? What, with you Taig businessmen?'

Rory stared at her, to see if she was joking. She was not.

'No,' he said. 'No, we're not in the Brotherhood.'

There was silence for a moment. A gulf had opened up between them.

Jessica said: 'If you mean that old guff about the Orangemen. If you still think there's some sort of secret ... Rory, that's all old boots, surely you don't think that?'

On the quay at Galway, with the warm wind breathing through the open windows, something cooled them. They both wanted, suddenly, to make it go away. Jessica, seat belt off, leaned across Rory's chest, drove her head into his neck and face, embraced him.

'Bloody nonsense!' she said. 'It's bloody rubbish, all of it! I love this country, all of it, and so do you! You don't think it's dying of corruption, do you, you don't believe the "criminal economy"!'

Smelling her damp hair, her stomach laid across his loins, Rory closed his eyes and believed in her, the pair of them, the breeze off Galway Bay.

'Have you seen the time?' he said. 'If I want to miss a pauper's grave I'll have to go.'

They went home via Connemara, because they wanted to, and despite the fact it would make her late to pick up Martin Parr at Aldergrove (perhaps because of that). They stopped at a small bar where everybody spoke Irish, which made Jessica feel very odd, as if she had wandered to a very foreign country, then drove out along the switchback road laid on the bog, through soil so thin and bitter that the white stone bones of Ireland protruded everywhere, mocking the tiny ancient farmsteads where generations had failed even to subsist. At Ballyconneely, with the Twelve Pins at their backs, they went down a track and faced the black Atlantic, left the low-slung car and scrambled out along the headland until they found, amazingly, a concrete pillbox, a relic of the war in which, surely, the Free State had been a neutral? They were high on a tumbling cliff, not the lonely strand of Rory's dream, but they wanted to make love. The trouble was, the clouds were piling in, the breeze was stronger, it was beginning to spatter down with rain.

'Inside!' said Jessica, grabbing him by the hand. 'Now that would really be a first!'

'It'll be full of shit and newspaper. This is where the tourists go, whenever they're caught short.'

'Surely it's too far out? It's only lunatics like us would make it this far.'

Apparently, Jessica was right. The earth floor was clear of everything, the place fresh from the constant winds.

'Not even any writing on the wall,' said Rory. 'So this was not the ancient site of Paddy Belshazzar's famous feast!'

'Have you got a felt-tip?' said Jessica. 'We ought to put something!'

'You're a vandal! This is the next coast to America!'

But Jessica, kicking round the floor, found a sharp piece of broken concrete. With the point, she scratched MUFC into the wall, in six-inch letters.

'You're cracked,' said Rory. 'Are you a fan?'

'No. You see it everywhere. I've even seen it on a Finnish bus-shelter. It's traditional.'

'It's nuts like you that put it there. Put it down, Jessica. Come here, now. Come here.'

They took each other's clothes off more slowly this time, and examined each other's bodies in more detail. Jessica was besotted with his crooked organ, and Rory discovered two moles inside her fine, rich pubic hair he claimed for the Pope in Rome. He apologised in advance if he should be too expert, but Jessica conceded graciously she had nothing against technique *per se*, it just got in the way of animal passion sometimes. After starting in the pillbox, they moved out into the rain on the grounds that they were Irish, and came wonderfully just as a shaft of sun broke through and warmed them, too poetical, too symbolic, too fucking marvellous for words, crooned Jessica.

'I knew you'd be great at it,' she carried on, whispering despite the mighty desolation in which they lay. 'I could tell by looking at you, I just knew.'

'It's not me, it's the place,' he said. 'D'you know, Jessica, it's impossible to do it badly on the coast of Ireland. Next time, we go south, OK? We'll make a trip of it. Better, we'll do the circuit, we'll fuck our way round the whole of it, we'll circumnavigate.'

'Jesus. How long do you think that would take? We'd be in wheelchairs. Walking frames.'

He got up on one elbow.

'Walking frames. Artificial limbs. Next – the Cork Leg! We'll do the south-east corner!'

'Ach, you're a fool. Ah Christ, Rory, we must do this again.'

The sun was back now with a vengeance. Steam rose from the scant grass they lay on, from their bodies and from the concrete of the pillbox. His face clouded, slightly.

'Was that in any doubt? Of course we're going to do it again. What's to stop us?'

Jessica thought of Parr. He had packed his dinner jacket. The ghost was back across her grave, in boots.

'You're never telling me it's because I'm a Tim?' he said. That made her laugh.

'Don't be ridiculous!' The laughter died. 'You know. You've got a girlfriend, too.'

Rory was shut up. He flopped back onto the wet ground. But the Wee Green Patriot could be sorted out. Would have to be.

'There's nothing else?' he said. 'No other reason? It's just your secret service man, is it?'

'My what?'

'Your man across the water. The one you might get married to, by default. He sounds like an agent to me. Joke, joke.'

She smiled, without great enthusiasm.

'He'd be more exciting if he was, maybe.' She sighed. 'Do you want to go with me again? Honestly?'

He sat up, scratched his naked chest.

'Nah, not really. Shut your mouth, Jessica, be serious!'

She put her arms around his neck, and rested her face on his shoulder, her eyes tight closed.

Be serious . . .

TEN

It was not far from Moira roundabout to Aldergrove, a half an hour or so, but by the time Rory dropped her at her car, Jessica Roberts had made up her mind. She would have been some forty minutes late, and as she had no intention of ringing home to leave a message, Parr would be in a quandary. She tried to picture him getting flustered, but conceded bitterly that it was not possible. He would wait for an hour or so, reading a newspaper or catching up on paperwork, then he would go to the McCausland counter and hire a car. They knew him at McCausland's, and would treat him reverentially. He took their biggest manual model, and he tipped at both ends, the ideal customer. If she was quick she could be at Holywood before him, to change and have a bath. To wash the smell and feel of Rory off her.

As she buzzed along the M1 back into town, Jessica's resentment grew to flame heat. She could picture him so clearly, sitting waiting at the airport, that she ground her teeth at one point, made spitting noises. At other times baffled amusement gripped her, at this bizarre reaction. What had she done, after all, that had changed things so very much? She'd had a wondrous time with another man, a time that filled her with remembered textures and sensations, that would have left her smiling now if Parr had not become so damned intrusive. It was not unique though, was it? She was going on as if she loved the fucking man, not just the fucking! And that was not so, surely, it wasn't feasible, it was ridiculous?

'Jessica, Jessica,' she told herself. 'Come on now, pull yourself together. It's just the novelty of the left-hand thread. It's just the doggy smile. It's just . . . oh Jessica, what are you *thinking* of?'

If I did love him, she thought more soberly, he'd be the first one that I have, maybe. She felt her mind draw back from that proposition. But how were you meant to know? Was there a formula? She remembered Karen saying something once (But was it Karen? About Tony? It seemed unlikely): 'When I'm with him, it's like a light goes on inside my head. When he goes, it switches off.' She thought of Rory's hand on her bare stomach, she thought of the two art students with their camera, she saw two brimming glasses of Beamish in the dockside bar, and the light came on. Oh shit, she thought.

Then: Stupidity! Utter and complete stupidity! It was the aftermath of lust, mixed up with tiredness, and too much booze. It's the hangover from twenty-four hours of daft behaviour. The afterglow of good food and sex and fun. He's a good-looking man, and he makes me laugh, and he screws like the angel of light. Love's got nothing at all to do with it, love's a stupid joke, God, how he'd laugh at me. Or run a bloody mile, more like. No – how he'd laugh.

When she swung into the leafy driveway at Cultra, she was relieved to find no other vehicle there. No alien car, no McCausland. She closed her door quietly, regretting not leaving the Polo on the road, and tried to sneak through the back way to her room. No chance. Her mother called her from the kitchen, then appeared, wiping her hands upon her apron.

'Jessica? Where in heaven's name have you been? I wish you'd ring in when you're staying out all night, you know you've said you will.'

'Sorry, Ma. It was the driving. I had a few too many.'

'Where were you?'

Jessica had not even thought. She screwed her eyes up. Her brain was tired.

'You won't believe me, I've forgotten. Just for the

moment. Nowhere exciting. A party, over near Newry. Belleeks, that was it.'

She said it because Rory was in her mind, and he had told her he lived not many miles from Belleeks, at a little crossroads in the lower hills. She regretted saying it, obscurely.

'In Armagh?' said her mother, as if she disapproved. 'Oh well. Martin's rung. From the airport. He said he'd got a car, not to pick him up. Wasn't that a little rude of you?'

Jessica was tempted to be obscene, but fought it back.

'He's a big boy now,' she said. 'I'm going for a shower.'

'Jessica.' Her mother's voice was sharp. 'Martin has come especially, you know. Your daddy's giving up important business. This is meant to be something special.'

Jessica bit her lip. She knew now where the hot resentment came from. She knew the trouble.

'Sorry,' she said. 'Yes, I know. But honestly – I'd better have that shower, hadn't I?'

'You see,' said Mrs Roberts. Then let it go, on a fading smile. 'Oh go on, then. But darling – do buck up, eh?'

'I'll be all right,' said Jessica.

It was fear.

There were messages awaiting Rory Collins when he got home, and his mother gave them to him with little interest. His mother was a strange, fey woman who had become odder since her husband's death. She had always been touched with religion, but as Rory had grown out of boyhood into his teens, she had been content to let him follow down his father's road to politely concealed indifference. Rory still went occasionally to Mass with her, and sometimes, as a kind of acknowledgement of how different he was from Michael, she would talk to him about the Church, and its importance in their lives. Her bitterness about her husband she kept well hidden, only letting the sharp edges show sometimes when Rory would be drunk and stupid. She allowed no liquor in the house, of any sort, and genuinely hated it. They were quietly fond of each other, and in the bungalow Rory went on often in a way his friends would have been surprised by, a TV and slippers man, or sharing the crossword with his Mam.

'Rosie has rung twice,' she said. 'I told her you were across on business, but she seemed impatient. Is it serious with that one, Rory? She's a firebrand.'

'Away with you!' joked Rory. 'Keep your meddling nose out of my sex life, mother!'

Mrs Collins smiled an uncertain smile. Rory had decided early to make a story out of sex, to lift it from the dark and violent mystery that he suspected had lain between his parents. He wondered if she confessed about the things he hinted at. He would not, indeed!

'She said to ring as soon as you got back. I told her I would stand over you, but nothing guaranteed.'

'Good. I might toss her a crumb. Mallachy?'

'Of course. He said he knew what you were up to and I would lock the door against you if I so much as guessed the half of it. I said I wouldn't ask.'

Rory made a kissing gesture with his lips.

'Very wise. Now listen, I need an hour's kip and a bath, so I'll settle for the bath. First I'd better speak to Tom. I had some success in Galway City. You'll have your mink stole yet.'

'Rosie said it was very urgent.'

He was on his way out.

'They're so impatient, these young girls. If only they knew what hot lust leads to for a woman.'

'Amen to that,' said Mrs Collins.

Tom Holdfast was sitting in his office before a computer screen. He had a stillness, as if he might be stone, or stuffed, or dead. Rory could see him through the open door as he crossed from the bungalow, through the yard of machinery and tractors, and into the business block. Holdfast heard him enter, but did not move, or speak. Rory felt his banter slip away. He was a desiccated stick, Tom Holdfast.

'Tom,' he said. 'I clinched it with your man. He wanted five per cent, we settled it for three point seven five. Don't tell me I did wrong?'

Tom Holdfast turned slowly in his chair, his finger still resting on the button which he seemed so loath to irrevocably press. He had a very Irish face, although he was a Protestant, pale reddened skin, white hair, hooded watchful eyes of green-flecked hazel. He did not smile.

'I expected four. Well done. The exchange rate's going our way too, it makes a change these days. If we order it in punts today and blast it through we'll save another point oh three. Massey's were on from Canada about those gear chains. They'll replace them free of charge, the lot. I have a buyer, too, for some silage. Is that a possibility?'

'Oh God,' said Rory. 'I hadn't thought of that.'

Holdfast swung back to his computer and pressed the button. The machine began to whirr.

'You'll maybe have to pay a man to do it, then,' he said. 'Now wouldn't that be an expensive pity?'

'It would,' said Rory. 'I'll try and make some time. I'll try and get some mates to help out for the crack.'

He went into the yard, yawning. The farm at Hackballs Cross had been neglected since the sun came out. He'd been off having fun too much. It would be great to take Jessica, to cut the grass with her, drink champagne in his little hidey-hole, make love. He wondered if she could drive a tractor. Rosie could. He dismissed that thought, impatiently. It would be great crack to teach her, on the Zetor.

He called out to Tom Holdfast: 'I've got a few hundred

in it, Tom. I'll do me sums. If I cannot make the time myself it might still be worth paying Dessie Clancy and his lad.'

Holdfast did not bother to reply.

Thinking of Jessica, Rory walked back to the bungalow. She had told him how Karen had gone half stupid over Mallachy, when it had been just a one-night stand, a one-night stand that did not, in the event, come off. Well, he'd had his one-night stand with Jessica, and it had gutted him, he knew how Karen felt. Jesus, maybe it was something in the water! He looked at his watch. Only about an hour since he'd left her. Jesus, he began to get a hard-on at the thought! They hadn't made an arrangement to meet, even, she had visitors coming for the night, official ones to see her father, she had to help him 'entertain', she'd told him not to phone at all. He thought of Rosie. He'd better get it over with. He tried to think of screwing her, but could not. It must be something in the water . . .

The house repeater bell began to ring, a different tone from the repeater on the business block. It stopped, his mother appearing in the window seconds later, gesturing to him. It was Rosie.

'Hi,' he said. 'I was just on my way to call you. How's it going?'

Rosie had a plan. The girls were going to a concert, so the house was hers that evening. She would get some Dublin Bay prawns and tons of garlic, if he could bring some great wine or other? Just the two of them, it would be wonderful. Oh shit, thought Rory Collins.

'Oh shit,' he said. 'I've just been on to Mallachy. He rang while I was reaching for the phone. I've arranged to pick him up.'

'Well unarrange it.' Her voice was steely.

'I'll try. He was on his way out.' It sounded implausible, even to him. He searched for inspiration. 'We've got to talk, he's . . . a . . . Look, we'll probably have to see him later, for a drink, OK?'

'Are youse trying to tell me something, Rory?'

'I'll ring him up. If I'm quick I'll catch him. Shit, I'm sorry about this. What concert are they going to?'

'Piss off,' said Rosie. She put the phone down.

He dialled Mallachy immediately, in case she should pre-empt him. Mallachy laughed like a drain.

'So I was right,' he said. 'You've been off screwing the rich-bitch. One word to the Wee Green P, old son, and you're dead meat. What's it worth?'

The details fixed, Rory rang Rosie back. He'd put off Mallachy until nine o'clock, he said. They were set for the garlic and the prawns, if they made it quick. He managed to sound quite hurt when she informed him coldly that she'd changed her mind.

'Ach well,' he said. 'A burger'll be fine by me. That way you get to save your cash.'

He was smiling as he sank into his bath.

Parr was smiling when at last he greeted Jessica, his usual rather wolfish smile. She had showered and put on a tracksuit, having been called down to help in the kitchen before getting into something more elegant. She had tried to curb it, but her tongue had been like acid. She had nagged at her mother for insisting on cooking everything herself, although she always did it, however formal the occasion or long the guest list, she had gone on and on until Mrs Roberts had snapped back in her turn, furiously. Given that the evening was meant to be so special, so significant, they could hardly have got off to a worse start, but Jessica refused to compromise. The whole thing stank, she said, the so-called surprise element was patronising, she was being treated like a child. Mrs Roberts advised her to mend her temper before her daddy came home, and asked what Parr would think if he caught her like a toddler in a tantrum. It was at this point that he turned into the drive.

'There,' hissed Mrs Roberts. 'Oh Jessica, what's got into you! For God's sake get that scowl off your face.'

She went to open the door herself, drying her hands on a tea-cloth. Parr, in grey slacks and sports jacket, kissed her on the cheek and came into the kitchen. The wolfish smile for Jessica.

'Darling,' he said. 'You do look beautiful when you're angry. Was it *very* difficult to let me down completely?'

He laughed, showing his white, sharp teeth, pleased with his joke. Jessica would not respond.

Mrs Roberts said ruefully: 'She's in a foul mood, Martin. If I were you . . . '

'Oh shut up, mother,' said Jessica. 'Parr, go and get a drink, or something. I'm sorry I wasn't there. I got detained.'

'In fact, a bonus,' he replied. He was in supreme good humour. 'I went down to the harbour airport without your beady eye on me. Useful.'

'The airport? But you've just got off a plane.'

'Something to pick up. Air freight. Not big, but quite significant. It's in the boot.'

Jessica caught a secret smile flitting between them. Inside her chest, she felt her heart grow heavier. It was their complicity, the suffocating weight of their complicity.

There was a realisation swelling in her, that her ideas of easy extrication were insane. No snap of the fingers was going to break this spell, her complacency and her inertia had locked her deep into the circle of assumptions. Why had she thought she could just walk away?

A picture slipped into her mind, inconsequentially, a vanload of religious freaks. Ulster Still Needs Jesus. Ulster needs a fucking break, Rory had added.

Oh God, and so did she . . .

ELEVEN

After six o'clock, when the cheap rate had started, Karen King let herself out of the side door of Aunt Jane's bungalow and walked the quarter of a mile to the public call box. There were two reasons not to use the phone at home – the cost to a generous woman living on a widow's pension, and the impossibility of talking in the open-plan downstairs without being overheard. She'd done it the night before when she'd tried to get hold of Jessica, but Aunt Jane had turned the radio up so loudly (to make it nice and private for her niece) that she'd hardly been able to decipher Mrs Roberts' apology for her daughter's absence. Tonight, Karen wanted to talk to Tony. The brevity forced on her by a pay telephone might possibly be quite useful.

The evening had turned fine in the past hour or so, although there were still dark clouds massed in the west, over where Ireland lay, but Karen had spent a useful day revising, and felt virtuous. As she fed coins into the machine, the irony of that struck her. Throughout the revising, to her surprise and her annoyance, Mallachy had obtruded. She had found herself, at one stage, lightly stroking the back of her hand across her breast, and had jumped with guilt. She would forget him, she had forgotten him, what the hell was going on?

Tony's voice, when it came through without a crackle, brought a reassuring flood of gladness.

'Phew,' she said, quite unaffectedly, 'it's nice to hear you, mate! Whose stupid idea was this separation, anyway?'

Tony was a Mancunian, a large stodgy boy a cut below

her, in her mother's 'humble opinion'. He had thought she needed a holiday while he was working to get some scratch together, although he had studying to do as well. He had suggested she take up Jessica's constant offer, considered she could do her revision on the beach or wherever, had smiled comfortably at her half-serious suggestion that Jessica might 'lead her astray', or at least have a good go at it. His first question was about the time she was having, his first statement that the cat – and he – were doing fine. Karen was all at once extremely pleased that she'd done nothing terrible with Mallachy. Well, hardly anything . . .

'Only another week,' she said. 'I miss you, Tony love. It's pretty boring here and I've only been at Auntie Jane's just over a day. Still, it makes a change after Jessica's. She's as mad as ever.'

'She would be. What's the latest?'

Karen limned it in, surprised at how easily she added lurid details. 'Balladic archetypes' sprang to her mind – a good phrase, she'd try to work it in somewhere when she got back to university. Wild black-haired boys and women who should be untouchable. To bring it down to earth, she ended with a pet joke phrase of theirs – 'tears before bedtime!'

'Bloody 'ell, it sounds like it,' said Tony. 'Romeo and Juliet, without the poetry. Typical Jessica.'

Karen barked with laughter.

'She'd murder you!' she told him. 'She hates the way everyone goes on in England. I'll tell you, she'll marry anyone she wants to. Not that her mum and dad would mind, they're lovely. It's just not like we think it is, it's completely different. Auntie Jane kept going on about the violence. She kept examining me for bullet wounds, I think. She expected my clothes to be bloodstained!'

Her money was starting to run out. She regretted, now, that she'd brought so little.

'I'll have to hurry, love,' she said. 'This thing eats cash.'

94

'I wouldn't mind eating you,' said Tony. 'You were all right there, were you? Honestly?'

'I did ring twice. I was only a hundred and twenty miles from Manchester.'

'But that was in another country.'

'And besides, the wench is dead! I'm running out! I'll ring you again! I love you!'

'I love you t—'

Outside the phone box, she shivered in the breeze. The clouds out to the west were thickening.

That night, Jessica Roberts found the ritual element she had always accepted in her high home life hard to bear. She dressed for dinner in a plain dark dress, then stared for ages in the full-length mirror in her bedroom, hating herself. She was the last down to the dining room, where the first course, a cold soup, was already laid. Her mother also favoured a small black number, while her father and Martin Parr were like twins, except for the differences in size and weight. Once, she supposed, she must have been impressed by formal evening wear on good male bodies, but now it annoyed her. Her father was a big man, broad-shouldered and stout with an important stomach, and Parr was strong and wiry, like a bundle of whips with an urbane face. But in their dinner clothes, they were twins. All three were sipping sherry, and her father handed one to her.

'You look lovely, darling,' he said. 'Your mummy says you had a mood. No more of that, eh? We're going to have a wonderful evening.'

'Of course,' replied Jessica. 'It was probably a drink I needed. I am my father's daughter.'

Parr, as ever, was the heart of social nicety. Ever since he had known her parents, he had had them in the palms of both his hands. At first it had amused her, because his Englishness could have stood out like a sore thumb, could have made them, indeed, appear inferior in some subtle way, less smooth, less cultured, provincial. Now even this annoyed her, the way her father toned down some of the roughness of his idiom, her mother increased the Holywood Hampstead in her voice. The thin, handsome face, grey-eyed and intelligent, no longer struck attractive as he made his small talk. The sense of dread within her grew alarmingly.

At table, for the first course, the three of them worked on her as if consciously. There was something up with her, something lacking in her mood, which needed patching, turning round. In the kitchen, preparing to bring in the meat and vegetables, her mother almost sniped at her, but pulled up just in time.

'Darling,' she said. 'You must try, for your daddy's sake. I know you're nervous, but try not to be. We all love you, here.'

Jessica, expecting a sharp dig as the tone had initially indicated, was put out, then relieved. She had been known to storm off sometimes, to take violent umbrage and depart. But she could not, really, let that happen tonight. This was a Big Occasion.

After the main course but before the pudding, her parents had decided that they could not afford to wait forever for the sunshine to break through. Things had improved — Jessica had been seen to laugh twice, and her hands around her knife and fork were less white-knuckled — but there was no guarantee they would go on improving. It was noticeable, among other things, that she was drinking faster than anybody else. Samuel Roberts, judging the moment to be ripe, rapped on the table with a silver spoon.

'Jessica,' he said. 'You're not stupid, and neither are we, although you might be doubting it at the moment. You know something's going on, we have a little surprise set up for you, and I think the time has come to let the cat out of the bag. Martin, I have to tell you, warned me you might take it hardly, done this way, and Martin's always right, damn him! But I know you'll forgive me, so it doesn't matter anyway!'

Martin smiled, Mrs Roberts chuckled, Samuel Roberts beamed. Jessica's mouth went dry, her hand reached automatically for her glass.

'Jessica,' said her mother. Jessica swallowed a big swallow, notwithstanding.

Martin Parr took over. He leaned back in his chair. He had a slight air of apology.

'This is the craziest thing I've ever heard of,' he said. 'Jessica – before it's all too late – will you marry me?'

'Oh fuck,' said Jessica.

'Jessica!' her mother snapped.

'Well,' said Jessica.

Parr stood. The tension in the room was palpable. He wanted to defuse it.

'I could go down on my knees,' he said. 'We've done it all wrong, but it's not irrevocable, is it? It's the wrong time and the wrong mood, maybe – but not the wrong question?'

'Surely not,' said Mrs Roberts, sounding reassuring. Trying to reassure herself.

'It's our wish,' said Mr Roberts, uncomfortable as hell.

'Our dearest wish,' echoed his wife.

Jessica breathed deeply, trying to get a grip. She was exhausted, she was close to tears or laughter, she was probably getting drunk, topping up on last night's alcohol.

'Give me two minutes.' She shot upright, her chair sliding backwards noisily across the polished floorboards. Her glass went over with a crystal *Ting!* Jesus Christ, she thought, fleeing to the lavatory across the hall. Even Parr can't still be smiling after that! What a disaster!

After five minutes in the lavatory, however, she was ready to return. She had sat on the seat cover, resting her head on the porcelain of the washbasin, licking dry lips and bringing her breathing down. She listened to footsteps in the hall, a muttered conversation. Shortly, she needed a pee, and had one, feeling strangely comforted by the act. The juddering in her ribcage was quieting, the panic dying down. Finally, she rinsed her hands, then dabbed her face with a cold flannel. Somehow, she did not conceive that the nightmare could continue. Somehow, the whole strange incident would have sorted itself out.

They were silent as she walked through the door to the dining room, as if they had a secret. They seemed to stare at her, examining her face minutely for her reaction. Across an easy chair that had been pulled forward, was something off-white and ancient, a cascade of silk and lace. A wedding dress. Jessica's heart rose into her mouth.

'What is it?' she said at last. As if she did not know.

'Oh Jessica!' Her mother almost fluted it, trying to sound pleased.

'It was my mother's,' Parr told her, gravely. 'And hers before that. She had it from another member of the family. It's an heirloom, in a way.'

Samuel Roberts said gruffly: 'It's a piece of tradition. A fine tradition.'

Her mother said: 'The trouble we had in keeping it from you, Jessica. We smuggled it across in a little plane from Blackpool.'

'But it's English!' said Jessica, surprising everybody with the sharpness of her voice. 'You'd never have me marry an Englishman, surely?'

They stared at her in silence. Parr's thin, keen face had narrowed, strangely. He was going bald at the front, she noticed. Had she never noticed it before? He was thirty, older than she was, but not old enough to go bald, surely?

'What are you blethering about?' said Samuel Roberts. 'We don't have any of that nonsense in this house.'

'Martin is a Protestant, dear,' said Mrs Roberts. 'Well, Church of England.'

'Good,' said Jessica. She was panicking, she had lost control, she was almost babbling. 'I'm glad you're not that way inclined, prejudiced, I mean, because I can't marry Parr just now, I'm sorry, Parr. Just now I'm going with a Catholic, who lives down in Armagh.'

Her mother had gone white, instantly. Her father began to turn a deep and dangerous red. Jessica held a chairback, her throat constricted, fearing she would choke.

'Joke,' she croaked. 'That was a joke. Please, Parr – I can't marry you.'

She had rendered him, at last, bereft of speech. She could not isolate his expression, though, because her eyes were swimming.

'But,' her mother said, 'you have got to, Jessica. Think of the sacrifices Daddy's made. Everything we've always . . . the way we've . . . '

'A Catholic?' Her father's sudden boom swept her mother into silence. His eyes were wide open, the pupils fearful black. He refilled his enormous lungs.

Jessica shouted: 'It was a joke, a joke, a joke! You can't just come along one day and tell me who I'll marry! Have you all gone insane? Do you know what year it is, what century? I don't want his mother's wedding dress! I don't want to be part of tradition, least of all that bloody one!'

'You'll shut your mouth, Miss!' roared her father. 'You'll shut your bloody mouth!' He stopped, fortunately, of his own volition. Father and daughter faced each other, breathing jaggedly.

'Jessica,' said Mrs Roberts, in despair. 'You just don't understand. We're not forcing you. We thought you wanted to. We thought . . . the culmination . . . all our dreams . . . '

'And now you're telling me,' Samuel Roberts started. But Martin Parr cut him off. He raised his voice.

'Sam! Jessica's overwrought, I think. Jessica, we'd better talk this over.'

There was a break. Jessica was standing on the polished floor, beside the polished table, in the elegant and lovely room. She was trembling, her face ash white, her eyes lost in dark caverns. Soon she would collapse.

Then anger swept her. Her colour heightened, instantaneously. Her dull eyes flashed.

'What a good idea!' she snapped. 'What a pity someone did not think of that before! But before you get around to it, chew on this: I'll do what I like, when I like, and with whom I like. Have you got that? Daddy? Mother? I'll do *anything* I like!'

As she flew up to her room, she thought her father might have killed her for that speech. But she had got out of the dining room too fast for it to happen. She locked her bedroom door behind her.

TWELVE

Rory Collins – with all the tact at his disposal, as Mallachy admiringly put it – took Rosie to the Amsterdam for their drink. To make his point, he had taken her for a burger, nothing more, and defied her to come on too strong about it. Then they had done a short walk along the Lagan, the mood teetering precariously between rapprochement and a set-to. He blamed it all on business, but could not resist taunting her for expecting him to be at her beck and call, while disapproving that he was rich.

'You bloody socialists are all the same,' he said. 'You hate me because I have the cash, you hate me because I'm not tied to a counter in a shop or slaving down the mines for it. You hate me when I turn up in the sexy German motor, you hate me when I can't turn up at all. You're schizophrenic, so y'are.'

Rosie, although small, could pack a hefty punch. They had some of their best times when they were close to fighting, they had both noticed it. She went for him now, on the grassy river bank, surprising staider strolling couples. Rory ducked and ran.

'It's not because you're loaded that I worry after you,' she shouted. 'It's that I think you're gay! Watch him, mister! He'll feel your arse as he goes by, I know him!'

He ran the faster, and got behind a tree. As she came towards him, he appraised her almost dispassionately, from her beautiful dark features to her nicely bouncing tits. Almost dispassionately. She had tangled brown hair, a small and lively face, a dress of dark red material that clung to her. Her legs were brown and shapely.

Rory jumped out and grabbed her round the waist. Soon they were kissing.

'Ach, you're not bad,' he said. 'For a wee wild Republican. When the revolution comes, will you string me to a lamp post with the rest?'

'By your balls,' she said. 'But only after I've made good use of them!'

'Tonight, Josephine, tonight!'

'Hah! You mean when you've tucked up Mallachy into his bed!'

The row was well over, however, and meeting Mallachy on the corner near his house caused no further friction. Mallachy, remembering the story they'd concocted, gave Rory a piece of paper which contained (he said) a 'list of the addresses', and Rory thanked him for his trouble. Rosie, by now, didn't give a stuff. There'd be a singer in the back room at the Amsterdam tonight, and the crack would be excellent. All she had needed from her man, she had decided, was an indication that he was still keen. Rosie, who had four brothers and six male cousins, very close, distrusted her countrymen more than most women of her age. And that, she reflected sometimes, was saying plenty . . .

They had poured out of the back room in an interval of the singing and were fighting for the bar with empty glasses, when Mallachy dug Rory sharply in the side.

'Fuck sake,' he murmured. 'Is that not Jessica's pushy wee cousin over there?'

Rory looked round quickly, taking in Terence Rigby and his pals, then seeking Rosie. Terence Rigby and his pals were eyeing him and Mallachy with clear intent, and Rosie's presence would have been a great embarrassment. She had gone to join the queue inside the ladies.

'If he blows his mouth off before the Wee GP,' he said, 'I'm for castration. Are you ready for a spot of fisticuffs?'

'Does Paisley piss pure orange?' Mallachy was delighted.

He hadn't had a good old fight for ages. He especially fancied Terence's thin good looks for rearranging.

'Are youse ordering, or just blocking up the bar?' said a smiling, thirsty man. Rory and Mallachy slid aside to give him preference.

Terence and his pals – Nick Day, the short one, Stewart Ross, the fat – found a corridor opening in front of them, on the surge. The bar was packed and noisy, bursting with good nature. Also on the surge, they were quickly face to face with Mallachy and Rory.

'Well well,' said Mallachy. 'The tide flows in and brings the shit. What are you drinking, lads?'

The main room in the Amsterdam is long and narrow. The surge that brought them forward had cut them off. In front the enemy, to their right the crowds at the bar counter, to their left tables and the wall. The door was thirty feet behind them, beyond a mass of people. Stewart Ross's face registered a minor panic. Mallachy had it, instantly.

'Don't shit yourself, son,' he bantered. 'You're among the civilised in this place. If youse keep your nose clean.'

Terence was of sterner stuff. He spoke to Rory.

'Why don't you put a cover on his cage?' he said. 'It's you I've come to talk to.'

Rory felt enormous pressure at his back. Over his shoulder he saw the looming shape of Arthur Dooley, the main singer of the group they'd been listening to. He was about six feet, went eighteen stone at least. He was a quiet man, they said, with black greasy hair and beard, a voice like rough-crushed granite when he sang. His enormous arm went over Rory's head, the empty pint pot hanging in the smoke above the counter. Beneath his armpit, at the same moment, Rory glimpsed Rosie returning from the ladies.

'Look,' he said, to Terence. 'I don't know what you think your argument with me is, but forget it. If you want to talk it over anytime, we'll arrange to meet.'

103

The little fat man, courage apparently returning, leered.

'Christ, Terence. He'll be hitting you with his Filofax in a wee minute.'

'I've left it in the BMW,' said Rory, the humour directed at himself. 'Should we go outside and talk this over? That would be sensible.'

It was a last throw, and it worked in part, helped by the situation. No one in his right mind would want to start a fight in such a place as this. But Rosie was pushing through the roaring crowd, she was only feet away. Terence, at that moment, decided on a bit of harmless menace.

'Listen, Taig,' he said. 'I'm not here to fight, I'm here to save your fucking life. Lay a finger on my cousin Jessica—'

'Go!' shouted Rory, and launched himself at Terence. His pot was in his hand still, it preceded him like the torch of justice.

It occurred to him, in that split second, to let it fall. He did not want blood, at any price. But in the same split second something like an iron band clamped round his waist, squeezing the breath from him and bringing him to a dead stop. Another band encircled him from the left, two massive arms had him from behind, his feet were lifted from the ground. Terence's face went from being startled by his attack to astonishment, then might have cracked into a smile. Mallachy, however, unfettered by the arms of Arthur Dooley, hurled his glass, which caught Terence in the face, just above the eye, and broke. A piece winged off and sliced a gash in Nick Day's cheek, while Stewart Ross, diving sideways, pushed a man into the table that he sat at, dislodging drinks into his girlfriend's lap.

'Bastards!' screeched Terence Rigby, his hand across his eye. Stewart Ross, pushed backwards by the man that he had knocked, rammed Terence into a gaggle at the bar. Nick Day, blinking blood, received a push that could have been for anybody, and went onto his knees.

Rory, still crushed, his face warmed by the flavoured breath of Arthur Dooley, was drawn backwards from the fray, inexorably. The Southern lilt, all broken glass and deep concern for human nature, murmured sadly in his ear: 'You're savages up here, you're just like savages.' The gigantic man turned him slowly, against the tide of people pressing to the epicentre, and planted him squarely on his feet. Behind him the noise was changing, rising, as the fight wound up to pressure. Before him was the face of Rosie.

'Jessica,' she said, her eyes like diamonds. 'So who's this Jessica?'

Rory, jammed sideways as Arthur Dooley walked back into the action like King Kong, managed to become separated for a while.

The fight was not a long or bloody one. There was no space to get a swing, for starters, and the mood was all wrong, anyway. Everyone had come for a good time, and they did not want it spoiling by some wildmen. Arthur Dooley's presence deterred the opportunists, and Mallachy was content to watch Terence and his sidekicks receive the odd punch as they were passed and bundled backwards to the door. Rather than following, he plunged into the passageway between the bars, seeking his mate. He was well satisfied – he'd drawn blood and not received a blow.

'Got the bastards!' he said triumphantly. 'What's with that skinny-gutted shitbag, anyway? Has he got some claim on Jessica, or something?'

'Tssch!' went Rory, explosively. Too late, Mallachy located Rosie, thin-lipped with anger, jammed against a wall. She came at them like a canoeist, breasting white water.

'Oh God,' muttered Mallachy.

'Rosie, where you going?' said Rory, seizing her arm as she powered past. She tried to shake it off.

'To find out who is Jessica,' she spat. 'He'll tell me, even if you won't, shite.'

He gripped more tightly.

'I'll tell you, there's no need for this, I'll bloody tell you.'

The big feller had struck up the opening chords of his set, the last one of the evening. The noise in the Amsterdam was settling to a pleasant background roar.

'You better bloody had,' she said.

Mallachy said, hopefully: 'Would youse want that other drink? My shout.'

'You're walking home,' said Rosie. 'We're off.'

'Is that wise, just at the moment?' He made a face at Rory. 'Someone could be waiting outside the door.'

It was a thought, but Rosie was already on her way, freed by Rory. The men followed at a small distance.

'Next time we'll kill the twat,' said Rory, quietly. 'He was in that car down on the promenade. He told Jessica you're in the IRA.'

'You *what*!'

'You heard. If I survive the Wee Green Patriot, we'll go for him.'

Rosie, in the doorway, was surveying them sarcastically.

'Should I go first, in case there's trouble? Mallachy, you are *not* invited.'

The road outside was clear. Rosie stamped ahead of Rory the two streets to where they'd left the car. For an instant, he wondered why he bothered. Maybe he should take the opportunity . . . but for the moment, that was not the issue. The issue was escaping with his eyes intact, with his skin still on his face. The central locking clunked, they both got in. Rory, letting go his breath, murmured: 'Rosie.'

She cut in on him.

106

'Is she a Protestant? Of course she's a fucking Protestant, a name like Jessica. Who knows this? How big a laughing stock am I?'

'For Christ's sake,' said Rory, angrily. 'If I'd been unfaithful, what matter if it was a Protestant or not? For Christ's sake, Rosie, let's have none of that!'

She went silent. Rory started up the engine and got the vehicle moving. He headed, automatically, towards her home. The traffic was quite heavy. They stopped at a red light.

'We've got to have this out,' she said. Her voice was dull. 'So you haven't been unfaithful, is that what you're saying? We can't go back to mine, the girls could be back any time. You've got to tell me, Rory.'

He set off jerkily. He saw an opportunity and did a screeching U-turn. Horns blasted, headlights blazed.

'I'll go along the coast,' he said. 'I don't know why I'm bothering, you've had this mood on you for days. Three lunatics come causing trouble, and you take their side. I've never bloody heard of Jessica. It was a misunderstanding.'

It was a lie so blatant, it brought out Rosie's anger. She turned on him, screeching and pummelling, but circumscribed by the fact that he was driving. Rory, using this, allowed the car to swing over the white line, invited all the hard lads and the death-wishers to flash and honk and snarl at him. Keep moving, that was the strategy. Keep moving till she burned it out.

In a few minutes they were on a smaller road, with the lough in view. Rosie, having shouted long enough, fell silent. After a while longer, Rory nosed the car onto a patch of spare land. There were a few lorry trailers parked there, a high wire fence along one side, nothing more. He killed the engine.

'Rory,' she said. Her voice was low. 'You'd not betray me, would you? Who is this Jessica? Tell the truth.'

'I will,' he replied, after a tiny pause. 'But first I need a piss.'

Then he did tell her, but he told her lies. He told her he and Mallachy had got involved 'through Mallachy's big mouth' in a late-club row up the Malone Road where some students had been blowing off their mouths over politics and religion, and it had almost come to blows. This Jessica woman – he assumed it must be Jessica, he'd never heard her name for sure until tonight – had been in danger of getting her face poked down her throat, was all. Mallachy had stepped into the breach, and—

'Mallachy!' Rosie interrupted. 'Now I know you're fantasising! Mallachy help a woman?'

'So would I tell you if I'd made it up?' he said. He knew her mood was changing, he could win. He expelled breath, ruefully.

'I knew you'd never believe it,' he went on, 'but it's true. Mallachy steps in, and takes a punch in the mouth. The girl takes a punch as well, and I hit some bastard with a chair. Mayhem. We're barred.'

Rosie was thinking, turning it over in her mind. He waited.

'Where is this club?' she said. 'What club?'

'I told you. Malone Road. The Parrokeet or somesuch, I can't remember. I'll take you there! Now! If you don't believe me?'

He reached for the ignition key, but Rosie stayed his hand. She was quiet.

'Mallachy had another brush with him later, another day,' he said. He was impressed with the quality of his invention. 'That thin-faced feller. He's got this *idée fixe* that Mallachy's a Provie gunman.'

He had hoped for a snort at least for this, but Rosie did not react. Rory pressed it home.

'Wonderful, eh? Mallachy the Mouth! I think he may have planted the idea that I was after her, for badness' sake. You know Mallachy, he never knows when to

108

stop. It's all above board, Rosie. You can check it out. A cock-up. A misunderstanding.'

It was so complicated, he did not understand it himself. Rosie said quietly: 'You're all such liars. All of you.' He thought that called for a reaction.

'Listen, I was up to here with him!' he said, vehemently. 'Why the hell else do you think I went for him? It was getting out of hand, the stupid innuendoes. I'm not lying, Rosie.'

Before she could reply, before she could sort out the details, even, he launched himself on her and stopped her mouth with his. His left arm went round behind her neck, his right snaked up inside the clinging fabric of her dress. She struggled momentarily but not, it seemed, with serious intent. There was spite there, a desire to hurt, but it was not unmixed. She bit the inside of his mouth, and grabbed a handful of his hair and jerked at it. Rory slipped the fingers of his right hand sideways underneath elastic, tangled with her pubic hair. With her free hand, Rosie dexterously rolled the seat knob and fell slowly backwards with Rory spreading over her, repositioning himself with his right leg. She released his hair and put that hand down between them, feeling for his buckle. As they scratched and bit and fought each other, Rory remembered Jessica, and worried about the marks his skin would bear, but he did not worry long. He eased inside Rosie with her pants still on, they rolled around each other like grotesques. By the time they had finished, they had slipped down off the seat, half in front of it, half underneath the dashboard. They lay there gasping, murmuring, Rosie with a piece of his lip still trapped, more gently now, between her teeth.

'Oh Christ, I love you, cunt,' she said.

'Yours too,' said Rory.

THIRTEEN

Inevitably, perhaps, Parr and Jessica ended up in bed together at roughly the same time that evening. Their love-making was far more civilised, in one way. There was certainly no biting.

Downstairs, when Jessica had stormed out, her parents had found themselves remarkably constrained by the stranger in their midst. Mrs Roberts, indeed, who felt completely disoriented, clung on absurdly to the reality of Martin Parr. If he had not been there, none of it would have happened, but because he was there, she had to retain control. Before, she had seen him comfortably as part of the family, so to speak. Now he was an audience before whom a front must be maintained. It kept her, very specifically, from breaking down.

'Martin,' she said, almost urbanely, 'you must forgive us for our daughter. That was the most appalling display she's offered up for years. I will quite understand if you want nothing more to do with her.'

Her husband, suffering in his own quite different way, looked at her as if she had gone crazy. It had not occurred to him that Jessica's behaviour might have put a suitor off, more that Parr would want to go and smack her cheeky face, as he would have done. Parr, however, walked rather stiffly to the sideboard and lifted a decanter.

'Oh, I don't think it will come to that, June,' he said. His voice was not noticeably strained, although he felt it must be. 'I wouldn't want to marry her if she wasn't wayward, would I? Will you take a spot of brandy? I think we all need something.'

Samuel Roberts did. He joined Parr at the sideboard and held out a balloon.

'But we haven't had the pudding,' said Mrs Roberts. Despite herself, there was a tremor in her voice. 'What should we do, Martin? Shall we wait for her to come back? To come to her senses?'

Parr poured brandy, glad of the mundane reality of the task. He was in a state of minor shock, as if someone had kicked the chocks away. Roberts gave a brief bark of laughter.

'We might wait a long time!' he said. 'I sometimes wonder if she's any senses to come to.' He threw back the brandy and held out the glass for more. 'God though, what a terror! June, let's forget the rest. We can live without your pudding, just for once. Why don't you clear away while me and Martin have a chat?'

He was assuming that it was a hiccup, only. That was the public stance. Despite his mighty hollowness, Martin Parr added to the edifice.

'June,' he said, 'he's right, let's call it off tonight. I promise you it will all turn out fine. I can tell you I've no intention of letting her slip away from me, and I'll bet my bottom dollar she's not going, either. It was all my fault, I did it wrong, all the psychology.'

She shook her head at that, denying it with vigour. The sense of him as alien was withdrawing.

'No,' she said. 'She's too wild, too headstrong, rude. I feel awfully ashamed.'

I feel sick, thought Martin Parr. He saw the wedding dress, across the chair. It had seemed such an easy, splendid gesture. Was there another man?

'You've nothing to be ashamed of,' he said. 'She wants her head, we'll let her have it. It's not as if she didn't warn me, is it? I should have taken notice.'

June Roberts went and touched the old silk fabric, tears filling her eyes.

'She loved the dress, though, Martin,' she said, hopefully. 'What woman wouldn't? I'll put it away. There were a couple of little bits, small repairs I thought I'd tackle. Perhaps I'll get Jessica to have a go at them, whenever she's calmed down.'

She stood there, looking helpless. There was a question on her lips she could not articulate.

'Martin? You don't think . . . ?'

She wanted to bring up the Catholic, he knew. He did not want to help her. He wanted to bring up the Catholic, as well, with Jessica. In a few moments, Mrs Roberts gave up. She sighed.

'Go you into the drawing room,' she said. 'I'll clear the things away.'

Before Parr knocked on Jessica's bedroom door, he stood outside and listened for a while. There was no noise, no radio, no light, but he could not imagine she would not be waiting for him. He had spent some time alone after talking to her father, had changed his clothes and had a shower, trying to clear his mind of all the stuff of history, the political necessities that ruled their lives, the reasons he must lie. He was coming as a supplicator, with an open pit inside him. Tonight he had expected to become engaged, and everything had collapsed. Most completely, all his certainties.

Staring at the elegant, panelled door, Parr was aware of the difficulties he was facing. He saw himself as cold in many ways, a match for Jessica in terms of their relationship. He knew that people thought them an ideal couple because they lived their mutual lives at arm's length, they complemented each other in self-containment. Now, he feared that he would not be able to express his real feelings. Jessica had exploded publicly, but in private he might not be able to summon up the words. He knew he could not plead.

The talk with Roberts, when it had come to it, had been quite short, and quite constrained. They had sat on opposite sides of the empty fireplace in the drawing room for some time without speaking, each wondering how the subject could be broached. In their dinner jackets, glasses of brandy in their hands, they appeared not unlike an uncle and his nephew in their London club – not much to say to each other, but quite content. Each was aware, in fact, that they had too much to say, rather than too little. Too many things they shared, too many secrets.

In the end, it had been Roberts who had spoken. He was smoking a cigarette – something he rarely did outside his office – and he looked at it almost with distaste.

'If there is a Taig,' he said, 'you realise we'll have to do something about it.'

The sentence seemed to hang in the still air with the thin grey smoke escaping from his lips. It needed no elaboration.

'Yes,' said Martin Parr. 'Of course.'

Inside, he still felt raw. Even by her own weird standards, he thought that Jessica's behaviour had been extraordinary. He still had no idea if the reference had been a joke, as she had almost desperately claimed. If it had been – what a joke indeed, to throw into the waters of an engagement party.

'On the other hand,' said Samuel Roberts, watching him through narrowed eyes, 'she said it was a cod. Do you believe that?'

Martin Parr drank brandy, and thought about betrayal. He realised that the religion of a rival would be the last consideration on Jessica's agenda. Such irony.

'It's possible. Not so much a joke as a rebuke, perhaps. For springing the surprise at all. She told me that she didn't like surprises.' He stopped. 'The upshot was, though, that she turned me down. That's my first consideration, Sam.'

The leather armchair creaked as Roberts shifted his bulk. He was reaching for the decanter. He let his arm drop.

'Of course,' he said. 'The wedding must take place. That's most desirable. If you still wish it, naturally . . .'

Parr curved his lips, a dry acknowledgement.

'Next time I ask we'd better drop the wedding dress, I think,' he said. 'If we should get a second chance, that is. The symbolism was a bit too much for her. The sand-filled sock of history.'

It was a kind of joke, but when their eyes met neither of them smiled. Roberts finished his cigarette, crushing it between broad thumb and finger. He flicked the stub into the fireplace.

'If it comes to it,' he said, 'a sand-filled sock would do as well as anything. I sometimes think a blunt instrument would do some good for her. To make her see what's going on around her. To make her know which side she's on.'

Parr did not reply. He thought of other weapons, and their deployment. He hoped that he would have no need.

When he knocked, Jessica was lying on her bed. She was calm, her breathing even, she had possibly dozed off at some time, a thought she found quite odd. She got off the bed and went to unlock the door without any trepidation, or any other strong emotion. She was tired, tired of the whole thing. She no longer knew what she was sure of.

'Hallo,' said Parr. 'Can I come in?'

'OK,' she replied, moving to one side. 'Do you want a light on?'

She turned it on, blinking at the sudden harshness. She had been meaning for an age to get a dimmer fitted.

'Jessica. First I must apologise. I'm not blaming them, but your mother and father thought it was a good idea, and foolishly I went along with them. I didn't realise it would get up your nose so quickly and so far.'

She sat on the bed. She drew her legs up underneath her, sat cross-legged on the duvet.

'You're lucky you didn't get a bottle smashed across your head,' she said. 'The whole damn trio of you. Look, Parr, what is all this holy shit, this anti-Taig shit? It was new to me, it was a shock.'

She had no shoes on. She began to pick a broken nail on her left foot. She picked up the foot in both her hands and nipped the jagged crescent with her teeth. Parr looked at the exposure of her inner thigh with a dropping sensation. She was talking Taig already. She was not interested in the rest of it. But his voice, his expression, remained detached.

'I think we were all wound up,' he said. 'We were all aware we'd made a total cock-up. There'd been assumptions, hadn't there, made very happily and very easily, and they smashed into the buffers. Your father's not a bigot, you know he isn't, he was lashing out.'

She raised her eyes to his, for the first time. They were bright with anger.

'So what was all this "sacrifice" stuff my mother mentioned? "You've got to marry him, Martin's a Protestant, Martin's Church of England"? What was *that* crap?'

Parr did not reply, let her grow calm once more. Jessica began to pick the other foot.

'I'm telling you the truth,' he said. 'As far as I know it. I imagine it was all part of the same reaction. Somehow — not unnaturally, I'd say — they got it into their heads that you'd be . . . well, I don't want to get my nose punched here, do I? You know what I mean.'

'That I'd jump at the chance of marrying you. That I'd be overjoyed.'

'That sort of thing. Not precisely that, but that sort of thing. Not just them, me too. Your reaction did come as a shock, you know. Rather like putting up a mouth to get a

115

kiss and getting a blow instead. A bucket of iced water in the face. Your father just lost his cool a little, I suppose.' He tried to leaven it with a minor joke. 'To be fair, you were babbling yourself, at one point.'

'But my daddy babbled out the truth.'

Her voice was still hard. She glanced at him, expecting a reaction. Parr did not react. All right, you bastard, thought Jessica.

'Is he in the Brotherhood?' she asked.

The eyebrows moved, at least. He dropped into a wicker chair too casually, among discarded clothes. He did not reply.

'Well?'

'I don't know precisely what you mean.'

Jessica had dredged her memory since Galway City. A part of thinking about Rory Collins. Rory Collins. Jesus, that was miles away, light years! Where was Rory Collins now?

'I think you know quite well. I think it's the sort of thing you'd make damn sure you know, despite you're English. You do business with my daddy, you're very close to him in that way. Is he a member?'

If he admitted nothing, she was done. She had vague memories, only, to build on. She had been out with a young lawyer once, a bumptious and ambitious man, and a boring one. He had told a self-regarding tale of secret arms stores, battle plans for if the Catholics should ever pervert the British government into some dreadful sell-out of the Protestants, a scheme of dirty tricks clandestinely organised by some of the highest in the land. The Brotherhood, perhaps? But she had hardly listened, dismissing it as tedious fantasy.

'I've heard of them,' said Parr, surprisingly. 'I hear lots of things in my line, naturally, I talk to so many people. They're meant to be a bunch so wedded to the mainland, so loyal to the English crown, that they'd even fight against the government if they thought it necessary.

116

It's a myth, it must be. I've certainly never come across any evidence that it exists.'

'What is your line?' asked Jessica. 'The truth, Parr. You've never really told me, have you? You've always been so very vague.'

You've never really asked, thought Martin Parr. You've never really seemed to care.

'At bottom I'm a conduit,' he said. 'My brief is to channel funds from Britain into the Province. There have been plenty of them. Millions. Billions. I prime pumps. Help industry. Oil cogs.'

For a moment it looked as if she'd ask him more, she raised her face to his. So Parr pre-empted her.

'Jessica, I've heard all this stuff before, it's nonsense, honestly, romantic bilge dreamed up by journalists, mainly. If you're talking moonshine, why stop at the Brotherhood? Why not mention the UCCC, the Committee? Why not the inner force, the inner circle? You could mention MI5, you could bring in Dublin elements. Everything that's happened here, everything that's gone wrong, is meant to be a part of some coherent plan – the overthrow of O'Neill, the destruction of the power sharing, the jamming of the Anglo-Irish Agreement works, screwing poor old Peter Brooke. It's not like that, you know it isn't. There are destroyers behind the wings, maybe, but they don't play a jolly little team game, it doesn't work that way. Ireland's complicated.'

Jessica was rocking herself, her arms folded in her lap. She felt desolate.

'Being Irish is complicated,' she said. 'That's true enough. You lot have never understood.'

Self pity now, she thought. He ought to pounce on that. But Parr said carefully: 'A cliché, but probably it's true.' And she thought, Smug, you English are so fucking smug.

'The problem is you think you have the right to try,' she said. She laughed, self pity over. 'The problem is that half of us think we're British anyway, so we can't complain I guess.' She stopped, her mood sagged again. 'Oh Parr, my daddy's not a terrorist, is he?'

'What!'

She stared at him. She could not read his face at all, that was the problem. Was that shock real?

'You know what I mean. If Britain gives us all those billions, to keep us going in spite of all the trouble, might not the cash dry up if we had peace? Might not some businessmen, for instance . . . oh, you know. He's not in the back room somewhere, is he, feeding funds and silent approbation to the gunmen? Somebody's behind them, Parr, the murderers and bombers. Someone's behind them.'

'Your cynicism's breathtaking,' said Parr. 'But that aside, I don't believe you're right. It's a class-based thing, the terrorism, it's not a lot to do with people like us, but I think you're underestimating them. Just because they're brutes doesn't mean they're not capable of doing it themselves, and very well. They're not stupid, however mad they are. They're tying down half the British Army, for God's sake. They're brilliant.'

'I think they have backing, still,' she said. 'I think . . . oh God, Parr, I don't know what I think.'

'Is there a Catholic? A man?'

The question was so sudden that she jumped.

'Of course there's not! Oh Parr, for God's sake! That's not the problem!'

He sat back in the wicker chair, and their eyes joined. A smile had formed on his lips, and it seemed to Jessica to be a rueful one. She felt rueful too. Oh God, the lies, the lies.

'Does it matter?' she asked him.

'It does matter. Jessica, believe me it matters very much. You know I find these things hard to say, but . . . but I felt destroyed. Just by the thought alone. It was horrible.'

118

He came across and sat beside her. He put his arm around her, awkwardly, because her legs were still crossed underneath her. He tried to pull her to him.

'You will marry me, won't you?' he whispered. 'If I ask you properly? I'm sorry for all the nonsense, I'm appallingly ashamed.'

She was ashamed in her turn. That dreadful scene at dinner. It was only now she began to understand her cruelty. To him, it must have seemed ice cold, indifferent. She allowed her head to sink onto his shoulder, knowing that sex would follow, knowing she had no reason to say no. I suppose I will marry him, she thought. It was a question of sanity, or madness.

'I'll think about it,' she said. 'But I make no promises. Any more bullying, any more moral blackmail, Parr . . . '

'Yes,' he said. He nuzzled her neck. 'Jessica . . . '

He moved gently round her, untangled her crossed legs. Jessica lay back, still hard, still seeking softness in her heart.

'This is not to seal a bargain. Any bargain.'

'Of course not.'

She saw his penis as he pulled down his pants, then closed her eyes. It was straight, as it always had been, no bias to the left, no bend at all. Oh Christ, she thought.

'I won't come, Parr,' she said, not unkindly. 'Just do it for yourself for once.'

Alone in her head, as he moved in and out of her, she brooded. There would be nothing in the Rory Collins thing, she knew that, it was just a wild flirtation. There was precious little concrete to it, and she had probably hurt her mother and her father quite enough. She felt Parr coming, trying to be quiet about it as a mark of respect for her lack of interest, she guessed. Ever the gentleman, he soon withdrew. She held his head upon her breast, she patted it. If we were married, she thought, all the lies could stop.

119

When he had gone, she turned the light off and lay back on the bed, still in her dress if not her knickers, staring at the ceiling. She thought of Rory Collins.

Then Rory Collins came. There was a spattering of noise at her window that could only be thrown gravel, although she'd never heard the sound before. She sprang off the bed and reached the window in a swoop of wild excitement. Looking down, she saw him beside a bush, only half concealed, laughing at her face. She was gripped by joy and terror.

She was gripped by something else, a truly strange sensation. Her body opened, she felt things pour from it. All the confusion, all the fears and doubts, all the crushing tension. She felt them pouring from her mind like dirty water down a drain. She felt that she'd been emptied.

At last her madman, surely.

FOURTEEN

It was a scene of joy and terror, it was fraught with danger, it was wild with possibilities. Neither of them, the trouble was, could take it seriously.

'You're mad, you're crazy, you're insane,' hissed Jessica. 'Before God, Collins, if we're found out there's hell to pay. Go!'

Rory, like a boy, drew back his hand and flipped another spray of gravel at her. Jessica had opened the window. Some rattled on the glass, some got her in the face, some spurted into the room. She almost burst, suppressing fear and laughter.

'I'm serious, I'm serious. Rory, everybody's up, they're walking round the house, they'll come out for a breath of air if they don't hear you, even. What do you *want*?'

'What do you think I want, you fool? Your cousin warned me off again, we had a little set-to in the pub, so I thought I'd better come and make me mark.'

'Terence? Oh Jesus. What did he do?'

'Nothing to write home about, forget it. Ach, Jessica, it gave me the excuse! Look, I'm coming up the wall, I'm rising on the lep! The lady in her tower of cold ivory!'

He had assumed a stage-Southern accent. He emerged from the shadow of the bush and scuttled to the wall. He scratched the red brick with his fingernails.

'No creepers! What sort of house is this itself, the way you said your da was rich!'

'Shut up, shut up! Oh Rory, please shut up, they'll hear you!'

There was a note of real anxiety in her voice. She

glanced behind her, as if her door might open. She wished she'd locked it. Rory, picking up the fear, stopped fooling quite so much.

'We'll be all right,' he said. 'Can I come up, though, seriously? There's not even a bloody drainpipe.'

His voice was quieter, but his schemes were just as mad. Jessica, despite her panic, knew she'd have loved him to come up. She remembered what she'd just been doing. Oh God, she'd have to wash, though.

'Of course you can't,' she said. 'I'm not joking, someone will hear us. Please, love.'

Rory considered. He'd have some explaining to do himself, if he took off his trousers. He looked along the house wall, counted lighted rooms. Two below, one above. Lucky they did not have a dog, indeed, but still completely dangerous. He'd had to come, though, after dropping Rosie off. He'd tried to fight it, to stay on the straight and narrow to the M1, but had turned off eastwards like an automaton. A higher power, he had told himself. Lust.

'I've got to talk to you,' he said. It wasn't lust, it must be more than that. 'I suppose it would be stupid to get arrested in the process, but . . . Can you come down, at all?'

Behind her, at the door, she heard a creak. God, if they should come in now!

'Jessica?'

'Sssssh!' It was no longer funny, no longer an adventure. She tried to shush without making a sound. Her head was half turned to the doorway. 'Oh please,' she whispered, in a second. 'Go, Rory.'

Her mother's voice called softly: 'Jessica? Darling, are you awake?'

'Jessica?' he whispered, from below. 'I've been lying to you, we have to talk.'

Jessica leaned half out of the window, waving at him frantically to be silent, her face contorted. Rory, catching a laugh, clapped a hand across his mouth. He put a finger there, solemnly — trust me, schtumm. She swayed her body back inside the room.

Her mother must have gone. Like a wrung cloth, Jessica peered palely from the casement for the last time, she told herself. She had to know the rest.

'Lying? What about?'

'Only the important things. Life, and sex, and rock'n'roll. I want to do the Cork Leg soon, I want to have you here and now, I want to fuck you, Jessica.'

There was another creak outside her bedroom door, perhaps imagined. Her heart was stopping up her throat.

'Lying about what?'

'About the Wee Green Patriot. Among other things. But never mind it now, we have to talk it all through. Tomorrow, can you make? You must.'

The wee green patriot. So Terence must be right! Jessica, somehow, was enthralled as well as horrified — and swept by desire. There *was* something concrete between her and this man, and with the knowledge fear flared inside her, biting, complex fear.

'In the morning,' she said. 'I might be watched though, sort of. Where could we go?'

The face below was almost split in two by smiles.

'I have a place. It's safe. I get lost myself sometimes, it's so hard to get to.'

'Fool. How will I find it?'

'I'll ring you in the morning. I've got some work to do, unfortunately, so it won't be till eleven. Eleven fifteen on the dot, wait for it to pick the phone up. I'll say I'm from the garage if someone else does, about the service. I'll give you the directions, we'll get there separately. OK?'

She swallowed. There was silence in the passageways behind her. She was tempted to go down. She knew it was stupidity.

'OK.'

They gazed at each other like a pair of fools.

'You'd better go,' she said, softly. 'Rory – I'm glad you came.'

'Aye,' he said. 'So am I, too.'

'Goodnight, then.'

'Aye. Goodnight. Jessica?'

'Yes?'

'Ach, to hell,' he said. 'I'll tell you in the morning.'

He bolted. Jessica sat, yearning. She heard a car start up.

I love you too, she told the scented air.

Martin Parr was not a hasty man, but before he went to sleep he made two phone calls. Despite the hour, he got replies immediately, and was transferred up through systems without delay. He acknowledged to himself that he was fishing, really. Jessica's father, like most men in his position in the Province, was watched much of the time, kept an eye on, lightly guarded. In the process, there was a spill-over, inevitably. Jessica swam in and out of the local scene, and would be noticed, if not recorded. Martin Parr had access. He was using it.

The guest room that he had was large and airy, and overlooked a different part of the garden from Jessica's. Parr kept his window open, and while he waited on the line, let the sounds from outside wash his consciousness. Wind noise, mainly, the gentle breeze from off the lough hissing in the trees, the occasional moan of distant engines. Between the calls, he went and hung out of the casement, in shirt and trousers, bare-footed, and breathed the sweet clean air. He thought of Jessica, thought of the love they had just made, and felt his heart go cold. The night had brought him shock and pain, so far. He feared it might end up in deep humiliation.

Parr did not consider himself a jealous man, in any way. When he had taken up with Jessica he had recognised her as a wild Ulster girl, and had respected her for it.

He had respected her lack of interest in what others might have called sexual morality, had respected the fact that she had slept with him and neither offered nor expected anything in return. When it had happened four or five times, and he had, perhaps, begun to feel some stirrings of a more disturbing passion, she had brought him up with a catalogue of the men she had had, and made it clear that – if she wanted it that way – there would be more. Parr, on the spot, had accepted that.

When love had come to him, it had been more difficult. However, he had slowly modified his lack of jealousy into trust. Jessica, after a time, had said she loved him too, and grew quite fascinated by his refusal to bring up the subject of fidelity. Sometimes she hinted at young men, she teased him, but more and more, Parr became convinced that she was faithful – as he was to her – because she loved him. Occasionally she let slip as much: that she went out with other men, enjoyed the crack, but that was all. Odd, he reflected, that now she had been forced to make a straight denial, he had lost his confidence. He drew in another breath of air, and it shuddered in his chest. He closed the window.

The second phone call, like the first, drew him a blank. Jessica had been observed on many occasions, he was told, and with many young men. Of whatever religion, whatever political persuasion, she did not appear to differentiate. But no, she had never been observed doing anything 'noticeable' in any way, she was just a woman going about her life, and apparently enjoying it. Parr put the phone down, and sat on his bed, and thought some more about her. He was relieved. He half contemplated creeping back to her room, trying to communicate something, trying to make things better. What things? For whom? He was not sure.

If there was a man, what would he do? Again, he was not sure. If it was a Catholic? He thought of Samuel

Roberts, of what that would really mean to him. Oh Jesus, there was so much at stake, such ramifications, such things as Jessica could never dream of.

Parr stripped his trousers off, then his pants, and sat contemplating his cock. Small and shrivelled, still a little sticky. Like a walnut, Jessica had once described it, lovingly. He touched it. Poor little walnut.

An idea came to him, and he went and got his Filofax from his briefcase. He looked up a number. Terence Rigby. Just on the off-chance. He looked at his watch. Late.

He left the number by the telephone, and rolled himself into his bed.

That could wait until the morning.

When Rory Collins let himself into the bungalow, his mother was still up. She met him in the hallway, in an old blue dressing gown. She had a cup of something in her hand.

'Egad, ould woman! You've caught me out this time. Is that Horlicks? Can't you sleep or something?'

'Hot milk. I can smell the drink from here. You should take a cup.'

Her face was lined and sour. She should be asleep.

'I've not had much,' he lied. 'With the driving and all that. Seriously – why are you up so late?'

'Tom Holdfast. He was in the office. I must have heard a car door slam, or something.'

Rory narrowed his eyes at her. She could be very vague. It was past one o'clock.

'Tom Holdfast? Are you sure?'

She moved past towards her bedroom door, forcing him aside.

'One of his little meetings. It won't be the last time.'

'Mother?'

She stopped. He sensed that she was angry, obscurely.

'Ach, Rory,' she said, impatiently. 'The men. You know. If you don't know at your age, you should work it out. Or ask.'

He was lost, entirely.

'I am asking,' he said. 'What men?'

She pressed the handle down, pushed her door open.

'Oh, don't ask me,' she said. She entered. The door began to close. 'Don't ask me.'

No point in calling out. He knew his mother. Rory bit his thumb.

FIFTEEN

He had business in the morning, accounting business, and Tom Holdfast was not the sort to let idle chitter-chatter get in the way of that. Rory was late for their appointment, and when he arrived, Holdfast told him dourly to close the door and join him at the biggest table. It was spread with computer paper and piles of accounts, with desktop calculators at both their places, both switched on. He raised his green-flecked eyes to Rory's, assessed his liveliness, the state of his attention. He grunted.

'I hope you didn't overdo it too much last night,' he said. 'We've a lot to get our heads round, Rory. None of it will wait.'

Rory said: 'I'm all right. But how about yourself, Tom? My mother says she saw you here. In the wee small hours. You weren't alone.'

Holdfast, hand on his calculator, raised his eyes again. Slowly, a smile came to his face.

'I'll tell you later. Now, business. That pile on your left, there. Aye, that one. Peter Fogarty, of Killeavy. We'll start with him.'

They worked solidly for nearly two hours, through the bad debts, the underpayments, the cash they themselves owed for plant and lubricants. Holdfast worked quickly, despite he hardly moved, ranging over the spread papers like some sort of croupier. At times he got impatient, if Rory failed to grasp a point, and on several occasions he glossed over figures that Rory raised a query on, assured him it was all in hand, there was nothing he need bother with. Rory, who had been told to trust him by his father, never pressed him.

It was just beyond eleven when they finished, and Rory was well conscious of his need to use the telephone. He was tempted for a moment to leave his questioning till later, till a better time, but Holdfast had his own ideas.

'Well,' he said. He was wearing a ginger sports jacket, and he thrust a couple of ballpoints into the breast pocket. 'So your mummy saw me with the boys, did she? I shan't apologise for waking her, however.'

He was a polite man, invariably correct and pleasant with Mrs Collins, so this was done deliberately to elicit a response. His expression reinforced the view.

'Go on then. Why?' said Rory.

'What were they here for, do you think? Think carefully, now. You don't imagine I was involved in anything that could be detrimental, do you?'

Rory thought.

'If you had been, I guess, she would have told me.'

'But for yourself? What's your opinion, Rory?'

'Me too. I don't think you'd do . . . I don't think you'd do any harm to us. I trust you.'

'So you'd be right and you'd be wrong. I was paying money out, illicitly. Your money. Your mother's money. Mine. I was paying money to the paramilitaries.'

Rory experienced a stab of anger. He leapt instantly to a conclusion.

'Protection money? The cheeky bastards! And my old man a—'

'Michael used to do the same,' said Holdfast. His voice was calm. 'We used to fight about it, when I first knew. You know my opinion of the gunmen, Rory. On either side.'

Rory's expression softened for a moment.

'The loonie two per cent,' he said. 'And Michael?'

'It was his firm, was it not? I wasn't even on the board till later. Michael was romantic, Rory, you know that. Even if he could have turned them down he wouldn't have, in my opinion. He could never see the danger of

129

such things, he could never see the way they'd drive the country down into the stratum of the beasts. When he was dead, it was far too late for me to opt out. A Protestant, indeed. There were some among them would have killed me for the hell of it. The principle, they would have said. We get on all right now.'

Rory digested that.

'Jesus,' he said. 'Hell, Tom, you should have said something. How much do we pay? Is it a big amount?'

'It's not a negligible amount. I can keep it hidden from the Vatman and the revenue. We can handle it.'

They stood in the office, Holdfast resting on the table-top, both lost in thought. Rory did not know how to take the information. He supposed it was all right, but then . . . He supposed it was inevitable.

Tom Holdfast thought about the rest of it. He had not told Rory everything, not by a long shot. Michael Collins had been an active sympathiser who had, he suspected, been well aware of some odd uses that the farm at Hackballs Cross had been put to, and who had, maybe, done more than sympathise. He had agreed to pay the money out, before Michael's death and after it, because they had had an understanding. Which had not included Rory, the gadfly son. But not even Michael had known about the other sum – smaller, but just as regular – that Holdfast had dourly diverted to the fighters on his own side of the great divide. Two per cent insanity could go a long, long way.

'Shit!' said Rory. 'It's eleven thirty-five! I've got to leave you, Tom. There's more to life than filthy commerce.'

He shot off for the bungalow and a private phone. Tom Holdfast sighed, and sat, and called for coffee from Loretta on his intercom. And two digestive biscuits, if she'd please . . .

* * *

Parr, throughout the morning, had been dipping into similarly murky pools, had heard, in fact, the name of Michael Collins mentioned. His first source had been Terence, who had intensified his own investigations after the humiliation at the Amsterdam. Indeed, he and his mates had driven to a house in East Belfast straight from the fracas, to try and tee some pals up for a quick retaliation. It had not materialised, sterner counsels had prevailed, but people had been consulted, people with files and knowledge as well as hatred, and Terence had gone to bed happy in the supposition that he would get revenge, and soon. When Martin Parr called him, at breakfast, he covered his surprise at being asked, and revealed that yes indeed, Jessica had got her own wee Taig — although he had to add, when pressed, that it was not known yet if it was more than an acquaintanceship or a flirtation. He was in awe of Parr, and so was glad to be the bearer of bad news, although the cold voice — demanding detail that he did not have — revealed no hint of anything beyond mild contempt. When asked for names, however, Terence had his triumph.

'I do know his name, as it happens. He goes around with another Taig, a bad wee feller who runs with terrorists, called Mallachy O'Rourke. Jessica's interest is Rory Collins, we're working on him at the moment. All I know for definite is he lives down in Armagh, not so far from Newry, in the hills. We're working on it.'

Parr made no comment. He neither liked nor trusted Terence, a young man full of braggadocio in his view, and there was a certain bitterness in receiving such information from such a source. He doubted it would add up to much, though, just another of her lads, the orange or the green. The terrorism link sounded similarly unlikely.

Terence said: 'If there's any way I can help you out on this?'

Parr grunted.

'I doubt it. But thanks for the offer. Bye, now.'

The name was useful, though – to himself he did not deny it – and as information came in from other places, more reliable, more official, Parr began to be disturbed. By the time he left the Cultra house, a picture was emerging of a young man with definite allegiances. His late father was an IRA supporter, believed to be a money source, believed to have strong cross-border links. There was some doubt – there were many doubts – but circumstantially it was strong. This young man . . . but Parr would not allow a final judgement yet.

Parr was not a hasty man, and he gave himself a lot of space to think in. When he left the house – Jessica had still not come down – he drove in the McCausland car to the heart of Belfast, where he went to an office in a grey, featureless building and followed up the leads. He used the telephone some more, he sat and concentrated. If Rory Collins were an activist, or even if his links with terrorists were palpable, then things were bad indeed. The daughter of Samuel Roberts, quite simply, could not be seen to be involved.

Something occurred to him, and he punched out Terence Rigby's number once again. Terence would not mention his own name to anybody, he was confident of that, but he must be told to say nothing about the rest of it, to anyone. Least of all his cousin Jessica.

He was too late. When at last she snatched up her bedroom phone and found Rory on the end of it, Jessica had already endured a call from Terence. Edgy as a cat on broken glass, she had gone at him like a power-saw, but had failed to silence him entirely. Wee Rory, he had said – he had shocked her with his knowledge of the name – was connected to the terror men, he now had concrete evidence. Tell me it, you lying little shite, she said repeatedly, and was partly reassured by the fact she had him floundering. But although she slammed the phone down in fine style, she was shaken horribly. And when she went down for a cup of tea, her mother mentioned casually that Parr had gone to Belfast, not to England as expected, although she did not know why. What was the matter, she then asked. Why do you look so odd?

'Jessica?' The voice was tentative. 'Can I talk? I'm sorry to be late. The business.'

Jessica drew in a great breath of cool air. She had decided to send this man to hell. His voice filled her with confusion and relief.

'It's all right. I've had a morning of it, too. Rory?'

'That's me.'

Let's call it off, she had been going to say — believing, maybe, she could manage it. She let it hang. She had been thrown by everything, today. Why had Parr not gone back to England? Where was he?

'Nothing. I'll tell you later. Look, this place. Give me directions quickly. I need to see you, I need to talk. Rory, this might not be on, we might have to—'

'Stop! Don't say another word. You'll need a pen and paper. How well do you know the land around Dundalk?'

'Dundalk! That's bloody miles!'

It was where the bars were stiff with wanted men. He had told her that himself.

'A far country. We have the motorway, then take the A1 at Hillsborough. It's sixty miles or so, seventy at most. How fast can you get up to in the green machine? I'll tell you what, meet me at the border and I'll bring you the ways myself. It's not an easy spot to locate, where we're going to. It's near a place called Hackballs Cross, a nothing place, a couple of houses scattered on the map. That's why I like it.'

'Oh God,' she said, distressed. 'What sort of name is that? What lovely little incident does that commemorate in our great history?'

He was taken aback.

133

'Jessica? What's up with you this morning? Look, we need to hurry this along. Will I collect you or do you want directions? It's nearly twelve o'clock.'

She didn't know, she didn't know. She didn't want to see this man again. But why deny it, she was going to.

'We'd need some lunch,' she said. A rearguard response, normality. Rory was severe.

'Jessica. This is my fucking heart you're using as a football. Be serious!'

Be serious. She remembered that. She remembered Connemara. They would have to talk. She would be serious.

'I'll find you in Dundalk,' she said. 'Just in case. Stop at the other side of town on the same road, the Dublin road, I think?'

'It is. The N1. Signs to Drogheda.'

'I can hardly miss your flashy car, can I? Look in your mirror for me. As near two thirty as I can make it.'

'The pea-green incorruptible. I'll be waiting. I'll buy you lunch, you madwoman.'

'Rory?'

'Yes?'

It was Terence Rigby. It was what he'd said.

'Nothing. It'll keep.'

'Jessica?'

'Yes?'

'Just in case of what?'

Martin Parr spoke to Terence Rigby, then to some other men, then rang to speak to Jessica, twenty minutes after she had left. He had thought he would invite her out for lunch, talk to her, try and work things out, assess things. He had thought that that might still achieve something. June Roberts said she'd gone out in the car, saying nothing except that she'd be back in time for cocktails at the Clarkes' as she had promised, a business thing for Samuel. Would Parr be interested? Parr, voice neutral, in a raging calm, declined.

He sat back in the leather office chair and tapped his fingernails. He had felt the knife blade turning in his gut as he had talked, and he acknowledged it. He thought of Rory Collins. Nothing crude or hasty could be done.

Crude or hasty. Parr was not a jealous man, he told himself, but he was at least a human one. Perhaps Jessica had not realised how much trust reposed in her, how confident he had been. Perhaps he had not realised it himself. But if she did not love him, if she was *contemptuous* of all the things they'd had . . . that was unbearable. He sat in the drab office, aching. For his self-esteem and her lost grace. For infidelity.

If that was true, when that was proved, then everything was changed, irrevocably. The hard things would be easy, the matrix would be smashed. The measures to be taken could be pitiless indeed.

He hoped to God that, so far, it had not been physical.

SIXTEEN

At Hackballs Cross that day, it was not. Jessica, when she arrived, was overwhelmed by too many things, lost in too many emotions, to even want to make love. Rory did, but Rory was immensely happy to wait for her, to go along with any whim. She had seen his crazy house, and she had loved it.

The drive from Dundalk was fast and furious, largely because Jessica was late. She had got stuck getting out of Belfast, and got lost trying to take a short cut round the traffic jam. On her way, out of shame that she would mess up the arrangements, she stopped at a small shop and got some fresh rolls and ham, some butter and some tins of Smithwicks bitter. When she finally drew in behind the charcoal BMW on the road to Drogheda, she brandished the plastic bag and gestured – lead me on!

It took a little time, and without the guidance she would never have found it in a million years. The country was green and flat and featureless as they got nearer Hackballs Cross, with high hedges and few signs of human habitation. Rory made left and right turns in quick succession, seemed to go back on himself, seemed at times to be driving blind. Jessica followed closely, watching the stop-lights and the curly hair she caught from time to time around the head restraint on his front seat. The concentration calmed her, soothed the worries that had surfaced on the drive from Belfast to the border. This was a crazy episode, but all was not lost. This man was a Southerner, in his heart, a Southern boy whom she could give up if she had to, whom she could forget. She was hungry, too, healthily starving. Things could not be all that serious.

Finally, Rory turned off a minor road onto a rutted track between high, uncut hedges. He slowed to almost nothing, but still the low-slung car needed guiding around each pothole and over every lump. Jessica dropped back a short way – the Polo handling the terrain without a struggle – and thus was in a position to take the view full-frontally when she rounded the last corner. Involuntarily she stopped the car, almost struck with awe. The BMW, like a crippled beetle, bucked slowly onwards to stop outside the house.

It was extraordinary, this scene, to Jessica – a surreal mixture of opulence and decay. The house was square, and Georgian and magnificent, in a setting of green grass, black gravel and great, mature trees. Except that it was dead as well, long dead, and blind and rotting. It was coloured in cement and grey, its slate roof dull with moss, great jagged lengths of cornice hanging down like broken fingers from its brow. Above the cornices, behind the parapet, the guttering was ablaze with colour, long waving grasses, cornflowers, a trailing rose. At some dark windows, filthy curtains moved in the breeze, lace ends dangled through the grey-crusted, broken panes. And all in a huge square courtyard, gravel, grass and flags, surrounded by tall trees, wild hedges, walls. Beyond it, and to both sides, were farm buildings, red rotting brick, lost in undergrowth.

Rory walked towards her, dressed in jeans and sneakers, a soft yellow shirt. His eyes seemed alive with joy to her, simple joy at her reaction.

'You love it, too,' he said. She nodded, dumbly. 'My great inheritance. My past and future. One day, Miss Roberts, all this could be yours!'

Jessica switched off her engine. Why bother to go farther? She got out and stood beside him, gazing at the house. It was enormous, ten bedrooms perhaps. She listened to the silence, beyond the shushing of the leaves and calls of beasts. It was complete.

'Rory, it's incredible. Is it really yours? What's its history? How long has it been derelict? Is it really from your past?'

'More from yours, I guess.' He made a face. 'Ascendancy. As far as my old man could find out, it was abandoned two generations ago, or more. Maybe you weren't so far out with the name. Hackballs Cross.'

'Oh don't. This fucking country, Rory. Why are we so bad? Oh Rory. I love the fucking place!'

Rory leaned down, reaching through the window of the pea-green car. He came out rustling.

'Tins of beer and sandwiches. Jesus, you're a princess. I've only spirits in the house, and wine. A Smithwicks'll do nicely.'

'Wines and spirits? Tonic, too? And ice! Ach, there's nothing like the primitive life, is there?'

'The ice'll take a little longer. Will I show you? There's a little bed, an'all. Well, quite a big one, actually. Well – nothing short of king-size, if it comes to that! Let's go and try her out!'

A cloud passed over Jessica's face, which puzzled him. He misinterpreted.

'You're not jealous? That it's been used before?'

'No, stupid! It's just that . . . '

He popped a can of beer and thrust it into her hand. He tore a roll open, stuffed it with cut ham and gave her that.

'Invitation withdrawn,' he said. 'Until later, anyway. Come on, Miss, the grand tour. Can you drive a tractor, by the way? I've an awful lot of silage to attend to.'

Outside the courtyard and the kitchen garden, beyond the barns and outhouses, were fields of rolling grass, cut by hedges. Jessica stared about in every direction, but she could see no other buildings, or sign of human life. Like the house, the impression off the landscape was schizophrenic, of richness and desolation equally. The grass rolled in waves, glistening and gleaming as it undulated. It was lonelier than the sea, somehow.

'But it's so vast,' she said. 'Is it all yours? What do you do with it?'

'I cut it and I crush it down. I screw it into the barns and I go mountain climbing with my Zetor. Oh, that's a big wee bastard, you'll love my Zetor, it's cheap, reliable, a monster. We used to sell a few of them. Then,' he added, 'when I've turned it into silage, I sell it. And get the grants. Like a proper Irishman.'

A slice of ham fell from his roll onto the ground. Rory picked it up, blew on it, put it in his mouth.

'Come on,' he said, and took her by the hand. 'I'll show you where it happens. We'll crack the Zetor up. I don't believe you wouldn't want a little go. There's some grass cut in the bottom barn already. We'll go and frighten it.'

The afternoon was slipping away, the afternoon was racing by. Sheltered from the wind, Jessica could feel her face begin to roast, the sun was like a hammer. Rory tore off his shirt, tying the long sleeves round his waist. Jessica had dickered about wearing jeans – doing a Karen, she had mocked herself – but had settled for a button-through with a longish skirt to it. She could have undone the top, let the breezes lick her breasts, but she did not think so. One lick led to another, in her experience, and that was not the idea this afternoon, there were serious things in train. At least, she told herself, that's how I remember it. Somehow, the details had got blurred.

Rory's Zetor was magnificent. He unlocked a padlock into a smallish barn – the key was in the padlock waiting – and got her to help him push the wooden doors back. The thing was gleaming red, bigger than a tractor ought to be in her opinion, with bigger front wheels than expected, and smaller back. It looked more like an animal than a tractor, a long low dangerous thing, crouched forwards with its shoulders hunched. It was clean, even the wheels were clean, as if it were put out on a drive on Sundays and given the old once-over like the family car. Rory patted the bluff bonnet, the Zetor badge, with pride.

'All it needs is two seats and we could go for a jaunt in it. You stand clear, I'll start the bastard up.'

He clambered up behind the long bonnet, onto the padded bucket seat. He bent and pulled a knob or two, turned the key. He gave the thumbs-up like an old-time aviator, grinning.

'Contact!'

After three turns, the engine fired. Black smoke poured out, quickly turned to blue. The smell of diesel, burnt and unburnt, filled the air. Jessica covered her mouth, but Rory breathed it in, as if at Scarborough on the poster.

'Smell the ozone!' he whooped. 'Come up here, me darlin'!'

Infected, mad herself, Jessica ran forward. The metal of the gear-casing vibrated before her eyes, rattling the spanners in an open toolbox. She reached her hand across the big back tyre and gripped Rory's. She put a foot on the machine, where the gear-case joined the engine casing, and her free hand on the steering wheel. As he jerked she launched herself, and stood beside him, his arm around her, his face in her stomach and her breasts.

'Grip on, my lovely woman! Leave go the steering wheel! Away we go!'

The engine barked, a harsh hacking sound, and they rolled out into the sunshine. The metal body jumped and bucketed beneath her on the ruts. Jessica swung, clinging hard to Rory, as they made for another barn. While he jumped down and opened the doors, she gripped the steering wheel, which shook her arms with its fast, rhythmical vibration.

140

'Hold on tight now!' He was back in the seat, having kissed her glancingly on the mouth as he swung down into it. 'If you fall, you'll lose a leg or something. But it's worth it!'

He moved a lever on the gearbox top, then gunned the engine in a lower range. The tractor surged forward, into the dimness. There was an overwhelming smell, dust and grass and malty-sour fermentation. Ahead of them, as her eyes adjusted, Jessica saw a mountain of cut grass, in a high-sided pen affair, a concrete floor-space walled in with wooden planks, thick as railway sleepers. They careered towards it, speeding up the while. Jessica, no idea what was happening, screamed in delighted terror.

As they hit the grass, Rory pressed the accelerator hard down, wrestled with the wide black wheel. The front tyres jerked and bounced as the Zetor bored into the pile and began to climb and crush it. As they reared backwards and ground further up the slope, a wild, sweet smell arose, sweet and rotten, mingling with the blasting smoke from the exhaust. They reared to an alarming angle, the tractor pointing to the roof, the wheels slipping in the juice cascading from the broken stalks. Then they reached the top, the tractor could go no higher, the wheels began to sink. Rory dipped the clutch, banged into reverse, accelerated as he let the pedal jump. As the machine leapt backwards, skittering off the wet green mass, Jessica was nearly thrown into it, over the bonnet, except she grabbed him, screeching, dug in her fingers. When he jammed the brakes on she was better balanced. As he surged ahead once more she was braced, her arm around his neck, their faces close, their shouts a merging roar. 'Hup!' they shouted, and the Zetor hupped, climbing roofwards, six feet off the ground and more, crushing grass beneath its belly, slipping, gripping, shuddering. After five charges, she was riding like a bronco-hand, willing them yet further up the pile, covered, like Rory, in a sheen of sweat and sap. And exhausted.

'No,' she said, as he backed into the sunlight. 'No, I don't want a go. You're crazy, so you are. You can teach me next time, maybe, whenever I come again. I want a gin and tonic now, or were you spoofing? I want to see inside your lovely house.'

They left the tractor in the sun and wandered to the crumbling mansion. The back kitchen door was unlocked – no one could find the place without a map, said Rory, and so what if they did? – and inside it was cool and deathly quiet, save only for the buzzing of a fly or two. After the rich aroma of fermenting grass and diesel, the smell struck oddly on the nostrils, unknown and yet familiar, the breathing of a house long empty – damp and dryness, and decomposing wallpaper, and dust. The room was furnished, but only by the neglect of the last inhabitants to take the stuff away. A wooden kitchen table with some crocks on it, a car battery split long ago, three chairs and a broken clothes horse, a pile of something in a corner that could have been a tramp's bed, or, indeed, a long-dead tramp. There were two pictures on the wall, pale washed watercolours, country scenes, and a broken mirror on a bit of string.

'It's sad,' said Jessica. 'It could be such a nice room to have breakfast.'

They had to pick their way around the rest of it, because the floors were mainly gone, although some big holes still had carpet laid across them. The main staircase was just passable, but the upstairs rooms were too dangerous to enter, Rory said. He showed her one, from the doorway, where the great plaster-covered beam had cracked right along the front wall of the house, pressed down by the roof, and sagged in a filthy, green-stained vee almost to the floor. Under it, where the rainwater ran down and gathered, the planking was a swamp of rot and funguses.

'Me father dreamed of putting it to rights,' said Rory. 'Can you imagine that? It would take a million.'

'You'd better make a million, then,' said Jessica. 'Surely it would be worth it, Rory?'

'That's the hardnosed Proddie talking, isn't it? The authentic voice. My father was the other sort, a romantic dreamer. God, what did he not dream of doing!'

'I just couldn't bear to leave it go,' she said. 'Can't you get grants, or something? If it was done up, it'd be worth two million.'

He shook his head.

'This is the South. We're across the border. No house is worth that down here. Anyway, where is it? What is there for anyone to do? It's Somerville and Ross territory, but with time moved on. If you put on the pink and rode to hounds like English gentlefolk these days, some wee feller with an Armalite would blow your head off. Quite right too, in my opinion. On this one I'd be on their side, I'd have to be!'

'I hope you're joking,' said Jessica. Despite herself, she felt the clouds roll back. It must have showed.

'Ach, sure I am.' He took her arm, guiding her across the broad landing towards another door. 'I wouldn't even kill the fox, and that's the point. A house like this has had its day, we're talking social wilderness, as well as the natural sort. Me father drove here once and found a dozen men in balaclavas in the yard, it's said. So the Armalite joke might not be far off, when all's said and done.'

Jessica stopped. Her face was clearly stricken.

'Is that true? Were they practising, or something? Training?'

He tried to joke it off.

'We'll never know. Me father wasn't quite crazy. He did a U-turn and buggered off to Dundalk. Better cirrhosis of the liver than a bullet in the head. Listen, that's enough ould morbid talk. I'm going to turn the key on Aladdin's cave. Shut your eyes.'

She didn't, but she cleared her mind of bad thoughts

143

quite successfully. She watched curiously as Rory rolled back a piece of carpet six feet away and pulled out an iron key. He winked at her.

'The secret spot. No secret to you from now on. Whenever you get here first you can go in and warm the bed up, can't you?' He put in the key and turned. '*Voilà!*'

The room was small, and like an oven. Jessica felt sweat break out fresh on her skin as they walked in. It was dark, heavily curtained in black velveteen, with a mustiness in the air. Rory did not switch on a light, but strode to the window and jerked back the drapes. It was a sash window, and he threw up the lower half. Fresh air followed the flood of light. There was no electricity, she realised. Of course.

'Good eh? The bed, the cupboard full of booze, the fridge. What do you fancy, Jessica?'

It was a nice room, a small surprise. She had expected opulence, baroque furniture maybe, rich drapes. But it was simple and plain, an ordinary junk-shop bed – although quite large, by no means king-size – two armchairs, a table with a Tilley lamp. Over in one corner was a washstand, with a big old jug, and beneath it, large and unwieldy, decorated in lurid purple flowers, an antique piss-pot.

'All mod cons,' teased Jessica. 'And I suppose the fridge is mythical, as well? Or does it run on steam?'

He twitched another curtain, a lightweight floral one. Inside an alcove was a fridge, and beside it a two-ring gas stove.

'Calor,' he said. 'Oh ye of little faith! That cupboard there has tins of food, underneath the pots and pans. On the other side, the wine cellar, the bottles specially selected by my importers, otherwise known as the local off-licence. Local at home, that is. Nothing's local here.'

'The bed squeaks!' said Jessica, sitting on it. 'But then, I suppose it doesn't matter here.'

'Open house,' said Rory. 'Anything can squeak, and

welcome. Jessica . . . what's troubling you? You know what I was going to say outside your window, don't you?'

Jessica felt panic rising. She knew, she thought she knew, but she could not bear to hear it. She knew because she felt the same herself, the whole damn lot of it, down to the last small detail. And that was bad enough, the appalling jumble of emotions, the appalling realisation that she was no longer free, but what was worse was all the rest of it, the things she'd learned, or guessed. It was Terence and his poison, it was Parr, it was her father, no longer just a patriotic businessman, a stranger in whom she'd glimpsed bedrock, the heart of so-called loyalism. She was afraid of everything, even, obscurely, for Rory's safety. How could she say all this?

'I'd like that gin and tonic,' she said. 'If you were serious.' Then, as he moved away, she added: 'You told me you were lying. About the wee green patriot thing. You said you'd tell me.'

'The Wee Green Patriot "thing"? That's no way to talk about a lady!'

'A lady? What?'

He stood there, and she sat. Her eyes were lifted to him, dark and unhappy, she was lost.

'Would you like a slice of lemon in your drink?' he said.

On the road, not far away, the Wee Green Patriot herself was driving. She too had had a call this day, and finally had told Mr Blaney in the shop that she was going, that she was unwell, could not go on. In one way, the plain, unvarnished truth. She had gone home to her room, she had debated fiercely with herself, she had rung up Rory's mother. Rory was not around, it was not known where he'd gone, but Rosie thought she knew. She would have put her life on it.

It was a long way to Hackballs Cross, and she hated herself for going, spat hatred at herself as she threw the Metro southwards. She had no idea what she would do if she should find him there. With her.

But surely he would not be, she told herself, waiting at the border to be cleared by the men in body armour. Surely he would not take another woman there, not to their place?

She could see the big old bed, that squeaked. She did not even notice when the soldiers waved her on.

SEVENTEEN

Jessica was late home, but only by twenty minutes. As she swept into the driveway, she met her father's Jaguar coming from the house. They both braked, Jessica flamboyantly, shifting gravel. She wound her window down to match the glide of his.

'Jessica!' scolded her mother, across her husband. 'You promised!'

'Whatever have you been doing, girl?' There was a new bite to her father's voice, an edge of worry. 'You're green!'

Christ, thought Jessica. Many a true word . . .

'I'll follow!' she said. 'Tell Mrs Clarke I had a puncture. I'll be there ten minutes after you.'

Her mother was staring, too.

'Is that grass seed in your hair?'

'I told you, I had a puncture. The car slipped off the jack and pushed me in a ditch. Go! I'll follow!'

Before they had the chance for more, she knocked it into bottom and leapt for the front door. The Jaguar sat for a moment, as if pondering, then ponderously moved towards the gateposts. Jessica realised as she ran into the house that Parr had not been with them, nor was the hire car in evidence. Odd. Maybe he'd gone back to England, after all. Maybe it was all coming out in the wash.

Within a minute, she had taken off her clothes beside the basket, folding in as much loose grass as possible, and got into the shower. She washed fast but thoroughly, emerging pink and warm without even a smell of the country about her, and no chance at all – she thought merrily – of a single solitary stalk or blade falling from her knickers at the Clarkes'. She whistled as she dressed, choosing the formal look, with tights despite the season and the warmth. She brushed out her hair and spray-gelled it into a neat, demure style, she'd do the whole thing properly for her ma and daddy. What did she care? She was happy.

As she hared back down the staircase, the phone rang. Jessica went past, went back, hovered, picked it up. She did not feel so confident, after all.

It was Karen.

'Jessica,' she said. 'How's things?'

She did not feel so confident at all. Enormous state-ments welled up inside her, like erupting lava. Jessica closed her mouth on them, squeezed with all her might.

'Amazing. Just . . . well – look, this is crazy. I can't talk, I can't possibly. I'm meant to be slurping cocktails down the road, I'm as late as hell, my daddy's going to cut me off without a shilling anyway. I've done a . . . I've been . . . '

'Rory! You dirty bitch!'

'Shush! You'll set me off! Oh, Karen—'

She saw the clock beside the front door click off another minute with its big black hand.

'Love, I've got to go! Cultra high society. Holywood, to be precise! I'll ring you later. Are you in?'

'Tell me! Is it Rory?'

'I'll ring you later. *Yes!* Oh Karen!'

She banged down the receiver, almost laughing, almost shrieking with exhilaration. At the Clarkes', she had consciously to compose her features before she rang the doorbell. The sight of Holywood High Society – Cultra Division, Echelon Number One – made her want to shriek anew. Her mind was full of gas fridges, and mighty tractors mounting compressed grass, and wooden floors with gaping holes in them.

'Jessica,' cooed Mrs Clarke, a fat old bag of only forty-six, dripping jewellery to match her insecurity, 'how *awful* for you to have a puncture. How *brave* of you to struggle through. I do *appreciate* it, my dear.'

Her husband, a businessman of sixty with a suffering face, compressed his lips into the imitation of a smile.

'That's right,' he said, his accent nowhere near so smart as that his wife achieved. 'It's amazing what you young girls can do these days. Imagine Andrea changing her own wheel.'

'Not in these nails I couldn't, anyway!' The tone was acid, disguised as tinkling amusement. 'What a pity Martin wasn't there, though, Jessica. Where are they when we need them most? What a pity he couldn't come tonight.'

I wonder where he is, thought Jessica. A waiter in a white coat brought her some drink or other, a salad on a pool of pink. He was about her age, and eyed her bosom hungrily. Fucking out-of-work actor, thought Jessica. Another Mallachy. She gave him a suggestive leer, then turned away. Something to worry him for weeks, she hoped. The great what might have been . . .

Half the party was in the house, half outside, so Jessica circulated efficiently without actually having to talk to anyone. She tracked down her mother, to be told that Parr had left that afternoon, which gave her great relief. Dodging the frumps in their best dresses, dodging the pursuing actor/waiter, she found secluded spots in which she could recall the gin at Hackballs Cross, recall the afternoon. Most of the time, she felt completely in control, with only little panics round the edges. When she and Rory had left – separately, in case of God knew what – everything had been settled, all the snags resolved. Everything in the garden, she had thought, turning the Polo Fox around to leave it, had been lovely.

They had not made love, in the end, for more than just time reasons. When they had started talking seriously at last, the possibility of sex had ebbed away. They had

149

talked sex, naturally – little else. But sex with other people, not real sex any more, not their sex. It had taken them ages to confront the truth, and now they had, they tried to tell each other it. Against the clock, for Jessica could not forget her promise to her mother. Now, more than ever, keeping such a promise was important.

'The Wee Green Patriot,' said Rory, handing her her gin, 'is a woman. If I thought anything about us, I thought you understood that. Her name is Rosie Kennedy, and she's wee, and she's hellish green. She comes from Derry, in the first place, or a Republican stronghold just outside it, and she lives in a Republican stronghold in Belfast and she works for a Republican chemist in Victoria Street, Blaney's, if you ever want to take a poke at her for messing with your man! She has the normal amount of brothers and cousins and so on for one of our sort, and if it's any consolation, she's the only connection with Republicans, or Republicanism, or the IRA I've ever had, unless you count Mallachy and his mouth, which I wouldn't recommend. What's more, it's over. I meant to say it outside your window but it wouldn't just come out.' He laughed, his eyes sparkling with sudden delight. 'Maybe because I'd just been screwing her in the car! Amn't I the swine!'

Jessica had a mouthful of gin and tonic, a big one. She kept it there despite the stabbing in her stomach, still just able to enjoy the cold sweet taste. She thought of fucking Parr, the times can't have been so far apart, but that did not count. Oh you bastard, Rory.

'I was just getting engaged,' she said, surprising herself. 'While you were at it. So I can't complain, I guess.'

Had it been a competition, she would have won. His face registered shock, he actually went paler before her eyes. And his eyes went wide, and dark, and fearful.

'Oh God,' said Jessica, quickly. 'Don't worry about it! There was a row, it was a horror tale! I was lying, too, when we came back from Galway. I knew he would be there, I thought he was going to propose at last and I knew what I would say. Well, I nearly knew, and I did, too. It was diabolical. The upshot is – no wedding plans.'

Rory had sat on the arm of one of the easy chairs. He blew air through tight-pressed lips.

'No wedding plans? Or no wedding? Jessica, I haven't said it yet, I don't know fucking how to. I love you, right? Is that understood?'

She screeched with laughter.

'Of course it bloody is! I bloody love you too! The problem is I don't know how to handle it, or I didn't, it's a new experience for me! I'm like you, Rory. One of nature's whores. Men are sex objects, they always have been. I'm not sure that I even *want* to love you!'

'Bring up the violins,' said Rory. 'It's romantic, isn't it?'

A grin split his face. He beamed at her, beamed like sunshine.

'I suppose we ought to kiss. To make it all official, or somesuch. Do youse want another gin, or what?'

They both began to smile a lot, and laugh. Jessica told him bits about the proposal, and they giggled like two kids. She told about the wedding dress, and they shook their heads in wonder. She almost told him what she'd thought when Parr had taken off his underpants that last time, when she'd noted with distaste the lack of left-hand kink, but she bit that back. She asked him about Rosie and he confessed it had been more serious than he'd said but still would be resolved because of his resolve.

'Everything is over,' he said. 'Whether I do it like an honest man, or it's done by stealth, the WGP has no dominion. Jessica Roberts – if you want me – I am yours!'

They still had not touched each other. Jessica was cross-legged on the bed. She glanced down, half-shy, and noticed the green grass on her legs, juice and stalks. Fear and excitement flooded through her.

'The dear knows what'll happen when I say my piece,' she said. 'Maybe you're right — stealth it ought to be. I don't care though. It's irrevocable. Maybe I'll plead insanity.'

'Much good that would do you where we come from! Why don't we force the issue, do a runner? Why don't we do the Cork Leg? Maybe we could get a licence, is that legal? Get married in the South!'

'Hey! Hey!' said Jessica. 'I don't marry anybody, Mister! I never said I liked you that much!'

'Well thank God for that — I thought you had me trapped there, for a minute! So what about the Cork Leg? Serious. Why don't we go tonight? Then we get out of even being stealthy! We just send them each a postcard! Having a lovely time, glad you're not here, fuck the lot of youse! PS — please send money!'

'Now if you're telling me you're broke, after all this, the whole thing's off. Just because I was easy, didn't make me cheap. Not tonight, though, I've got a date, did I not tell you? Cocktails in Cultra. I've got to dash, I promised.'

'The fiancé?'

'He was never that. No, the local *nouveaux riches*. Half the population'll be there! Parr might be, I suppose. I hope not. I'll jump that hurdle if it comes to me.'

'Was easy?' said Rory. She was blank. 'Just because I was easy, past tense. I quote.'

'God, a pedant. OK, you've got me bang to rights, guv, that's what I said. I wouldn't put too much trust in it, though. Don't trust me as far as you can spit. I always could revert.'

Rory got up off the chair-arm and came towards her. Jessica jerked her legs from underneath, and swung upright off the bed. They stood silent for a moment, chest to chest, then embraced. They squeezed hard, they nearly crushed each other. It was enough.

'The dear knows what I'll tell them,' she said, quietly. 'Especially if Parr's still there. But tomorrow, I'll say I've got to go to Dublin, I'll make one of my girlfriends up, who wants to see me. I wouldn't bother with a story normally, but I get the feeling times have changed a little. Maybe I'll tell my mother I've got some special shopping that I want. I could hint about the wedding!'

'Jesus, you wouldn't? What a bitch!'

'You'd best believe it. It'd have to be an overnight, naturally, if I'm buying me trousseau! We could meet up at the cottage on Lough Swilly. I'll give you the directions or we could meet at Rathmullan and I'll bring you there.'

They moved apart. Still touching.

'I already know it. Has it got a tin shed and a water butt?'

'No. Just the house, blue window frames, you could see it from the strand that day.'

Rory clapped his palm to his forehead.

'Jesus, me and Mallachy damn nearly raided it and raped the occupants. The other one.'

'You're joking? On that night?'

'We did. I'm ashamed to say it. We sat up on the slope and fantasised.'

'We lay three hundred yards away and ditto! Poor Karen. It would have made her holiday. Not if you'd got old Mrs Doyle, though! I think that's the cottage with the water barrel. She hangs her corsets on the line to dry.'

'Your glass is empty,' Rory said. 'Look, Jessica, I'll find the place, but we have to fuck now or I think I'll die.'

Jessica stepped back and checked her watch. She tapped him lightly on the fly.

'You'll have to die then. Look, let's say tea-time tomorrow, give us both plenty of leeway to get clear. No paying off the Wee Green Patriot tonight, though, mind.'

'Please. Just a little one. Just five seconds for myself. I'll make it up tomorrow in the cottage.'

'The hell you will, you selfish bastard.' Although to tell the truth, the idea appealed most strongly, even for five seconds, this was not like Martin Parr. Jessica moved in, squeezed him harder, moved back. God, it's big, she thought.

'Rory,' she said. 'I've got to go.' She put her arms around him, he round her. They kissed, the greatest luxury in the world, both felt that they were melting.

'God it's big,' she whispered afterwards, feeling it against her groin. 'God, I love you, Rory.'

He watched her get into the green machine and turn around and head slowly for the avenue of thick bushes. In the way of young men in love, he still had the erection as he climbed into the low seat of the BMW. He had locked up the room, he had thought over the arrangements for next day, he had put away the Zetor and hung the padlock (still with its key) on the hasp. Perhaps Dessie Clancy and his boy might be sent to do some silage, it seemed unlikely he'd be around here for a little while. The Cork Leg, the two of them together, whatever the consequences or embarrassments. He started up his engine and began to crawl across the ruts. Perhaps he'd catch Jessica up on the big roads, he'd given good directions but she might get lost and lose some time. After Dundalk he'd take the Kilcurry route while she'd head straight up the N1 to the border, then for home. He had a sense of loss, keen, although they would meet again tomorrow. From now on, it was the two of them.

After they had gone, Rosie Kennedy emerged from the bushes where she had been hidden, her eyes and heart like stone. She had not seen anything of the farewell, because she could not bear to look. After the grumble of the BMW had faded, she lay on a patch of rich grass as if asleep, aware that flies were landing on her face, unmoving. At first she felt as if she felt nothing, as if she had been disembowelled, but then that passed. Then she felt as if she had been kicked while she lay there, kicked repeatedly, in the stomach. She wished she had not come, wished she had not hidden the Metro down the road but had driven boldly in and found them at it and exploded. Now she was unsure that she could ever explode again.

But she did. She went into the house, and got the key, and went into the room. She pulled the curtains back that he had closed, and she stared round it, as if she had never seen it in her life before. Then she destroyed it. She broke every bottle, every plate and cup, every glass and every piece of glass. She pushed the fridge over on its face, door open, and smashed the ice trays with her heel. She tore the burners off the cooker, and smashed the gas valves, and the earthenware jug and the ornamental chamber pot with them. She broke the legs off the washstand, and wrecked every other piece of furniture she was strong enough to wreck. She broke two mirrors and the Tilley lamp and tore up eight books. She threw all the bedclothes on the floor and pulled down the curtains, which she added to the pile. She scooped up broken ends of wine bottle and emptied dregs of wine on them. She was sweating, her skin burning, her breath coming in great gasps. At times she thought she was enjoying it.

Soon, however, she was at a loss. For anything worse to do, for any explanation. Although she had been home, she was still in her workclothes, and she had a lipstick in the pocket of her duster coat. She took the lid off and went up to a wall and held it up to write something. Something final, something awful, something hurtful, perhaps a threat, even. She stared at the wall until it appeared to move towards her, but nothing came.

Then she dropped the lipstick and turned blindly to the bed. She fell face forwards onto it, great cries tearing through her throat, dry, awful, racking sobs. The mattress was quite new, pale chocolate brown with flat white buttons. She smeared it with her tears and snot.

EIGHTEEN

Jessica did not get round to ringing Karen until next morning. The cocktail party – through a subtle tension between boredom and social nicety – sustained itself far longer than anyone would have hoped, and the Roberts were among the last to leave. This was not normal, but Samuel Roberts seemed to have a need to show how dutiful his daughter was by parading her to all and sundry, involving her in 'conversations' with people whom she (and he, indeed) would have run a mile from in the normal way of things. It had come on him, this need, when Mrs Roberts had pointed out that their daughter was more or less invisible, and unfortunately he had tracked her down to a quiet spot behind a clump of evergreen which the waiter had discovered half a minute previously. Judging by the way his face had darkened, he may even have thought that this was the offending Taig . . .

Cornered, and reading the signs of incipient anger, Jessica had followed him demurely, and played her part. She had talked tennis to the tennis set, sailing to the Strangford Lough brigade, and sewing, God forbid, to a stalwart of the ladies' sewing circle. She may even have agreed, she told a startled Karen in the morning, to make a sampler for the church bazaar in autumn. When they finally got home, things got a little worse. Her father, ponderously concerned and slightly drunk, wanted a wee chat with his wee girl, but he did not know how to express what he would have liked to say. It was only about eleven, but Jessica feigned tiredness. The topic, she well knew, was Life, the Universe and Everything – and she did not want to play. Her mother, who was as anxious as her husband, knew her daughter better. She tried to let her go to bed, she dropped in inanities, then she hung around in case things got nasty. But Jessica could handle it, despite some moments.

It was the specifics that were difficult. At one point Mr Roberts, fed up with the gentle fobbing off, cleared his throat and said: 'Jessica, Jessica, you know what I'm driving at, why not be straight? Are we to hear wedding bells or not?'

Mrs Roberts made a tutting noise.

'Samuel,' she began, until a black look passed across his brow. Jessica moved in lightly, with a small laugh.

'It's all right, Ma. Daddy's right, I'm being coy. But please, Daddy, don't ask me for an answer here and now. I've talked it over with Parr and we understand each other. We'll sort it out.'

'And did you sort out the particular?' he asked. The darkness had modified into a flush. Jessica allowed herself a snap of temper, although hers was simulated.

'If you mean the crack about another feller, I'm off to my bed,' she said. 'I told you I was joking and I won't go into it again. Hell's teeth, father.'

My, she thought, amn't I the cute dissembler! Stealth or truth, Rory had said. This time tomorrow night she'd be with that other feller, for good and all, maybe. Then what would Daddy say? What would she say, come to that?

He was sitting in an armchair, half belligerent, half upset, and Jessica was swamped with affection and regret. How could she do this to him? What was she doing? The third question nudged hatefully. And would she do it, come the crunch? She would, she would, she had to!

'Sam,' said her mother, cautiously, 'you've to be in Coleraine for eight, you know. No more whisky, now.

158

We need some sleep, the lot of us. Jessica, have you got any plans?'

'I have.' She got up, smiling brittly. 'I'm off to Dublin to do some shopping. Sonia rang.'

'When?' said her father. Wow, thought Jessica. The affection receded. Suspicious old swine.

'As I got down the stairs to go to that wonderful cocktail party you sprang on me,' she said. More sweetly, to her mother: 'Karen rang as well. She sends her love.'

'You were all covered over in grass,' said her father. The belligerence was on the ascendant.

'Oh shut up,' said Jessica. 'I'm for my bed. I won't be home tomorrow night I expect, Ma.'

'Oh,' said Mrs Roberts. 'All right, dear. What are you looking out for?'

The wedding lie was in the forefront of her mind. Her mother's face was wan and tired, her cocktail frock ridiculous. The party's over, thought Jessica.

'Oh, nothing special. Sonia's a bit depressed, that's the truth of it. She just needs to break out, I think.'

That's the truth of it. Thus are made good lies. It was too late to ring Karen at her Aunt Jane's when she reached her room. Jessica climbed into bed a bit depressed. Tomorrow she'd break out . . .

In the morning, when she rang, her mood was up and down. Twice in the night she'd woken up, which she never did. She'd woken with the horrors, and the fears. She'd exorcised them with thoughts of Rory's curly head, and his long brown fingers. She'd put her own fingers, her whole hand, between her legs but had not been sexy. It had comforted her, the knowledge that his would soon be there. Pondering on the problem of love, the shock and worry of it all, the glory too, she had drifted off. She'd listened to her father start the Jaguar, early, then she'd gone downstairs and had some toast and tea. She and her mother had only grunted to each other, both embarrassed in obscure ways.

Karen's voice was an instant lift. It was alive with prurient excitement.

'Jessica! You dirty little tart! Tell me, tell me! Christ, it's peak period!'

'Oh shut up, my old man would never mind. Can we talk, is Auntie Jane listening? Anyway, it could be the last call of mine he ever pays for.'

'What! Yes, she's out. What do you mean, has he kicked you out into the gutter?'

'No such luck. That would make it easier. He might do, though. Karen, shut up and listen for a minute. I'm running off with Rory.'

'Wonderful!' said Karen King. Her voice was breathy. 'Oh Jessica, that's just wonderful. You are insane, aren't you? You're the Great White Hope.'

'The Great White Dope, more like it. Oh Karen, can't you give me good advice, can't you kick me up the arse and tell me to snap out of it? Where's the sensible English girl I used to know and love? What would Tony say, for instance?'

Karen laughed.

'You'd kick *his* arse. He mentioned Romeo and Juliet. You said an Englishman could never understand.'

The mood dipped slightly.

'Well it's not just the English who are having difficulties in that department,' Jessica replied. 'I'm having more trouble than anticipated, I will admit. I never thought it would be easy, but . . . '

But Karen's excitement would brook no setbacks.

'You don't have to bullshit me,' she said. 'I've got over my mad jealousy. Tony's just a working-class romantic, I told him on the phone. You get off and do it, girl, you can always buy your way out of trouble if you need to. Christ, I've a good mind to come and join you, I'm still jealous after all! D'you think Mallachy would take me on?'

'Listen, you daft cow, this is serious!' said Jessica. 'I'm burning my boats! Parr turned up with a wedding dress and I'm running off to the Republic. This is not just a dirty weekend, you know.'

She had to tell about the antique wedding dress and the proposal. Karen, who knew her Strindberg and her Henry James, was round-eyed at her end of the telephone.

'Good God,' she said. 'I thought it was a marriage that was arranged. This is genocide! When are you going? Where? What are you going to *say*?'

They both paused to think. Perhaps sixty miles apart, on their islands. Both thought, oddly, of Martin Parr.

'What indeed?' said Jessica, at last. 'We're meeting at the cottage, early evening. What indeed?'

Another pause, a shorter one.

Karen said: 'Jess, if you need me.'

'Yeah,' said Jessica. 'I know.'

Mallachy O'Rourke, having failed to winkle out his friend the night before, was on the blower first thing in the morning. He got Mrs Collins, who characteristically forgot the story she had agreed on with her son.

'Oh yes, hallo Mallachy,' she said. 'I'll just see if he's up yet.'

'Back yet,' said Rory, seizing the receiver as he came out of his bedroom, wearing only underpants. He gave her a look. 'Hi, mate, I've just stepped in this minute. You know how confused the old trout gets.'

'You shouldn't sleep in your underpants,' said the old trout, loudly. 'I've told you before, it's unhygienic.'

'What's going on?' said Mallachy. 'Were you in last night or out?'

'Ach, you know the form,' said Rory. 'It was just a cover in case a certain person rang. If you'd tempted me out for a drink we might have run into her in a bar so I extended it to you as well. Nothing personal.'

'Is the fight still on with Rosie, then? She's murder that one, Rory. You'd be better off with the Prod, when all's said and done.'

'Aye,' said Rory, cagily. 'Look, I've got work to do this morning, I've to drive to Larne to pick a part up off the boat. Shall I drop by for you, we could have a sandwich and a drink.'

It was agreed, and Rory went to have some breakfast and a bath. He went back to his bedroom and stood there naked, deciding which clothes to take for his rendezvous with Jessica. The thought alone gave him a hard-on, so he slipped on his pants and trousers to show it who was boss. Then socks and slip-ons, and a knitted shirt. He left the overnight bag empty on the bed. He'd come back, plenty of time. For once, in fact, it did not seem to matter what he wore. Jessica had marinaded happily in sap!

When he picked up Mallachy, he still had not decided how much he'd give away. Not that he mistrusted him, but he could grind on a little when he was in the mood, and Rory did not want any Proddie rich-bitch hassle. As it happened, Mallachy was more interested in Terence.

'That feller,' he said, as they nosed off the M5 at Newtownabbey onto the coast road. 'The one that started the punch-up in the Amsterdam. You said he said I was a terrorist. Was that a cod?'

Rory had an inward smile. In his present mood, he thought Mallachy would be pleased by that idea.

'No cod,' he said. 'If Jessica's to be believed. He's her cousin, he's called Terence Rigby. I think he tried to fuck her once but got seen off. He reckons to be connected. Him and Bill and Ben.'

'God,' said Mallachy, 'even the UFF would have nothing to do with such riffraff, surely? He dropped you in it, though.'

He turned his head and grinned. Cheeky bastard.

'As I remember it, you did the dropping. You mentioned Jessica in front of Rosie. I've got the scars to prove it.'

'Lucky you,' said Mallachy. 'I thought you'd end up in the sack. He did it as well though, did he not? It's a good excuse, as if we ever needed one!'

The traffic was light, and Rory had the needle up at ninety. Belfast Lough was gleaming in the sun. A good excuse for what? He knew.

'Nah,' he said. 'Let's leave him be, unless he starts it off again. Let's face it, he might be family soon. Bad form.'

'You *what*!' Mallachy twisted in his seat so fast his seat belt almost choked him. He tore at it, across his throat.

'Now that *is* funny,' said Rory, his Garfield impersonation. 'Joke, Mallachy old son, *plaisanterie*.'

'Bastard,' coughed Mallachy. 'You fucking would, you bastard.'

My mouth's too big, thought Rory. When Mallachy dug at him, nagged for details, any little snippet, he insisted it was fantasy, pure cod. And Mallachy did not believe him.

They met the Stranraer ferry and waited for the engine part at the agent's office. Small but vital, wrapped in greaseproof paper, ninety pounds plus Vat. It was time to eat, so they found a drivers' cafe, had an Ulster fry. After a mug of tea each, they were thirsty, so thought they'd find a bar. Mallachy suggested heading northward up the coast, where he knew a couple, but Rory had things to do.

'I've got to drop this off,' he said. 'It's a farm near Mayobridge. Then there's things I've to pick up at home. We could have one in Belfast, maybe. The Amsterdam?'

'I'll come with you,' said Mallachy. 'I don't mind the smell of cowshit. We could try one in the country, do the business, bum some tea off of your ma, then you could bring me back to the big city. Don't tell me you're not drinking tonight, as well? Or are you still afraid of meeting Rosie?'

Rory considered. Quicker from his home to get to Derry by another route, but he was in no hurry. Jessica said late afternoon and he could do nothing until she arrived. He checked his watch.

'You're a bloodsucker,' he said. 'A scrounging, work-shy little shite. OK.'

On the way, he began to tell the story. He told about the fucking in the car with Rosie, and the rattling of the gravel off the Cultra window panes. How had he known which window? The powers of deduction, my dear Watson, and a pair of legs wound up and ready to go if he was wrong! He told of the day at Hackballs Cross – the farm near Dundalk, he called it – where Mallachy had never been.

'God,' said Mallachy, 'you have no sense of history at all, have you? To roll an Orange woman on good green hay! You ought to be ashamed.'

'Grass isn't hay, nor is hay green, you city ignoramus. In any case, I did not roll her in anything, we were as chaste as virgins in a nunnery. It's a meeting of the minds, my boy!'

'Oh aye, like the trip to Galway, I suppose? So if we meet Rosie for a drink tonight, I can tell her all about it, can I?'

They were in the country now, not far from Dromore. Rory was intending to take a left, get off the main roads. He had a little bar in mind.

'I'll not be there tonight. I'll bring you to your house and then flash on, I have a date.'

Mallachy contemplated his friend in silence for a while.

'Old son,' he said. 'This sounds serious. You can tell your Uncle Mallachy, so you can.'

'I wouldn't be surprised,' said Rory, 'if it hadn't crept underneath me stone at last. The love toad. Mark you, I could be wrong. I surely hope so.'

'I'll sing amen to that, at least,' said Mallachy. 'Well, I'll be doggoned.'

They were talking about other things when Mallachy first brought up the car. They had exhausted Jessica — or Jessica was exhausting Mallachy, he said — before they left the pub, and he had first spotted it two miles before, tucked into the entry of a field, almost hidden. He had caught a glimpse of it, accidentally, in the wing mirror on his side of the BMW as they slowed for a crossroads, and after that kept craning in his seat.

'What are you up to?' Rory asked him, on the fourth or fifth time. 'Have you got fleas, or something?'

'We're being followed,' said Mallachy. 'What car does Cousin Terence have?'

Rory was inclined to laugh.

'How should I know? You're paranoid.'

'I caught the outline of the one on Cultra promenade. A Toyota. This one's a Toyota. White.'

Mallachy was hot on cars. Because he could not afford one, he would have said. A little tension crept into Rory's stomach.

'Coincidence,' he said. 'For Jesus' sake, who in the world knows where we are today? No one followed us from Belfast, did they?'

'Not that I noticed. Slow down!'

His voice was urgent. Rory braked. Round the bend behind, a sporty white saloon appeared.

'He's slowing down as well,' said Mallachy. 'Shit.'

Rory watched in the mirror. The white car had definitely slowed. There was nowhere for it to go, no reason for the action.

'It was hidden in a farm gateway, past the pub. Somebody's on to us, mate. Put your boot down.'

Rory did. The white car hung back, dawdled, disappeared.

'This Terence,' said Mallachy. 'He's a spoofer, isn't he? He's not for real?'

Rory licked his lips.

'He was lifted once. According to Jessica. Guns, or somesuch. She thinks he's a bullshitter.'

He remembered. 'My Mallachy equivalent' or something, she had said. But how had he found them? Could it be him? It couldn't be.

'Guns,' said Mallachy. 'That's all we need. Never brought to trial, don't tell me. All hushed up. The Orange Mafia. Favourite sons.'

'It can't be anyone,' said Rory. His voice was strained. 'Who knows we're here? The middle of fucking nowhere. Nobody.'

They rounded a curve onto a longish straight stretch. Mallachy touched his arm and Rory braked, hard. A second or two later the Toyota nosed into sight. There were three men in it. Even in the mirrors, they were familiar. Mallachy craned round, stared.

'Germany v. Japan,' he said. 'I wonder how many pints your man has had. Floor it, Rory. I think we'd better go.'

But how the hell, thought Rory, as he jammed down the accelerator. How the bloody hell?

NINETEEN

The country roads of Ireland – designed for carts, laid on bogs, snaking like wild things round rocky outcrops – are either just the thing or not the thing at all for car chases. They are almost traffic-free, and therefore very dangerous. Racers – young men, most of them – get used to flying round blind bends at sixty plus, trusting to Providence that nothing will be coming the other way. Providence, with great regularity, lets them down.

There was a joke that Rory knew, and since his father's death it came to him from time to time. It was about two Englishmen who'd come across to southern Ireland to escape the traffic and restrictions and have a burn-up in their new Ferrari. They'd wound her up to a hundred and thirty-five in the middle of nowhere, in the wilds of County Kerry, and had screamed around a corner to be presented with the arse-end of a donkey cart, piled with hay, that had just come out of a field and blocked the road completely. The Ferrari driver had jammed on the anchors, gone into a skid, bounced off the verges, then steered into the field, missing the cart by inches. A few good bounds over the tussocks, up into the air, a nosedive – and a ball of fire. Two incinerated English. 'Ah, thank God,' said one Kerryman, looking back across his shoulder. 'If we hadn't got out of that field just in the nick of time, that bastard would have killed us both!' In the first few minutes of the chase, he could not free his mind of it.

The long straight stretch, however, began to iron out the kinks. Braking, he had dropped to second, which was a good accelerating gear. The BMW surged forward, the back end settled down onto the wheels, the exhaust note crackled. As the needle nudged towards the red he dipped the clutch and slipped into third, hardly allowing the engine speed to drop. Mallachy, twisted in his seat, was whooping.

'We've got the bastards on the hop! Go on, Rory, this is your patch!'

They were doing seventy as they approached the bend. The hell it is, thought Rory, I've no more idea what's round there than the next man. He braked savagely, knocked off too much speed, muffed the gear-change.

'Fucking hell,' said Mallachy, mildly, but said no more. The reproach was clear enough.

Inevitably, it was an easy bend. As he beat the vehicle forward, encouraging it with the muscles in his arms, Rory saw the white Toyota in the mirror. He had thrown away the advantage of surprise. They had made up twenty yards.

'Just testing,' he said, more joke than lie. 'Now we know for certain, don't we?'

'Well now we know, please Granma – do something about it, eh! Ziss iss not how Chermany vun ze var!'

Rory got towards the red in third before the next curve leapt at them. He hit the brakes late, then transferred to the accelerator to drive out of trouble if he needed. He did. The bend was tight, and progressively got tighter. By the middle of it (he hoped it was the middle!) his tyres were howling, they were leaning on the offside nose. The road narrowed, they were between high dirt walls, a gully. And nothing came to meet them . . .

'Better,' said Mallachy, tersely. Rory grinned. He had caught a whiff of sweat, that was not his.

'You'll beg for mercy, Mister Christian,' he said. 'Before I've finished with you.'

The next two bends were too close for a sighting of the pursuers, but Rory kept the pressure on. On the next good straight, winding up to nearly ninety, they assessed that they had gained fifty yards at least. Two long right-handers, a section of the wiggles, then more clear, straight road, and the race seemed won.

'Japanese lubbish,' Mallachy said. 'I wonder how they'd be on the open road. It'd be a pity if we got away too easy.'

Rory had his lip between his teeth. The road had dropped suddenly and steeply away from him, at the same time making corkscrews. Opposite a farm gate halfway through the sequence there was liquid manure spread across the tarmac in a greasy lake. He braked, accelerated, went into a sideways glide. By the time he had command once more, he was down to twenty miles an hour.

'Although,' Mallachy added, conversationally, 'there's not much chance of that!'

But the Toyota found the same patch of slurry, and made worse weather of it. The next time they saw it they had gained more ground and Rory – although sweating himself – had found his rhythm. He took the next crossroads blind, piling on the power, driving on the edge. As his confidence grew, so did his pleasure. He was almost disappointed when he saw a major road ahead.

'Ah well,' he said. 'Fun over. We'll lose them easy on the straight.'

But Mallachy had different plans.

'For Jesus' sake,' he said. 'Who's talking about fun? I want to tell these bastards once for all, it's time they got the gipsy's warning. Go across.'

Rory hesitated. The main road was clear, he could turn left and be away, he could be in Mayobridge with the spare part in twenty minutes. He slowed up for the junction.

'I'm telling you,' urged Mallachy. 'I'm sick to death of them. We'll draw into a field and have a little word. You're not afraid, are you?'

It was stupid provocation but it worked. As the Toyota

turned up in his mirror, Rory drove across onto the minor road.

'I'd like to know who told them where we were,' he said uncomfortably.

'Well then, we can ask. Give her the juice, though, mate – let's not make it obvious. Let's find a nice wee spot and get the drop on them.'

Rory's discomfort grew. He supposed it was all right, all this, he didn't imagine it could end in any harm. But Mallachy's excitement was disturbing. He stepped on the accelerator, felt the car respond, but his heart was going out of it.

'This is a waste of time,' he said. 'In any case . . . '

'In any case,' snarled Mallachy, 'you're prepared to be walked over, is that it? You're prepared to let some mimsy Proddie bastard tell youse what to do? Tell youse who you can stick your dick into and who you can't? Wake up, man, these prats are after us. If we're in front they're chasing and we're running, aren't we? If we stop we're not running any more '

There was an entrance, a green field, a clump of trees.

'There!' said Mallachy, and almost despite himself, Rory braked. The ground was flat, it did not look too soft. He made for it.

'Jesus,' said Mallachy, as they left the road. 'There go your shock absorbers. Here they come, they'll think we're after hiding.' His satisfaction grew. 'They've spotted us. Get in towards those trees.'

The field was not much worse than the drive at Hackballs Cross. Rory jounced along, keeping an eye open for major ruts. He watched the bonnet of the Toyota dip as it came through the gateway. He was breathing shallowly.

'Mallachy, you're an aggressive shite,' he said. 'You're cracked.'

'If the worst comes to the worst,' Mallachy replied, cheerfully, 'we've got the English popgun, haven't we?'

'No!' said Rory, violently. Involuntarily, he stepped on the brake, throwing them both forward. 'No,' he repeated, less fiercely, letting the car pick up once more. 'Forget it, Mallachy, just forget it. No stupid games.'

He curled round behind the clump of trees, and switched the motor off. On second thoughts, he restarted it. Mallachy made a small noise of amusement.

'Nervous, are we? Switch it off and save the gas. Let's get out and meet them man to man.'

He pushed his door open, unclipped his seat belt, and swung out. Rory, wrong-footed, cut the engine, followed suit. They stood on either side of the bonnet, looking through the trees. The Toyota, just visible, had stopped.

'A tenner says they bugger off,' said Mallachy. 'A tenner says they're scared as you are. Come on, Rory! Just a wee shot across their bow! Put one through the undergrowth!'

'Shut up. They're moving.'

The Toyota was going slowly forward. Mallachy was wrong, the men were on their way. As it dipped and rocked into full view it became clear what they had stopped for. All three were masked, in cotton balaclavas worn back to front, with eyeholes scissored out.

'Good God,' said Rory. 'Mallachy.'

'They're fools!' said Mallachy, furiously. 'They're playing games out of their league! By Christ, Rory, stand your ground, man, stand your ground!'

The balaclavas were blue, edged in white piping, the sort that mountain-climbers wore. Even to Rory, they did not look professional. He dearly wanted to be back in the car, but he stood his ground.

'Remember in the pub,' said Mallachy. 'What did Karen call them? Boddice and Bean, or something. They're cartoons.'

The Toyota stopped some thirty feet away. Behind it, green fields stretched into the distance. No roads, no houses, only grass and hedgerow. The man at the wheel –

Terence, from his size and build – left the engine running. Three doors were opened, almost simultaneously.

'Ach,' shouted Mallachy, his voice ringing with confidence. 'Here we are again, the three wise monkeys, fresh from their triumph in the Amsterdam!'

He stepped forward from the car, a short, explosive figure. He emanated aggression, like a fighting dog, waves of something came from him, almost palpable to Rory. Hatred, probably. Certainly not fear. Anything but fear.

Rory was afraid. The driver had come out empty-handed from the car, but the passengers both had iron bars. However, after four paces, all in a line, they came no farther.

'Shut your mouth, you,' said the driver. It was Terence, however low and gritty he had tried to pitch it. 'Keep your nose out and you'll take no harm. Collins, I've got a message for you.'

'Fuck your messages, you strutting peacock,' yelled Mallachy. 'I've got a message for you – get off our backs while you've still got the chance. We're losing patience with you, can't you understand?'

Rory hated both of them. He put a hand up, a sort of helpless gesture to make Mallachy stop mouthing off. It reminded him of the playground, this. But Terence's anger was growing to match Mallachy's.

'Call him off,' he roared at Rory. His voice had risen. 'Surrounding yourself with thugs won't help you, bastard. I'm telling you you've gone too far, there's people want your blood. There's—'

Mallachy, in a movement too quick for Rory to properly comprehend, had bent and snatched something from the grass beside his feet. As he straightened, a large stone left his hand and caught Terence Rigby on the shoulder. He gave a cry and staggered backwards. The two sidesmen each moved a step away. They raised their bars, a most unmenacing effect. Mallachy gave a hoot of laughter.

172

'You prats!' he yelled. 'Pathetic fucking prats! Come and get me, boys! Why don't you come and get me!'

Fat Stewart Ross and short Nick Day looked at each other. Rory could almost see the shock and fright behind the eyeholes of their masks. Suddenly, the adrenalin flowed in him, suddenly he found it comical.

'Mallachy, knock it off,' he said. 'Leave them alone, it's cruel.'

'That's it!' yelled Mallachy. 'Get you home to your mammies, boys! Get you home and have a think! Because if youse don't get off our backs, you're going to run into some proper people, know what I mean? If youse don't lay off of us we'll be giving names out. Do youse take my meaning, boys? I hope youse take my meaning!'

The laughter ended on a shot, the shot cracked out so unexpectedly that Rory yelped, sharply, like a dog. Mallachy rose backwards in the air, his feet came off the ground, then he tumbled sideways, spraying blood across the bonnet of the car before hitting it with a dull tinny thud and sliding out of Rory's sight. The fat man in the balaclava mask screamed once, like a little girl, and dropped his iron bar. Terence was leaning on the Toyota, supporting himself with the open door, looking like a broken puppet with white eyes. Rory noticed, bemusedly, that there was a pistol in his hand. There was smoke. There was an echo, still, from off a distant slope.

'Christ!' he screamed. 'What have you done! You bastard! What have you done! Mallachy!'

The fat man started being sick, inside his balaclava. He tried to rip it off, he doubled over, making an appalling noise. The small man jumped away from him, horrified, still holding his iron bar.

'You cunt!' he shouted. 'You stupid cunt!'

Rory started to move round the bonnet to Mallachy's side. Terence made a high noise, waving the pistol at him.

'Stop! Don't move! I . . . '

'You'll have to stiff him,' screeched the fat man. He had got the mask off, it hung full of vomit from his hand. His face was white, smeared with lumps of sick. 'He's a witness! Stiff him!'

Rory glimpsed Mallachy's dead face, which had a hole in it, a tear in the cheek, turned inside out, pink and livid. He stepped backwards.

'Stand still!' screamed Terence. He took a step towards him, the pistol at arm's length. 'Stand still.'

Rory jumped sideways, banged his hip on the BMW, scrambling to get inside the door. He could hear a noise, a constant groaning that he realised must be him. He dived inside the car head first, cracking his knees on metal, bellowing with pain. He heard a crack, a bang, a shout. He jammed both hands underneath the dashboard, frantic to get at the Webley, tearing at the box. When he had it he jerked his shoulders sideways, raised his head to see through the windscreen, sick with terror. There were shapes, a man was nearly at the bonnet, he saw the black shape of the gun.

Something told him to get out. He scrambled backwards, feet first, his knees banging on the sill then slipping to the grass. The edge of the seat caught the corner of the pistol butt, nearly pulled it from his hand. Rory lurched towards the back wheels, outside the car, then got behind the boot. He half stood, half blind, the Webley pointing roughly to the front. There was a bang that shocked him with its loudness, and his hand flew upwards. A whiff of smoke caught him in the nostrils, pleasant, indescribable. Ahead of him, away somewhere, there was a scream. Rory dropped onto his knees, one hand across his face, the Webley on its side in front of him. He noticed with surprise how warm the metal was, the metal of the car.

There was shouting, words he could not make out. Then slamming doors, an engine revved insanely, then an engine stalled as someone dropped in the clutch too hard, too fast. A starter, then more revs. The car moved off, more gently but still fast, then speeded up. He could hear it crashing as it bottomed on the hummocks, he heard springs jounce and squeak. Every now and then the clutch was slipped, the engine screamed, then settled down. He saw a flash of white beyond the trees. Soon there was silence.

It was perhaps two minutes before he lifted himself from off the ground. He used the boot as a handhold, then as a crutch. He leaned on it, taking comfort from the fact it was a car that he could see, and nothing worse. He listened to the birdsong, then a high plane curdling the air. When that faded, he stood fully upright.

There were two dead bodies in the field, not far apart. There was Mallachy, whose face had been torn open, and Terence Rigby, who looked peaceful and untouched. Someone had pulled his balaclava up, to see if he had life, presumably. There was a tiny scratchmark on his cheek, where a nail had caught, perhaps. Rory crossed himself.

'I hope you're satisfied,' he said. Was he talking to his God, he wondered . . .

TWENTY

Because she had to get to Dublin for her shopping spree, Jessica had to leave Cultra quite early. Her mother seemed to be a larger presence in the house than usual, mooching about in a somewhat sulky way, watching her. Jessica sat up in her room packing a small overnight bag, wondering how she could explain even that away. Normally, she travelled light, she was famous for it. A night in Dublin would usually involve a pair of knickers and a toothbrush if she remembered it, if not she'd borrow one or go without. This morning, foolishly, she wanted to take some special things, a flowing print dress in soft cotton she knew he'd love, a peasant slip she'd bought in Hungary six years before, a couple of sun tops that made her look terrific, some wild silk underwear. Even a flannel and a tube of toothpaste – Miss Superfresh!

When she heard her mother in the passageway outside, she panicked. She pulled back her duvet and thrust the bag under it. As the door opened she leaned on the bulge, looking guilty and absurd. Her mother, naturally, did not notice.

'Jessica,' she said. 'It's awfully late, but I suppose you couldn't drop me off at Molly's could you? It wouldn't be much out of your way.'

Molly lived at Downpatrick. Not many miles, but at least a half an hour extra. And to someone really heading west . . . Jessica forced a smile.

'OK,' she said. 'I'm dithering, in any case. Look, you go down and get your coat or whatever on. I said I'd take some clothes to Sonia, stuff that I don't want. Give me five minutes.'

She had had a growing plan, before her mother had come, to abandon everything and stop in Belfast to get some sexy gear at Anderson and McCauley's. She had had an idea that she ought to be ashamed of herself in any case, she was behaving like a wee girl with some sort of virginity to lose. With her excuse manufactured for her by the circumstance, she retrieved her bag from under the covers, jammed the items in any old how (now she could have them she cared not how they ended up) and skipped down to her car. The pea-green incorruptible, he called it. She looked at it with love. She even contemplated checking the tyres and the oil to give it a treat, but did not bother. Come on, Ma, she thought – let's be having youse!

Both of them, on the move, recovered their moods. They chatted about Sonia – Jessica lying easily about who she was and what she'd said – and about Molly, a schooldays friend of Mrs Roberts who had married a cattleman and lived in scarf and wellingtons, barrel-shaped and happy with it. Jessica joined the two unlikely intimates at the farmhouse for a cup of tea – she turned down the chance of roast lamb, mint and buttered spuds – then headed off, as if for Dublin. She figured it might be quickest to drive back north to the M1, but could not resist the Newry road, then Keady and Armagh, purely because it took her through Belleeks. She knew that Rory lived near Belleeks, although she did not know where, and the silliness of the whole expedition pleased her mightily. Wouldn't it be great crack to run into him in the BMW! Ah no, though, wouldn't it be better still to warm the cottage up, put a fire in the grate to take the dampness off, if any, make some food and set some wine to breathe? It was overcast in the west, but that would be no trouble to them. They could sit and watch the waters for a while, and drink and chat, then retire to the great big feather bed.

Before Belleeks and through it, she saw nothing that

could be the Collins business, neither sight nor sound of John Deere tractors or any other kind, and resisted the temptation to stop and ask. Five miles the other side she found a little pub that announced hot food on a roadside blackboard, and had a plate of sausages and beans with bread and butter and a pint of Guinness. Time was drifting by quite nicely, so she flowed along with it. At Keady she took the minor road through Maddan, went down to Middletown and up to Caledon, following the River Blackwater – and the border – to Aughnacloy before committing herself irrevocably to the A5 and Omagh, a town she quite disliked. She crossed at Strabane, then slowed her pace still further until she reached Letterkenny, where she shopped. They had some lovely lamb-hearts, they had some queenies, she was spoiled for choice, so she bought both. Thank God for time, thank God for money, thank God for the education and the mother that she'd had. Karen King, a staid and bookish girl, could not even cook an egg. English, you see . . . Jessica, laughing with pleasurable self-mockery, even knew about fine wine. Letterkenny, itself, had come on in that department in the past few years!

She found the cottage just as she had left it, cool, dark, slightly damp from its position in the trees and its proximity to the lough, and went round firstly opening all the windows and the doors. She switched on the immersion heater, boiled up a kettle, made some tea. She ran round the inside of the fridge with a cloth, turned that on, filled the ice-trays, put in the milk and white wine and the queenies and the double cream. Then she raked out ashes, brought in coal and wood and a few briquettes of peat (for the smell, mainly), and lit a fire in the sitting room. She'd left the beds unmade when she and Karen had done their runner in the rain, so she sorted out the big one, sniffing the fresh undersheet and duvet cover for signs of damp. Amn't I the lovely little housewife, she thought. I hope this wee Tim appreciates it! By six o'clock or so she had made the stuffing, prepared the hearts and vegetables, decided just how to present the scallops. She poured herself a glass of red wine, which she thought a pity, she would have preferred to wait. She took it outside into the coolish evening air, listening for a car engine. Apart from a motorboat on the lough, she heard nothing. She sipped, and sat down on a stone. She remembered her bag, in the boot, her plan to dress up like a princess (or a courtesan!) for him. At present, she was in jeans and tartan shirt, nice and thick and warm. Perfectly adequate for the job, she told herself. Especially if the bastard didn't come!

By seven thirty she was getting edgy, as well as hungry. She ate some bread and butter, noted that the red was down below the halfway mark, banged things about the kitchen a bit. At eight she turned the radio on, channel-hopping, trying to find some news. Inane DJs with mid-Atlantic accents. She did get news, about the Pope planning a visit somewhere, an air crash in Sweden. The Northern Ireland stations led with the crash, followed with some Parliamentary stuff from London, the Pope was never mentioned. The TV offered no news at all this early in the night. By the time the sun broke through the cloud – just powerful enough to redden up the lough-view windows on the other side – Jessica was getting badly worried. She kept looking at the silent telephone, wishing it would ring, wishing there was someone she could get in touch with. Oh God, she thought, my love. Surely nothing's happened to you?

It was ten past ten when she heard a car nosing down the gravel track, and by now Jessica was almost frantic. She leapt out of her seat as headlights glowed on the lower branches of the trees, and was outside waiting when the BMW stopped. Anger fighting worry, she half expected him to be smiling drunk. One glance at his face ended that idea. He was pale, appalling.

'Jessica,' he said. 'Something terrible. Mallachy's been shot. And Terence. I've killed Terence.'

A kind of groan escaped him, literally, as he pressed his fist across his mouth. He moved forward, the door left open, stumbling towards her. Jessica, horrified, still lifted her arms, as if automatically, and they embraced. For a moment she looked across his shoulder, stared down the slope across the lough towards the lights of Fahan. She did not understand, she could not take it in, she hoped – ridiculously – that it was some dreadful joke.

'Terence?' she said. 'My cousin Terence? But that quarrel wasn't serious, was it? You hardly knew him.'

'It was an accident,' he said. 'A kind of accident. Things got out of hand, it wasn't meant to happen. We ended in a field, and . . . '

'But you hardly knew him,' she repeated.

They moved apart, Rory dropped his keys, and picked them up.

'I couldn't come till dark,' he said. 'I didn't dare, in case. Oh Christ, Jessica, what has happened to us?'

He really did not know. Jessica led him into the cottage, made him sit down. She brought the whisky bottle to the kitchen, poured him a slug into her dirty wineglass, the nearest one to hand. Rory raised it to his lips but did not drink. He seemed bewildered.

'It happened in a farmer's field,' he said. 'This afternoon. I took a part to Mayobridge, afterwards. Jessica, they'll soon be after me.'

He was hungry, his face skin stretched and white. She divined this, made him eat a piece of soft cheese and a hunk of bread. The lamb-hearts, stuffed and purple, still uncooked, mocked her from the work surface. He tried to explain, but for the moment she would not let him. She made a cup of tea, opened a second bottle of red wine. She went and closed the BMW door, and looked it over. In the light spilling from the house, she saw stains across the bonnet, dark rust on the charcoal, and guessed what they must be. She went and got a bucket, hot water and detergent, found a cloth. Rory watched with haunted eyes, but did not comment. When she returned she sat opposite him, at the kitchen table.

'Go on,' she said.

At first, very little would come out, in sequence. He started telling her about the spare part, the job he had to do in Mayobridge, how he'd picked up Mallachy and gone to Larne. She asked questions about where they'd first seen Terence and his friends, but found his obsessive worrying at how it had been engineered, and by whom, irrelevant. These things happened in this country, he knew that. Maybe Terence had had links with the terrorists, as he'd liked to hint. He'd had a gun, presumably, she probed: it had been he who'd murdered Mallachy?

Rory dropped his forehead onto his hand.

'He had a gun. I didn't see it before he fired it. Mallachy threw a stone at him, a big one off the ground, and the next thing was a shot. It hit him, Jessica. In the face or neck. His blood . . . his blood . . . '

Went on the car, thought Jessica. And you lied to me, you said you didn't have a gun.

'Was it Mallachy?' she asked. 'On your side? Was it Mallachy that had the gun?'

His voice was low.

'No. It was me. Hidden in the car. Terence was going to kill me too, the fat one was shouting it, being sick and shouting it, that I was a witness and he should kill me, quick. I got into the car and banged one off. I didn't look, I swear to God I didn't, I just fired it. I didn't even know I'd hit anyone till everyone had gone.'

'You lied to me about the gun. You said you never had a gun. As we drove down to Galway.'

'Yes. I told lies, Jessica. We both told lies, I thought we understood that. If I hadn't had the gun I would be dead. Better maybe.'

They sat in silence for a short while. Jessica reached a hand across the table and touched his.

'No,' she said. 'No more lies between us, Rory, that's rank hypocrisy. I'd rather Terence dead than you.' She tried to smile, but her lips began to wobble. 'Oh fucking hell.' Her voice broke, she gasped in air and sobbed. 'Oh fucking hell, Rory, what can we do, what can we do?'

Later, crazily, she put on the lamb-hearts. Rory she sent to have a bath, bringing him a gin and tonic, the only bathtime drink, she said. The strain around his eyes was easing, and the radio had still made no mention of any gruesome discoveries in lonely northern fields. Their other comfort was, that of all the places in the world he would be safest for the night, this cottage must be number one.

'No one knows you're with me, if anyone even knows you know me,' she told him. 'My mother thinks I'm in Dublin – I dropped her on the way, for God's sake – and she doesn't know Sonia's surname or her phone number because Sonia's a myth! We're across the border, and both cars are hidden. If we'd been trying to escape, we could hardly have done better!'

'We were,' said Rory. 'Don't you remember?'

As he soaked, listening to Jessica in the kitchen, he felt as if his sanity might return. It was the tractor part that bugged him most, the fact that he had taken it to Mayobridge. When he had driven from the field he had been like a zombie, he had been unable to touch Mallachy even to cover him, he had not looked for a second time at Terence Rigby's corpse. But he had taken the part to Mayobridge, afraid that Tom Holdfast would be disappointed if he didn't, as natural as you like. The farmer had been in his meadow when he'd arrived, and Rory had left the parcel and the invoice in the porch and waved, thinking, as he had driven off, that it might even be an alibi of sorts. But it was the fact of having done it that ground down on him. It was inexplicable.

The border crossing, too, had become a huge issue. He had contemplated going home for his bag, but had rejected that as dangerous. Then he had set off at high speed for Donegal, heading first for Belfast to go north round Lough Neagh the Derry way, keeping as far away as possible from his own home territory and the bloody field. Quite suddenly, as he had roared along the M2, it had come to him that if he used any of the crossings close to Derry, he might easily be remembered when the hunt was up. A black BMW with a young man in it, going into Donegal. Not many days before, the same car had come the other way, and words had been exchanged with a British soldier, which might jog memories, also. At the next roundabout, sickly, Rory had turned back on himself, back to Belfast, back down south. He had crossed at the busiest point, Killeen, then struck out west on a tortuous, lonely route that had taken several hours and brought him through towns he'd only ever heard of, and hoped not to see again. Dying of hunger, he had not stopped to eat, dying of thirst he had gone up a hilly track and drunk from a stream. Then, parked out in that wilderness, he had waited and thought before he'd moved on, worried that Jessica might drive him out, or even turn him in.

'I even thought of crossing on an unapproved road,' he told her when they faced their steaming hearts, 'but I figured what would happen if they lifted me. In the end, I only wanted to get to see you. I guess they'll lift me in the end, I'll never get away with it. But I had to see you. I couldn't have you believing I was just a dirty little terrorist. You do believe me, don't you?'

She smiled at him. They were capable of smiling now, the immediate strain had gone. They both thought it was odd, the sense of almost well-being, but they cherished it, they nurtured it, they hoped that it would last.

'A dirty little gunman, but not a terrorist,' she said. 'The question is — how do we get you out of it?'

By daybreak, they were almost in the realms of fantasy, but they also had a base from which to hope. Jessica, who had a need to state a credo, declared that as their land was full of unhung murderers, there was no benefit to heaven from Rory going under. They were both convinced, they had convinced themselves, that no guilt could be attached to what he'd done (although the law would not agree, no doubt) and that escape was the imperative. As the light began to grow across Scalp Mountain, picking out the glimmer of moored yachts, they even considered them as possibles. If Rory could not get away by air, or on a ferry, he could get a boat and sail across to Britain. From Lough Swilly, or Dundalk, or even from Strangford Lough, where both he and Jessica knew yachts owned by their friends, although it would mean returning to the Six Counties and great danger. They went outside to watch the sun come up and chase away the mist, and talked about the navigation. That, he said, would not be difficult.

Throughout the long night, they had worked out the permutations. The fact that they were already across the border was their greatest comfort, for in truth he could only really hope to escape from the Republic side. Even that though, once the hunt was started, would be just about impossible. He could hide, but how long in an underpopulated country without the sort of network the professionals must use? He needed money — which meant bank transactions or a courier — he needed somewhere to live and with a reason to be there, and if he had to move — what price a charcoal BMW! At times, they both had the conviction they were doomed, the tendency — almost overwhelming — was to hang on and get caught. At other times they fought it valiantly, they spoke of other Irish fugitives, it was, at least, a great tradition . . .

It boiled down to this: Jessica would return to Holywood, because if she failed to once the bodies had been found, the balloon would go up with a vengeance. Rory would get back to Hackballs Cross, lock the car up in a barn or outhouse, and go utterly to ground. He had tinned food, booze and water, and more would be provided, somehow. Jessica, as soon as feasible, would sort things out for them in England, probably in London. If need be, she would run away to do it, but she could see no reason why that should arise. And she would get a message to him, work out how they would do the crossing, everything would be all right. Most of all, whatever happened, she would be in touch.

When the sun had warmed them, they went to bed. They made love, but their passion was of love and desperation, not sex, they drew comfort from each other's bodies, they were not seeking ecstasy. Rory went to sleep immediately, and Jessica watched him sleep. A tiny dribble escaped from the corner of his mouth, he was like a little boy. She loved him.

TWENTY-ONE

When Rory Collins woke, he knew immediately where he was. He was lying on his back, and he could hear the screams of seagulls. He had a slight backache from the soft, old-fashioned bed. He turned his head, and his faint fear was confirmed. He was alone. That's it, he thought, she's gone and left me. She's gone to turn me in. The doorknob rattled, and Jessica's head appeared, tousle-haired. She had two mugs of coffee in her hand, and wore a tartan shirt.

'It's on the radio,' she said. 'Two bodies in a field some miles from Rathfriland. No names, no clues, no idea of anything. I think we should get moving.'

Rory sat up, taking his coffee. He put it on the bedside table as Jessica climbed in, turned to embrace her. They lay like that for some moments, hugging hard. Then they sat back, hutched up to the bedhead, and drank.

'I thought you'd gone,' he said. 'Amn't I the cynic? If you want to go, Jessica, I'll understand.'

'Go fuck the Pope,' she said. 'Listen, gulp it down. I've got a feeling we've been given a reprieve. Let's go for it.'

While they dressed, they talked it over, oddly dispassionate. They'd decided there was just a chance that Terence's companions would keep out of it altogether if they could, there was more than just a chance.

'They'd be mad to get involved if they can wriggle out,' said Jessica. 'Is there any way Mallachy and Terence could just have killed each other? Did anybody see the cars, d'you think?'

'It was a hellish lonely spot. Bad luck they've been

found so soon, in fact. In fact, maybe it was Bill and Ben that blew the gaffe, I don't know. Was it Terence's car? He was driving.'

He remembered the noises it had made on leaving. Driven by someone who did not know it, unless they'd gone entirely to pieces.

'He's got a white one, Japanese. What about the gun?'

'I left it in the field, I think. I don't remember, but it isn't in the car. It would be near Mallachy, if I did drop it. It would have my fingerprints.' He stopped. 'His as well, though. Mallachy's.'

'That's something,' said Jessica. 'And they don't have your prints on record, do they? If the others just deny all knowledge . . . They will, won't they? They'll have to.'

Parting was the hardest thing. They kept the radio on, the next bulletin adding nothing new, but time was mocking them. They had only vague ideas about cross-border co-operation by the Garda and the RUC, but they knew the danger grew as the seconds ticked away. Problem was, the thought of facing that danger, however nebulous, made it seem incalculably more real, unbearable. They wanted to be together: they almost wanted nothing more.

It was the telephone that unglued them. As they stood in the doorway looking out, arms jammed around each other's backs, it began to ring. They both jumped, Jessica gasped. Their eyes met, panicky.

'Don't answer it.'

It rang for ages. They did not move, but each could feel the growing tension in the other. They did not speak, as if they might be heard, somehow, down the wires. As soon as it stopped, they went into the garden.

'Who could it have been?'

'Search me. Rory – go.'

He started up the engine, then got out for a last embrace. They held each other fiercely, then touched their lips together. Their smiles were small and hollow as he moved slowly up the gravelled path.

Jessica, when it came her turn to go, cursed her father for his choice of colour for the birthday car. Rory's charcoal was uncompromising enough, but the strange green of the Polo Fox was like a sore thumb. The only permanent near neighbours were Mrs Doyle and her halfwit son, but unfortunately neither of them was blind and deaf. There were also other people who might recognise it on the local roads.

However, Jessica, having tidied through and checked that there were no traces of Rory Collins left, locked the door and started up the little car determinedly. She drove it up the gravel fast, turned left, and made quickly for Ray, where she took a right onto a lonely little road and held the moorland and the mountains until she joined the major road to Donegal at Stranorlar. It was a pity, she reflected, that she'd shopped in Letterkenny so openly the afternoon before, but there was no help for that. This morning she had disappeared like some wraith (she hoped), and memories were uncertain things. There must be other pea-green cars . . .

To stay well clear of the border, she went right down to Sligo before heading off south-east to Longford then to Mullingar. Sligo gave her a pang of misery – lobster, chilled white wine – but also left her wondering. That all this could have happened in such a short time, and to her, Miss Ironsoul, as her Uncle Neil had called her once. She thought of Rory, and thought of love, and wondered. For a while, spinning past the sparkling waters of Lough Bofin, she was happy. Deliriously, she told herself bitterly, a few miles further on.

She crossed the border at Killeen, having ached from Dundalk onwards, with the knowledge she was close to Rory's hideout. She felt, while waiting at the checkpoint, like a dutiful daughter returning from a trip to Dublin – a shopping trip, she realised, and I've not bought a thing. Which reminded her to empty the rubbish gathered so carefully at the cottage into a roadside litter bin. She smiled. Three empty wine bottles – sure evidence that she had spent the night there, if anyone had found them. She didn't even have a headache . . .

On the last part of the road, though, she developed one. It was concentration, fear, anticipation. Three miles from Cultra she was aware that she was getting slower – indeed, she got horn-blasted twice, and had not the heart to snarl or V-sign back. They had found the bodies. Terence had tormented her with Rory's name, someone had made connections. She had absolutely no idea at all what she would find when she got home, but the first thing she saw when she nosed into the drive made her stomach clench. The McCausland car, surely the same one as yesterday. And her mother had said that Parr had gone . . .

Jessica closed her car door quietly, but knew she had been seen. A face at a downstairs window, glimpsed then gone. She looked around her. Another car, one she did not know, a dark blue Vauxhall. She waited.

After about a minute, the back door opened and Parr came out. He walked towards her slowly, his face blank. Jessica suddenly felt like crying, she had to fight back tears. She touched her car for steadiness. The pea-green incorruptible.

'Your mother's inside,' he said. 'She couldn't face you with strangers about, she's gone to her room. You do know, don't you?'

Jessica had decided to deny all knowledge. But she fell straight into the trap.

'Of course I do,' she said. 'I heard it on the radio. How are Uncle Pete and Aunt Sarah?'

'What radio was that?' asked Parr. 'I didn't know that names had been released.'

'I met some friends as I came through town,' she answered, steelily. 'They flagged me down. What is this, Parr? What strangers are about? Why aren't you back in England? Who do you think you're talking to?'

They were six feet apart on the gravel path, surrounded by lush shrubbery and grass, breathing scented air. The bleakness grew. Parr's face had turned to stone.

'I'm talking to a liar,' he replied. 'You haven't been to Dublin, have you, Jessica? You knew the man they found with Terence, didn't you? Mallachy O'Rourke. You know the man who left him in the field, who murdered Terence. You know Rory Collins, don't you?'

Jessica ran past him, crashed into the house. Downstairs were two men in suits, one in his forties, one much younger. They looked at her with faces blank as Parr's had been, as she rushed up to her room. Three minutes later her mother knocked.

'Jessica.'

'It's not locked.'

She was standing by the window, pale-faced but composed. Mrs Roberts ran towards her, hugged her. Her face was awful, her make-up wrecked. Jessica responded half-heartedly to the embrace.

'Oh my poor girl,' wailed Mrs Roberts. 'Oh Jessica, oh Jessica. What's been going on, what terrible things have been happening to you?'

Jessica could see herself in the full-length mirror, enveloped by her mother's back and hair and arms. She was detached, indifferent.

'Parr seems to think I'm involved in Terence's death somehow,' she said, drily. 'What is it, mother? What's it got to do with him, all this? You've never been trying to marry me off to some awful fucking spook or something, have you?'

Her mother began to sob.

'Terence knew the dead man, apparently,' she got out in the gaps. 'The Catholic. He was concerned because

190

they'd been seen with you and Karen. They were gun-men. Oh Jessica, I've been so worried.'

'I'm sure,' said Jessica. 'How did he know them? How did Parr know? Can't you work out anything, Ma?'

'Darling?'

Ah, fuck off, thought Jessica.

Rory had a sense of something wrong as soon as he stepped out of his car in the yard at Hackballs Cross. He killed the engine and listened to the silence of the place. He unlocked a shed and pulled the creaky wooden door open to get the BMW inside, then listened more. He stared narrowly around, trying to remember everything, to locate anything out of its place. The curtains to his secret room were open, surely he would not have left them so? But maybe, with Jessica there, he had forgotten, just for once. He started up and drove the car in, his stomach oddly hollow.

Outside, the door locked, he walked carefully all about the place. Maybe this would be the day he'd meet the lads in training! The possibility sickened him, he knew he would never be able to touch a gun again, or look one in the face. Still feeling odd, he walked through the ancient, dusty house. Upstairs he found the key, then went to the end of the passageway and stared over the trees, across the wide green rolling fields. He orientated himself, faced where he thought Belfast ought to be, turned slightly right for Holywood. Cultra, to be precise. I love you, Jessica, he said aloud, sad and solemnly. I love you, Jessica.

The room horrified him. He opened the door and stood and stared. The curtains were not drawn, but torn down. His eyes took in the mounds of broken glass, the pools of wine and spirits, the shards of ornamental glaze among the ruins of the wash-stand. He walked over to the gas stove, his eyes searching for the missing burners. He lifted up the small fridge, noted the twisted hinges. There wasn't even a cup intact so he could draw some water from the well and have a drink. He was dazed.

So someone must have tipped off Rosie, too. Or perhaps she'd done the sums herself, and come up with the answer. Rory stood in front of the message she had written on the wall at last, and thought nothing relevant. Rather he thought how odd that she should have done all this, then locked the door so carefully and put back the key under the carpet, how very odd.

The message had none of the hate-inspired brilliance that she had wished for before her grief had overwhelmed her. It was smudged, where the lipstick had broken in half. It said: 'Goodbye Rory. I love you.'

Rory wished he could make a cup of tea.

As the day wore on, things got worse for Jessica. She had walked back into her own home, and had found herself alone. Her mother's tears and blandishments were all one-sided, and when her father came he made no pretence. Jessica had sided with the enemy, and the fault must be corrected. Information was the first requirement, and only she could give it.

The trip to Dublin seemed to be their key. All three of them were sure she had not been, although they would not say why. Her mother, who had been party to such small deceptions in the past, provided ammunition, although she had not the fibre or the heart to lead the attack.

'Tanya,' said her father. 'Who is this Tanya? Your mother says she's never heard of her.'

They were in the big sitting room, a view onto the lawn. In the driveway now the Jaguar was added squatly to the cavalcade, but the Vauxhall had gone. Its occupants had not been introduced to her, or mentioned.

'I'm not surprised,' replied Jessica. 'I've never heard of her myself.'

She treated them with contempt. They must think that she was stupid. Sonia was the friend she'd conjured up. Daddy looked at mother, quizzically, keeping up the act. Her contempt grew.

'Sonia, was it?' said Mrs Roberts, timidly. 'I've never heard of Sonia, either.'

'Look,' said Jessica. 'What are you suggesting? That I didn't go to Dublin? I dropped you off, mother. I brought you to Molly's at Downpatrick. Where do you suppose I went after?'

They looked uncomfortable. Screwing with a murderer, was it? They could hardly say that, could they? Parr cleared his throat.

'Jessica, please,' he said. 'We're talking at cross purposes. We're not accusing you of anything, we're trying to flesh something out. There's been a murder. Your cousin—'

'*A* murder!' she shouted, furiously. 'Just one, Parr? Just a Protestant, is that it? I thought there were two men dead! I thought one of them was Mallachy O'Rourke!'

'You knew him!' shouted her father.

'I did not know him! How dare you! Parr told me his name in the garden! The point is he's dead as well and you're not interested!'

Her mother had gone white. Jessica wondered if she would be sick. Her father, on the other hand, was brick-red, breathing badly, fighting for control.

'Girl,' he said, his breath rasping. 'Jessica. Can you not grasp it? We're talking about savages here, gunmen, murderers. This country's being destroyed by savages. All possibility of rationality, it's going out the window. Every little dispute, every little disagreement, someone pulls a gun. Someone gets shot, or blown up, we're sinking in the weight of it. We've got to stop the savages, or we lose the lot, the place is finished.

193

Can you not just grasp that, we've got to stop the savages.'

The hypocrisy of it almost blocked her throat. She stared at her father and she almost hated him.

'But you're the savages,' she said. 'We're the savages, as well. *Two* men were murdered in that field, two.'

'That's right!' he shouted. 'Two! And now we need to find the murderer! To track him down! We need the law, girl, can't you understand? We've got to rule by law, not terrorism! And you withhold your help!'

She began to realise the blindness she was facing. Her father's face, strong, handsome, dark, was like a wall to her. She turned her eyes away to Parr's with something like relief. Now this man she could hate indeed.

'And I suppose you are the law,' she said, her voice quite even. 'A conduit, you said you were. A sewer, more like. A sewer and the sewage, all in one. You lied to me.'

He held her gaze. His face was calm, his colour normal. She hated him.

'Rory Collins is a terrorist,' he said. 'His father was a godfather who provided funds and refuge, both here and in the South. He had a farm somewhere near Dundalk, where they made bombs, stored arms, held weapons training sessions. Rory was certainly involved, he's almost certainly an active member of a group, as was Mallachy O'Rourke.'

'As was Terence Rigby, I suppose?' sneered Jessica. 'It's bullshit, Parr, the whole damn lot of it. It was just some fellers in a field, some he-man antics that went wrong. I've never heard of them, you're whistling up your arse.'

'Jessica,' began her mother, as if saddened by her daughter's capacity for coarseness even at a time like this. Then she cracked. Tears came in floods, she choked and coughed. Samuel Roberts threw a glance of rage at Jessica, put his arm around his wife and patted her.

'Jessica,' sobbed Mrs Roberts. 'Oh Jessica, if you know him, help, help us, help. We'll forgive you.'

So they've spoken to Terence's companions, thought Jessica, coldly, they're sure that Rory was the killer. But what about the gun? Have they found it, do they have any evidence? And Hackballs Cross, they did not know, they could not know, where that was. A farm near Dundalk – well, that was safe enough, indeed. She wondered who in the world, apart from her, might know of it. Rosie, of course. Apart from her and Rosie.

'Who were the fellers?' she said to Parr conversationally, as if her mother's sobbing form were not even in the room. 'Your men in the smart suits. Special Branch? Little spooks like you? You're the ones that's ruined this damned country, Parr. You're the savages.'

It was his turn for contempt. His fine clear eyes filled with it. He stared at her until she began to tremble.

'And you're a fool,' he said. 'If you believe that, Jessica, I pity you, you're a fool.'

She was beginning to break down. The shaking in her hands was obvious. The colour was draining from her face.

While she still could, she blundered from the room and ran upstairs.

By the middle of the evening, Jessica had got into a state that had her parents worried enough to call the family doctor. For herself, she was not sure how much of it was real and how much seized opportunity. It got them off her back, it got them off her back . . .

But alone, she still had fits of shaking, and she could not bid her thoughts. They were twisted, jumbled, horrible. Visions of Rory and the rusty bloodstains on the bonnet of his car, a misty picture of two bodies in a field, compounded more of film-clips than of anything real, perhaps, images of businessmen in bowler hats, of government officials, of millions of banknotes pouring down secret conduits that she could not understand. When the doctor offered her a sedative she was glad to accept, despite her normal scorn for such crutches. The doctor, assuming it was grief at her cousin's tragic death, offered quiet sympathy.

At about ten o'clock she called her mother up and said she was ringing Karen in the Isle of Man. She had to see her, she wanted her to come and stay if possible. Mrs Roberts could only agree, and took the news downstairs. Jessica burst into tears on hearing Karen's voice, and croaked out some of it, while managing to mention neither Mallachy nor Rory by their names. I wouldn't put it past you, she thought, of Parr. I wouldn't put it past you in the slightest.

Five minutes later Mrs Roberts returned to the bedroom and found her daughter apparently asleep. Jessica was feigning, and 'woke up' long enough to say that Karen would come over as early as she could next day, there was a morning boat. Then Jessica smiled wanly, and drifted off again.

'She's sleeping,' Mrs Roberts told the men downstairs. 'She looks so tired. Oh God, I hope she'll be all right.'

'She will,' said Samuel, awkwardly. 'Be sure of it, she is a tough wee child.'

Martin Parr said nothing.

196

TWENTY-TWO

Tom Holdfast, it was observed by Mrs Collins, enjoyed some sort of vogue. Mrs Collins knew only that her son had not come home one night, but there was nothing new or very strange in that. Late on the following day some men in suits arrived to talk to Holdfast, and maybe would have liked to talk with her, except that he forestalled them. The knot of them were standing in the yard as she came from the bungalow, and he half introduced her across the intervening space.

'These are men from Belfast, Mrs Collins,' he said, loudly. 'They were seeking Rory on some business matter but I've said he isn't here. You haven't heard from him, I'd guess?'

She smiled, and the men smiled back at her, not broadly.

'It would be a wonder if I had,' she said. 'He hardly ever rings when he's off gallivanting. He'll turn up some time when he's ready.'

The men in suits glanced at each other, as if deciding something.

Then one said: 'Oh well, thank you, Mrs Collins, it wasn't important.' He had an English accent, and Tom moved them away. She thought afterwards she should have suggested Mallachy, or even Rosie – to ask them if they knew. But she supposed it did not matter.

That night, though, Tom had one of his meetings, which she found surprising. Her memory was not of the best, but she was sure the men had come not long ago. Uncharacteristically, having got out of bed on hearing the vehicle, she stayed to watch them from a window. It was his own lot, the Protestants, the ones that her clever Michael had not even known about. She was slightly disturbed by this, she hoped they were not about to make unreal demands, but she trusted Holdfast. It was a case of having to.

The men were not after money, they were after information. They had been asked to find out things the back door way, things that Parr's official channels could not uncover. They were talking of a farm in the Republic, a place not too far from Dundalk. Tom Holdfast listened carefully to their theories, and their requests, nodding from time to time. Nearly forty minutes passed before they left.

It was after a third night without her son, and another visit by the English to her manager, that Mrs Collins began to worry. She still did not know that Mallachy was dead – the news releases had been deliberately minimal – and Holdfast could not see any gain in telling her. He would have to one day, out of pity, he supposed. But in the meantime, because neither of them had rung, he suggested that her son had gone a'roving, probably, with Rosie and their friend . . .

Karen King's arrival in Cultra caused great tensions. Both Samuel Roberts and Martin Parr were worried that she would prove an ally to what they saw as Jessica's stubbornness and duplicity, while Mrs Roberts was afraid her daughter might be heading for a breakdown, and hoped that Karen would prove the balm she needed. Jessica – more heavily drugged than her doctor had admitted to her – slept late, and Parr himself drove to the harbour to meet the Douglas boat. Karen was surprised and wary when he approached her – a lone young woman clearly seeking someone who had not turned up – and the feelings increased when he introduced himself. She did not play games, however. When he had proved to her satisfaction who he was, she got into the car. She was prepared to listen with an open mind. She was also aware she might be lied to.

Parr had thought out his strategy with care. He told Karen frankly that he was in love with Jessica, and that he was afraid she might have become infatuated with another man. Not to beat about the bush, he said, that man had murdered somebody.

It came as a cruel shock to Karen, crueller for the way he timed it. She gasped, she almost choked.

'You didn't know?' said Martin Parr. 'I'm sorry, I imagined Jessica had told you, on the phone. It was Terence, her cousin Terence who was killed. We had to put her under sedation, we called the doctor. She was in a bad way, as you can imagine. We're all so glad that you could come.'

Karen felt ill. Jessica had gabbled out that something bad had happened, that the shit had hit the fan, but nothing so terrible as this. And Karen could not ask this man, could she? She did not know how much he knew, names even. He rescued her on that, at least, immediately.

'The murderer was Rory Collins,' he said. He pulled smoothly away from a set of traffic lights, accelerated hard. 'I think you know the name?'

Karen shook her head. She croaked something, inaudibly.

'I beg your pardon?'

'No,' she repeated. 'No, I don't think so. We met so many people. Are you sure?'

'Of what?'

'Well, that he . . . That Jessica . . . '

Parr changed gear. His hand was long and slim, brown and rather beautiful. For some reason it revolted her.

'Maybe I could jog your memory,' he said. 'He had a friend called Mallachy O'Rourke. As I understood it, you and Jessica had been out with these two, as a foursome. Once, at least. The Amsterdam. He's dead as well.'

Karen was gasping. She had her mouth open, fighting for her breath. The car purred sweetly down the road to Holywood but she saw nothing. Mallachy was dead. How horrible, appalling. She could not remember, even, what he looked like.

'The point is,' said Parr, 'that Jessica can't see it straight, inevitably. There was some bad blood between this Collins and her cousin Terence, and it all came to violence somehow, down in the country. There was some shooting, and Terence and O'Rourke were killed. I could have lied to you, I could have said this information came from Jessica, but I don't want to deceive, the fact is she doesn't understand, she seems incapable of accepting that Collins is a paramilitary. You know PIRA? The provos, as we English call them. Over here they're called the provies, and Rory Collins is a member. Our problem is that Jessica won't admit she knows him, let alone that he's a murderer who must be brought to book before he kills again. We're pretty certain that she knows where he's in hiding, but she denies she's ever heard of him. Like you do, in fact. We'd be grateful if you'd think that over, incidentally. We'd be grateful if you'd think it over very carefully.'

He stopped talking, as if that were part of some plan. As indeed it was. He flicked his eyes to Karen's face now and again, as she digested, as she thought. Neither of them spoke until the Cultra turn-off was in sight, the left turn down towards the lough.

'You say "we",' she said, at last. 'Who are "we", exactly?'

'Oh, it's just a form of words, it's not significant.' He glanced across at her as he made the turn. 'Look, Miss King, I'm an Englishman. I have no interest in their problems over here, the whole sectarian thing. Like most English people I think it's a tragedy, a vile irrelevance, a nonsense. My only interest is in Jessica and her family, because, quite frankly, I'm in love with her despite this self-delusion, and I still hope they'll be my parents-in-law quite soon. Terence is their nephew, and he has been murdered, and I want to help to solve the crime, that's all. Please – if you can – help too. Don't simply side with Jessica because you're her friend, I honestly believe real friendship, in this case, would mean . . . '

He let the thought hang. They pulled into the drive, and in a moment Mrs Roberts was in the porchway. She looked rather terrible, to Karen, older, pale, shrivelled, as she hurried forward. Karen got out of the car and they embraced, then Jessica appeared, in jeans and jumper, and the three of them were soon in tears. Martin Parr stood awkwardly for a moment, then went into the house, ignored, untrusted.

Cruelly, however, June Roberts was not trusted by her daughter either. After two or three minutes, when Jessica led Karen to her bedroom, she shooed her mother brusquely off, told her to sort Parr out, get lunch prepared, do something useful. The pain on Mrs Roberts' face was terrible, but Jessica was hard and brittle. When she closed the bedroom door behind them, she locked it.

'Christ,' said Karen. 'Oh Christ, Jessica. What has been going on?'

Her tears expended in the garden, Jessica was like a diamond. She explained the story from her side, her side and Rory's, and said she'd called her friend across to help, nothing more nor less.

'I was in a state,' she said, 'but underneath that I'd already worked it out, which is why I didn't really tell you anything. I think Parr is in the secret services, he's something like that, anyway. I doubt if the phone's bugged yet, but it may be and I couldn't take the risk. Rory's in hiding, and Parr's going to pull out all the stops to get him. I'm going to save him and I couldn't really bear it on my own, I needed you. You should see your face, Karen. You think I'm raving, don't you?'

That was untrue, she was merely seeking reassurance. Karen's face, if anything, showed no doubt at all. Was it because of Parr, his questions and psychology, his slim brown hand on the gear lever? She believed Jessica implicitly.

'He told me you were bonkers, more or less,' she said. 'Infatuated with this murderer, but he could handle it, his nobleness was amazing. What did you ever see in him, Jessica? How could you have ever . . . ?'

Jessica grinned, quickly.

'Ach, go on Karen, tell me you didn't get a little buzz whenever you set eyes on him at last? He's like Mack the fucking Knife.'

Karen considered. In fact the air of easy superiority, the penetrating gaze, the self-assurance seemed to have turned her off, if anything. Maybe, she thought uncomfortably, it was a class thing.

'Anyway,' said Jessica, 'what about my mother and my father? Am I not to have loved them, too? They're involved, Karen, they're all a part of something I don't understand, I'm not a party to. But they still love me, don't they? What am I meant to do?'

'It was the coldness I found the oddest bit,' said Karen. 'He kept dropping awful facts in, so deliberately. It was inhuman, somehow.'

'Yes,' said Jessica. 'That rings a little bell.' She drew a noisy breath. 'Look, honestly, I don't know how he works at all, though. He's cold, OK, he's like an icicle, but he's alive with jealousy, Karen, he's burning with it. Hurt pride, maybe, humiliation. It's killing, really, I always thought he hadn't a jealous bone in him, I always tried to level with him about the other fellers.' She stopped. 'Oh, who knows, maybe that's not true,' she said. 'Maybe I'm kidding myself, maybe he thought it was all cod. But it's not cod over Rory and he knows it.

202

Rory's love, Karen. It's not like anything before. The dear knows what they'll do if they should ever find him.'

Karen said: 'He wanted me to help. All I've got to do is find out where Rory is and turn him in. That's what I'd do if I was really fond of you. All for the best, you know.'

They moved towards the bed together, and sat down. They held each other awkwardly. The skin beneath Jessica's eyes was brown and smudgy from the drugs.

'I was afraid he'd pump you in the car,' she said. 'I was petrified. I'm pretty sure they've nothing concrete to go on, he hasn't confronted me with sightings at Letterkenny or anything like that, but they'll be watching us like hawks, and they'll be fighting dirty. I still don't understand it, that's the hardest thing. Everything I'd been brought up to believe, all the old crap about sectarianism being evil, how intolerance would destroy our land, and then they go insane. I don't want to hate them, I don't want to treat my mother hard, but what can I do? They're going to kill him if they find him, and my parents are a part of it. Parr's going to kill him.'

She extricated herself from Karen's arms and stood. She yawned, a hungry breath to fight the sleeping pill.

'He said he loved you, in the car,' said Karen. 'He said he wants to marry you, still.'

For a moment, Jessica's eyes were venomous.

'I'd rather kill myself,' she said.

Then she yawned again, and pulled Karen briskly to her feet.

'It won't be true, will it?' she said. 'It's all a part of what they're up to. Look, let's try something, shall we? Let's go out to lunch, see what they say about it? Let's go to the Amsterdam, and stuff the lot of them.'

It was a nice idea, they told themselves, a neutral one that no one could object to – and it would be the perfect test. As they walked downstairs Mrs Roberts met them, a false smile on her face. She was in an apron, and announced that lunch would be five minutes – daddy was parking, he'd come home from Belfast specially to say Hallo to Karen. When Jessica said they were going out her mother went bright red, and very soon Mr Roberts added his weight. It was not an overt thing, no one came out and said 'You can't', but anyone could see which way the wind was blowing. Jessica grew tight about the lips.

'What is this, Ma?' she said. 'House arrest? I'm not a pregnant teenager, you know.'

Her father flushed.

'Jessica,' he began, his voice already with a dangerous edge. Mrs Roberts touched his arm.

'Darling. Jessica's been . . . the doctor . . . '

'Your mother's gone to trouble.' His voice was thick. 'It's a special lunch to welcome Karen back.'

'We'll have it in my room,' said Jessica. 'I won't be ordered to.'

Karen intervened.

'Oh come on, Jessica, let's eat down here. It smells wonderful. We can go out later, maybe.'

'Any time I like,' Jessica gritted. 'Any time I damn well like.'

'Yes, dear,' said her mother faintly. Her father's back was disappearing into the dining room. 'Come on now, darling. Please.'

Karen tried hard at small talk, as did Martin Parr, but still the lunch was terrible. Afterwards, Karen said she thought that Jessica should lie down, and led her up the stairs again. Jessica threw herself onto her bed, face down, and balled her fists.

'What can I do?' she said. 'Karen, what can I do? They'll drive me mad in the end, no kidding, they'll really drive me mad.'

'Why don't we work on that?' said Karen. 'It's not bad, when you think about it.'

Jessica rolled over. She was interested.

'What?'

'You know. You're doing it already, you can't fool me. It's not bad at all.'

Jessica sat up, and hugged her knees.

'Go on,' she said.

In the normal way of things, Rosie Kennedy would have known as much as anybody about the deaths of Mallachy and Terence Rigby. But after her destruction spree at Hackballs Cross, she found she could not bear to return to her apartment full of girls in West Belfast, or indeed her job. She left messages that she had picked up an infection and gone home to Claudy for some nursing by her mother, but went south instead, to a houseboat on Lough Ree owned by a man she'd once gone out with, a man in his fifties with money and compassion whom she knew would never mind. She had to break a window to get in, but he'd accept that also, if it ever came to it. For uncountable hours she licked her wounds, sometimes lying on the stateroom bunk, sometimes staring at the quiet waters of the lough, sorting herself out. She did a lot of crying, but she also lost three pounds, she found out later. It was a funny sort of compensation.

Rory, in the farm at Hackballs Cross, was leading a similar existence. Mallachy was his main ghost, his face was everywhere, the sound of his voice, his vile aggressive humour, the picture of his torn cheek, inside-out and bloody on his jawbone. Jessica flitted in and out, and Rosie turned up, too, darker and more reproachful than she was in life. Most weirdly, he kept meeting her in erotic dreams, her large, hard breasts and curving belly obliterating Jessica's leaner, flatter form. Several times Jessica, ousted, left the room and left them to it, and they would fuck each other tenderly, until Rory woke bathed in guilt and sweat and with an erection that, in wakefulness, he would deal with desperately for Jessica, only Jessica. He picked among the wreckage for tins and tin-opener, and lived on cold ravioli and cold water, a diet varied sometimes with skinless sausages in beans. For a long time he could not bear to start a clear-up, moving only to go outside and urinate or defecate, and to listen to the radio in the car, which worked reasonably even in the shed. He was amazed at how little news there was of Mallachy and Rigby, how quickly it was forgotten altogether. There had been no mention of himself at all, or the two Protestants, or a manhunt. He worried interminably as to whether it was manipulation of the news, or whether, in this sad country, it was just of no importance. He could not make up his mind which would have been the worse.

When Rosie heard about Mallachy, back in the house of girls, it was mentioned only because one of them thought she might have known him, vaguely. Rosie was shocked but hid it, and escaped to her room as soon as possible. The pay-phone in the house was relatively private, so when she could she went and rang Rory's number. Break-up or no break-up, she had to share commiserations, find out details. She got Mrs Collins.

'Hallo? It's Rosie. Hallo, Mrs Collins, could I speak with Rory, please?'

Three minutes later, sick with shame and hatred, she hung up again. As far as Mrs Collins knew, her son was ranging through the countryside on one of his jaunts. The only surprise was that Rosie was not with him, so perhaps he'd gone with Mallachy O'Rourke — would she make sure to have him ring, whenever she should find him? Rosie promised. Back in her room, she raged. She had no doubt at all about the truth of it.

You bastard, she told herself, you awful, awful bastard! Off screwing with the new one, and your best friend hardly cold. He was probably down at Hackballs Cross, she thought, he was probably fucking in the wreckage, underneath her message on the wall. While his poor daft mother did not even know that Mallachy was dead. What a bastard.

Mrs Collins, though, was not as daft as that. After tea that night, when all the men had gone, she went to the business block and found Tom Holdfast still working on his books as usual. She told him that she knew something was wrong and she thought that he could tell her what it was. He led her to a larger room and sat her down, taking another chair himself. He told her about Mallachy and the disaster in the field, he told her that Rory was involved somehow and that he'd disappeared, presumably into hiding. He did not think, himself, he said, that Rory would have done anything bad or evil, he was not that type of man.

She listened to it all in silence, her face revealing nothing. She had a handkerchief in her hand, which she had taken from a pocket in her dress. She folded it, intently.

'Where is he, Tom?' she asked, at last. 'Is he in that farm of Michael's, in the South?'

They held each other's eyes.

'I think he might be, Margaret. It seems the ideal place.'

Mrs Collins rolled the handkerchief.

'Those men who visit you. Have they been asking?'

'The Englishmen. Yes, they have.'

'And the others, Tom. I know about the others, too. The Orange murderers we finance.'

Holdfast did not alter his expression. Margaret Collins moved her head.

'You know where that farm is, don't you?' she said. 'No one else does. I never cared to. Have you told them? Will you?'

His green-flecked eyes appeared to change somehow, beneath the snowy brows. He stared at her, but did not reply. Margaret Collins, finally, bunched up the handkerchief.

'You're a good man, Tom,' she said, quietly. 'Keep me in the picture if you can. If you should hear anything at all.'

'We might somehow try a message. I thought about it. It might be dangerous, though. One could be followed.'

She stood, slowly. She had a hand upon the chairback.

'We'll bide our time,' she said.

TWENTY-THREE

It took more than two days for Jessica and Karen's plan to mature, but they were careful not to spoil it by hurrying. The evening of the first day, Jessica came downstairs dressed as if for dancing, and threw a violent scene when her parents kept up the stubborn pressure for her to 'stay in and recover'. She shouted and threw crockery, with Karen joining in the efforts to calm her down. When the doctor was suggested – threatened, bellowed Jessica, threatened! – Karen had to stop her from jumping on her father with nails unsheathed, and finally led her up the stairs to bed. With the door safely locked behind them they recovered in two minutes, then soberly assessed performances. Agreeing that they might have overdone things, Karen went downstairs after half an hour to apologise on her friend's behalf. Mrs Roberts was later allowed to see her daughter, tired and contrite on the bed. She told her husband things were bad.

Martin Parr, in the first instance, played it very cool. He did not need Mrs Roberts to tell him to be careful with her daughter, and was prepared each time he visited to make a tactful exit. He tried at first to engineer more talks with Karen, but she was not good enough an actress to pretend she liked or sympathised with him, so he did not press the point. He told her once, meeting in the garden, that he was worried about Jessica's state of mind, and thanked her for her support and sympathy. The investigations, he could not resist adding, were going very well – Jessica's green car had been seen near the family cottage in Donegal. Karen took the news to Jessica, and they wondered why he'd let it out. To worry her, they decided, it was the only reason possible. Now wasn't that a queer way to protect the one you loved?

In truth, despite the clues that had been pieced together, despite his rational blandishments to Karen, despite many hours of work by many men, Parr was little farther on. Because of Terence Rigby's crude and foolish intervention, whatever had inspired it, Parr's target had gone to earth irrevocably, and his frustration was immense. Terence's death mattered nothing to him, but from now on he was determined there would be no more amateurs, no meddlers, no mistakes. More immediately, certain that Jessica realised she was virtually a prisoner in her home, he waited for her to devise a way out. So that she would lead him to his goal.

There were no more scenes, but Jessica went downhill. She began to keep to her room, refusing even to come downstairs to eat, and demanded that her daddy should bring in Karen's bed so that she would not be alone at night. She frightened her mother one morning by tearing out her telephone (not unplugging it) and throwing it on to the lawn, bouncing it off the head of a stone statue of some minor goddess. While Karen's tray meals got bigger, Jessica's came down largely untouched, however enticing Mrs Roberts had made them. She was so wan these days that no one noticed she lost no weight. She lost no weight because she ate half what Karen had.

It was Karen who took the formal proposal to her parents, one night that Jessica had gone to bed – supposedly to sleep – not far past nine o'clock. She found them sitting in the dining room, the table still uncleared, not even talking. She said that Jessica had expressed an interest in going with her to the Isle of Man, and she wondered what they thought of it. They would stay with her Aunt Jane, who could be telephoned at any time if they had any qualms, and the very fact that Jessica had suggested it she thought of as a good sign: these days she hardly spoke. Mr and Mrs Roberts needed no persuading, although Mr Roberts wondered, privately, how Martin Parr would react. With Jessica out of Ireland, how could she bring him to his prey?

Martin Parr reacted well. Samuel Roberts phoned him late that night and he was cockahoop, although he did not show it. He had known that Jessica was far too smart to think she could sneak out of the house and contact Rory Collins undetected, so this would be another stratagem. Unless she'd really given up, but that he could not honestly believe. Next day he came round by appointment, and Jessica heartened everybody by being up, and dressed, and lively. She was even friendly, she touched Parr's hand and kissed her father on the cheek. She liked the Isle of Man, she told them, she had always liked it. It was peaceful, unhurried, calm, it would help her find her feet again, it would take her mind from off the Province. This sounded rational, and grave, and sensible. Karen kept her expression straight with difficulty.

But Jessica had another shot. With everybody settled and relaxed, she announced that she would take the wedding dress with her. *Her* wedding dress. Parr and her mother grew tense.

'But why, darling?' asked Mrs Roberts. 'It's so bulky. It's so old and delicate.'

'Hah!' said Jessica. 'It fitted in a car boot well enough! What's up, Parr? Don't you trust me with it? I'm meant to love you, aren't I?'

Her eyes were snapping, and Karen saw the blows strike home like bludgeons. Parr, and Mrs Roberts, and Jessica's father stared at her as if she was quite mad. Karen realised that there was no quarter any more, no mercy for this man. She thought she knew what Jessica intended, for the dress.

'Of course,' said Jessica. 'If you don't intend to marry me whenever I get better, just say the word. You told Karen you did, though. Didn't you?'

Parr spoke. He had recovered, but his lips were thin as knifeblades.

'If you want to take it, Jessica,' he said, 'it will make me very happy. It's precious, but then you know that, don't you? It's robust enough, I'm sure.'

'And there must be no surveillance, Parr,' said Jessica. 'You understand that, don't you? No phone-tapping, no men in funny raincoats watching us while we're peeing in the bushes? No, I'm not joking, Parr.'

'Darling . . . ' began her mother. Jessica quelled her with a glare.

'OK,' said Parr, finding again he had no choice. 'Agreed.'

'No surveillance?'

'Nothing.'

Parr gives his word, thought Karen King, and Parr is lying. That is understood.

She wanted to get out of this house now, rather badly. And Northern Ireland.

There had to be a message carrier, or the whole thing was a wreck. Jessica had worked it out with the phone book, although she had not dared to make a confirmation call. Some things were best done cold, she agreed with Karen, the shock element might save the whole damn enterprise. On the other hand . . .

Parr was told that they would catch a certain ferry, and that he was not allowed to take them to the docks — although he was at liberty to have them followed if he did not trust them! Mr Roberts was told he had to go to work, and Mrs Roberts that she could ring them in Port Erin, kiss them goodbye at the gateway, even, but could go no farther with them. Jessica was brisk and businesslike, and organised her bags as if she were off on the Grand Tour. There were a lot of bags, for her, one of them the large, square, solid case that held the wedding dress, and they

212

were marshalled in the hall. Parr, ironically withdrawn, offered to call the taxi and was politely thanked. The driver, when it arrived, helped them move the baggages, and did not watch them as they made farewells.

Karen kissed Mrs Roberts on the cheek, and got a hug. She and Parr touched hands, and said goodbye. Jessica embraced her mother coldly at first, then gave her a big impulsive cuddle. She held Parr's hand for a moment, then offered him her lips. It was a peculiarly warmthless gesture.

'Goodbye,' she said. 'Don't mind me, Parr, I'll be better soon. I'm sorry if I'm giving you hard times. Goodbye, Ma, I'll ring whenever we arrive and if I don't it doesn't mean I don't love you, I'll have got seduced by alcohol on the boat. You ring me at Aunt Jane's, eh?'

The doors slammed and the diesel grumbled and they left. Karen turned in her seat and waved before they took the bend. Jessica did not.

As agreed, they did not speak much in the taxi, and indeed there was nothing much to say. They did not expect that Parr would really have them tailed, but they kept their eyes open without chattering about it, in case the driver thought them cracked. It was overcast and warm, but they had little interest in the weather. The road from Holywood looked just as normal, nothing changed, nothing that required comment. There was a snarl-up at the flyover, but not enough to hold them back. However, as they crossed Queen's Bridge they both grew tense.

The taxi, across the Lagan, entered the one-way system and bore them away from their goal. They glanced at each other, touched hands on the seat between them. Jessica had checked and rechecked in the phone book, she was confident that it would turn out right. The lights stopped them, they held their breaths. They moved on, turned right, turned right again. They were in Victoria

Street. Unless she'd got it wrong completely, in two hundred yards they should see –

'Stop here!' said Jessica. It came out as a sort of squawk. It was too early, anyway, but she had seen it. Blaney Chemist, the name in large black lettering edged with gold. The driver glanced over his shoulder.

'Do what?' he said.

'The chemist. Just up on your left,' said Jessica. 'Pull over, will you? Please.'

They were in a stream of traffic. The driver showed no sign of slowing down. They were almost there.

'I can't stop here,' he said. 'It's a control zone. The Brits would come and blow my cab up.'

There was humour in his voice, but not much. They were going to drive past. Jessica's voice changed.

'Listen,' she snapped. 'I'm not asking you to leave it unattended, I'm telling you to stop for a wee while. I've got to buy something, OK? Just do as you're told.'

Karen, recognising the put-down of the lower orders tone, was embarrassed. The driver was of sterner stuff.

'Look, Miss,' he said, 'it's a control zone, it's a main road, it's a racetrack. I'd like to help you, but—'

Jessica leaned forward in her seat and hissed at him.

'Youse can fucking stop and fucking drop us altogether, then,' she said. 'And youse can whistle for your fare. Have youse never heard of women's things? Do youse want a mess on your back seat?'

The driver, face dark with shame and anger, pulled across the carriageway and bounced onto the kerb.

'One of you stays,' he said. 'And I'm going in two minutes. If I get moved on you've had me.'

Jessica threw Karen a twisted smile as she got out and headed for the door of Blaney Chemist, but as she pushed it open, the smile faded from her lips, the courage in her died. She saw a girl behind the counter and knew immediately that it was Rosie Kennedy.

Rosie knew something, too. As the elegant young

woman came towards her, she read her face and knew that some disaster had tracked her to her lair. At Hackballs Cross she had not looked, she had hidden herself when Rory and his new lover had come out to their cars. But some disaster had tracked her to her place of safety. Jessica watched the full, dark face grow pale, saw the freckles stand out orange on the pretty nose and cheekbones. She knew that she was paling, also.

'Rosie?' she said. Her voice was faint. 'I'm Jessica, I'm Rory's friend. I'm sorry if he hasn't told you properly, but . . . '

There were several people in the shop, and behind the counter, through an open archway, a fattish man was visible, making up prescriptions. The two young women were aware of all this, or they might have broken down. Rosie suffered a wave of shock, that she should be put to this, that she should be confronted. She could not speak.

'I know where he is,' said Jessica. 'They're after him, and I have to go away, I'm going to organise for him to get to England, escape. You've got to help.'

The second shock was even greater, but it was different. Rosie was bemused. But he's with you, she thought, he's run off screwing you!

'Who's after him?' she said. It was only words, because as she spoke she knew, it all fell into place, she understood. Mallachy and the Prod were dead, and they were hunting Rory. 'Is he at the farm?'

'He's safe,' said Jessica. 'He's got food and everything – well, you know all that. I'm going to the Isle of Man, Port Erin, then I'll make arrangements. I need your number, you'll have to pass on messages. Will you do that? Rosie, please.'

Rosie's face was like a waxen mask, her eyes enormous, black. She could only nod.

'He'll have to get a boat,' said Jessica. Another customer was approaching them, a woman with a box of something in her hand. Jessica glanced at her, agonised. 'We've already talked about it, he'll understand. There'll only be one message, they'll be watching me. He must get it, you must pass it on.'

She was pleading, they were chained together by their eyes. The woman was beside Jessica, almost nudging her.

'He's not to move until he hears,' said Jessica. 'He mustn't move an inch, an *inch*.'

'Excuse me,' said the woman. 'Are you serving?'

Rosie turned her eyes to her as if she was not there. She bent quickly, took a pen, wrote on a piece of paper. As she pushed it across to Jessica her hand was shaking violently. Tell him that I love him, Jessica screamed inside her head. You must tell him that I love him, if you can.

'I'm sorry, Madam,' Rosie said. Her voice was grotesque. 'Can I help?'

Jessica turned and stumbled from the shop, the piece of paper screwed tightly in her hand, as if a wind would come especially to steal it from her. She threw herself into the taxi before she could collapse. The driver banged the clutch in and jumped it savagely into the stream of vehicles. Karen looked at her.

After two minutes, Jessica unscrewed the paper with both hands. On it was a Belfast phone number.

They went and caught the boat.

TWENTY-FOUR

Martin Parr, when he received the call, was not consumed with fury. The taxi driver was not a fool (he was not a taxi driver, either) and as he presented it, could not have turned down Jessica's demand without blowing his cover and his master's. In any case, Parr had been half expecting something, and admired Jessica and Karen for the execution. So she had visited Blaney's chemist's shop for some tampons, had she? And emerged with nothing in her hands, to boot. Parr dismissed the man's suggestion that he should return there to suss things out, because he thought there would be better ways. 'What would you ask for?' he said, satirically. 'Something for the weekend? We don't even know who she went to talk to, do we? Get back to base, man, I'll call you if I need you. You've done all right.'

Through the official channels — tapped unofficially, of course — it took him just over an hour to discover Rosie Kennedy's name and details as an employee of the shop. There were only she and Joseph Blaney, and he knew which one he'd put his money on. Soon after that he had her number at the house of girls in West Belfast, and had arranged a phone tap, top priority. There were lacunae in his information — there always were these little gaps — which again did not annoy him because he expected them. She was not known as an associate of anyone, for instance, least of all Rory Collins, and even her family connections had not made the records. She was not marked down as a driver, either, which might have helped. As an afterthought, therefore, he put a tap on Blaney, too.

One never knew with Jessica and men, one never knew.

But Parr was satisfied he had his girl. He would have liked to talk to her immediately, he would have liked to know what the connection was. But he could wait. He rang the operations centre and organised a watch and tail, plus a clandestine photograph as soon as possible. She was a courier, most probably, and there was just a chance she might move quickly, even after work that afternoon.

His business done, he went downstairs and said goodbye to Mrs Roberts. She was still subdued at parting from her daughter, but he told her to be brave, he told her it would all come out well, very soon. He was not even very perturbed, twenty minutes later, when he was bleeped, and stopped his hire car at a phone box. A team had gone to Blaney's, he was told, but the bird had flown. One of them had asked where the nice assistant was, because she'd given him some help that morning, and Mr Blaney had got quite irate. She'd gone off with another headache, he had said, and he was getting rather sick of her and her bad health. Although this time, he did admit, she had looked pretty shaky.

Ah well, thought Parr, back in the McCausland car, not much harm done. Assuming that she was carrying messages from Jessica to Rory Collins, it was unlikely that this first one was more than a goodbye, or news that she was going to the Isle of Man. Jessica could not know the deal was rumbled, she'd have to use the phone sometime. And if Miss Kennedy only had a headache, she'd be back at work tomorrow, wouldn't she?

At Hackballs Cross that afternoon, Rory had got the Zetor out, intending to do some silage work. He had dickered about it for more than a day, afraid that even in the green heart of the country someone might hear and wonder.

As far as he could tell from the radio no one knew that he was on the run, and in any case he was in the Republic, and in a part not noted for its sympathy to Englishmen or Northern Ireland causes. But he was afraid, he did not deny it, afraid of what forces might be ranging out for him. He remembered Mallachy and his Sperrin Mountain tales. Even in the stoutest part there were informers. Touts were just another element in the richness of their history. He remembered Mallachy.

But if he did not do something he would go stark staring mad. He had recovered from his deathlike, shattered state some time ago, he had blitzed the secret room like fifty washerwomen gone demented. He had hauled out everything beyond repair and put it on the tip. He had cleared away all messes, carrying water in a billycan he'd rooted from the ancient kitchen and fixed the handle of. He had scrubbed the sticky bits off his mattress and his curtains and his duvet cover and put things out to dry on bushes. He got baling wire from a barn and bound up chair and table legs until he had a little rudimentary furniture, he'd picked up broken glass until he could have eaten a hot dinner from the carpet. Hot dinners, though, he could not have, because Rosie had banged in the cooker valves. He could have boiled water for his tea outside, but – for all he knew – she'd pissed among his tea bags and into his instant coffee jar. Certainly, she'd poured something in them, they were ruined.

Once he'd started, Rory worked to stop himself from brooding. Despite the dreams of Rosie, when he was awake his mind was filled with Jessica. He had never been in love before (if he'd thought so, this lot had proved him wrong, and with a vengeance) and sometimes the obsession drove him near to hatred. He could not get her from his mind, not for a second, he missed her as if physically, he found himself reiterating her name, Oh Jessica, Jessica, over and over again, and looking towards Belfast and closing his eyes and lowing like a beast. Once or twice he dozed off and woke up with his mind clear of her, it was conscious, like rebirth, then as he rejoiced, it would slam back, a blow to mind and stomach, and he would curse, and mock himself. He was enslaved.

When the room was done, he turned to the farm. He repaired some broken slates, he fixed two door catches and some hinges. He checked the air and fuel filters of the Zetor and greased and oiled her as necessary. In the end, he started her and sat in the steel sprung seat, bouncing rhythmically. Even that reminded him of Jessica, and sex, but that was not too bad. After a while, he backed into the sunshine, and thought. Yes, he would do some silage. Jesus – what if Tom Holdfast sent the Clancys down? Jesus – further – what did Tom Holdfast think, or his mother? Oh God, how could he get in touch with them?

He nearly had a heart attack when he saw a flash of red among the bushes of the drive. He cut the engine, willing it to die more quickly than the heavy flywheel would allow. He began to slither down, his hand still on the cut-off, when he saw more of the car. Oh God, the heart attack was real! It was Rosie, Rosie in her little Metro. Oh God, it could not be.

Before she had left Belfast, Rosie had gone shopping. She had walked quickly to the car park where she left her car, not considering for a moment that she might be watched. The shock of meeting Jessica had left her stunned, but in some ways she was coldly rational. There was no mistaking Jessica's fear and pain, no possibility that it was some foul plan to betray Rory. If she'd wanted to, she could have led the RUC, the Brits or anyone to Hackballs Cross, but she had come to seek her out and ask for help. Rosie was sure that for the moment she could move in safety.

She drove blindly, but with a clear idea of what she needed, and where to get it. At a yacht chandlers she bought a handlamp and a butane stove, a set of pans, a sleeping bag. Farther down the road she found a minimart and got tins of food, longlife milk, candles, salt and matches. Next an off-licence, for cans of beer, bottles of wine, two bottles of John Powers. She spent money like a sailor, largely on her credit card, and hardly discriminated. Her mind was out of focus much of the time, swimming with her thoughts of Jessica and fears for Rory. There was hate and there was misery, confusion on confusion. As an afterthought she bought jeans and underpants, some socks, some shirts, some shaving foam and chuckaway razors. It was getting out of hand, she was like some crazy mother. She even bought some thrillers and a yachting magazine. Oh God – and would he sail away from her, from her and Ireland? She blasted down the M1, her vision blurred with tears.

Now, climbing from the car, she hugged some of the smaller items to her stomach, like offerings, or perhaps more like talismans to ward off a rebuff. Rory, behind the tractor, thought of coloured beads and natives. She'd destroyed his place, betrayed him. And here she was equipped with baubles, to entice him out into the open.

At first, he did not move. He watched her coldly, trying to snake out of the little car clutching her parcels. She was in her workday clothes, he could see her white coat flung across the back of the passenger seat, he could see her face was flustered. Then a package dropped onto the flags, and burst across her shoes and ankles. It was milk, in a waxed cardboard carton. A look of such misery turned up on her face that he felt his heart go out. He stepped from behind the Zetor, showed himself. Rosie, in a gesture of despair, dropped the rest of her first load into the mess, and began to cry.

They moved together slowly after that. No race into each other's arms. Rory covered most of the distance, while Rosie got just beyond the bonnet of the car. He saw the butane stove in the white puddle.

'Well,' he said. 'Better late than never. Would you like a cup of tea?'

Rosie wiped her face.

'She sent me,' she said. 'Rory, I'm sorry about the place. I'm sorry about Mallachy and everything. Oh Christ, Rory.'

She rested on the bonnet of the Metro, perched. Rory stared at her.

'*She* sent you? Which she? Do you mean . . . ?'

'You can say it. Jessica. Oh, we're old pals now, my love. I'm the messenger. That's funny, isn't it? Me running messages for the high-born Proddie lady. I must be cracked.'

Rory moved round, careful not to touch her, and picked up the stove. He noted all the gear inside the car.

'Did she send the stuff? God, there's a lot of it. Rosie – what can I say?'

'Sorry? Thank you?' She made a gesture, low down by her knees. 'No, she did not send it. I did, I bought it for you. I was sorry for you, God knows why. I want you to escape.'

Stupidly, Rory wanted to talk about Jessica. He knew it would be stupid, cruel. It became perverted into an accusation, almost. Something that had nagged at him.

'How did you know?' he said. 'That I was here, that afternoon? That I was here with Jessica?'

There was another thing, as well. How had Terence Rigby known, when he'd followed him and Mallachy? Under his gaze, Rosie reddened, although not wildly.

'I guessed. Well, I guessed the place. I had a call. A phone call.'

'Who?'

'No one you know. A friend in Connemara. You had been seen. It was thought you'd jump again.'

Rory reddened now. Rosie waited.

'There's always friends,' she said. 'You ought to know that, Rory. You will not be safe here long.'

No point, then, asking about Terence Rigby. He was ashamed he'd even thought it. Why reveal that shame, to add to all the others?

'You made a damn fine job of smashing the old place,' he said, smiling. 'I can't say that I blame you, Rosie. For what it's worth, I'm sorry about all this. I know you'll disbelieve me, but it's been a shock to me as well. I don't know what happened, I don't know what is happening. She's a—'

He was at it again. He'd been about to call Jessica a 'fine girl'. Fine girls ye all are, he thought. More's the pity.

'Just don't talk about it, right? I said I'd bring you messages, but I never said I wouldn't ... oh, I don't know. Rory, get this stuff out of my car, will you? I want to get back home.'

She turned away, twisted sideways off the bonnet, looking at the ground. He made to say some more, but caught himself, thought better of it. He was able, strangely, to recognise his crassness and her pain almost indifferently, as though all emotion belonged to someone else, was not a part of his experience. Rosie kept her back to him, her shoulders forward, as if she had a stomach ache.

She did not help him with the gear. She straightened up at last, went over to the Zetor, rested against an enormous tyre. The heat from the engine, newly run, radiated on her skin. She loved the Zetor, she drove it often. No more, no more.

Rory was sweating when he had the car unloaded. Some of the stuff he'd carried straight into the kitchen, to keep it off the flags. Also, to get away from Rosie's presence, she irked him, pained him in a peculiar way. Other people's suffering, an awful bore, he told himself – especially when you were yourself the cause. He wondered, hot and finished, if he should offer her a can of beer.

'Look,' he said. 'Rosie. Let me pay, at least. I mean, it's great of you to . . . Oh Jesus, you know.'

He had approached within ten feet. Rosie stayed against the tractor, eyes on the ground. He could go no closer.

'I don't want your money,' she said. 'I don't want anything. Put it down against the damage.' She glanced up, she laughed, short but genuine. 'Jessica told me you had food and everything. God sake, if only she'd have known! She made me guilty for a wee moment. Rory?'

Her face was calm and serious. She was on her feet, no longer leaning on the Zetor.

'Yes?'

'I'll get over it. All this. You're an appalling bastard but I'll get over it. She looks quite . . . you know. For a Protestant.'

She grinned, and Rory's face almost broke into two. She's wonderful, he cried inside, she's wonderful!

'Christ, Rosie. You're fucking marvellous.' He surprised himself, he meant it. 'For a Catholic!' he yelled.

They moved towards each other, touched for the first time. It was not gone, though. Rosie's pain was still there, the laughter had not lasted long. She hurried round the Metro's stubby front and dropped in sideways, snatching in her feet, automatically reaching for her seat belt. The engine started at a touch.

'She said to think about a boat,' she told him. 'She said she'd be in Port Erin and there'd be just one message. I could help you, maybe? With the boat?'

Her door was open. He held the top of it.

'I think I'll be OK,' he said. 'I've worked that out. There's a friend down in Portmarnock who'll not mind it if his goes missing in a good cause, I'll square it after. He never locks the bastard.'

'There's always friends,' said Rosie. 'Tell no one anything will you, Rory? Never trust the friends.'

Her face was sad. There were tear marks underneath her eyes.

224

'I trust you,' he said. 'It's desperate, isn't it? After all the things I've done. Rosie – can you ring my mother for me? I feel terrible about her, she must be getting frantic, even her.'

'Tom Holdfast told her you'd be off with Mallachy, she didn't even know that he was dead. Maybe I'd best have a word with him first, see what she knows? Oh God, Rory, the Brits are after you. Holdfast is a Protestant. Another of the friends.'

'He knows about this place, too. If he'd a mind to tell them, they'd have lifted me already. He's a good skin, Rosie. Speak to him. If he asks you, tell him. He won't ask. You've got to trust somebody, Rosie. There's no other choice.'

There seemed little left to say. Their eyes met, and Rory closed her door. The window was already down. Rosie put the Metro into gear.

'I'll not be back,' she said, quietly. 'Not until I bring the message. I'll ring your mother.'

He nodded.

'You don't hate me, do you, Rosie? Why are you doing this for me?'

'I hate you for a child,' she said. The car was rolling forward. 'Don't let the bastards grind you down.'

He watched the Metro bounce slowly along the rutted track, until it went from sight. She'd never even asked, he realised, if he'd murdered Terence Rigby.

TWENTY-FIVE

Her first task, Jessica decided on the Isle of Man, was to see how obviously they were being watched. On the ferry they had practised spotting spooks, fixing on a woman who appeared to leave the bar each time they walked into it, and a man of fiftyish with a fawn raincoat who kept staring openly at them. By the time they were halfway across they had found the woman fast asleep in a deck chair, and they saw the man warned by an officer after a teacher from a tripping convent school had told him publicly to steer clear of her girls. They stood at the ferry terminal for ages after everyone had left, until they stood alone. The bus they later caught was empty after seven stops.

Aunt Jane knew 'all about' Jessica, and they had agreed beforehand to do the giddy types on holiday routine, so that they could stay out late or disappear at will. When Jessica had first phoned up in trouble Karen had kept it from her aunt, and when she'd gone across to pick up pieces had lied about a folk festival. As far as Jane – an ex-civil servant who loved the sea and peace – knew, this was a return trip, a chance for Jessica to get out of the rat race. Like most ex-patriate English people, especially escapees from London, she had a view of city life that tended to the lurid and the racist, with brass knobs on in Belfast's case. She was no trouble, though, she fed them when they wanted food and smiled a lot. In fact, they were not in much.

They were, of course, convinced that Parr was watching them. On their first clear morning they took another bus to Douglas, separated for an hour, then remet at a pub when Karen had hired a car. After that they drove around like tourists, setting traps up lonely roads to see if they could smoke out followers. They even booked onto the ferry for Liverpool, using their real names, then did not board. As on the afternoon before, they found themselves alone, unwatched and wondering what to do.

Although they found it hard, they had to take it seriously. Jessica had to phone friends in England, London friends, and organise some cover. The more they talked about it, the harder it began to look, the more ridiculous, the more impossible. But if they did ring – when they got round to it, when their courage let them try – they had to be sure they would not be observed, or listened to. They found themselves sitting in cafés, or in pubs, sympathising with criminals. The whole thing was hideous, when you thought about it, there was nothing simple about a life of crime. All they had to do was get someone from Ireland into London and hide him. A wanted someone, a someone known to the Army and police and secret services. They found it very difficult not to get depressed.

'Or Manchester,' said Jessica, hopefully. 'Manchester would do for a start. I've hidden a few men there in my time. I had seven in my old flat in Rusholme once, all thinking that they lived alone with me!'

They laughed, but their laughs were not so frequent these times.

'Anywhere you'd been would be the first place they'd look,' said Karen. 'They'd question anyone you'd ever known. Cuts out half the male population of north-west England.'

'Don't laugh,' said Jessica. 'It isn't funny.'

'I wasn't laughing.'

'The sad thing is, it isn't even true these days. Oh Karen, if I get away with this I'll be so fucking pure, even you'll be bored with me.'

227

'Thanks.'

'Even Tony, then. You know what I mean. How about Tony? Is there anything he might do to help?'

'What, let Rory ride free on his bus? Tony couldn't hide a needle in a haystack, love. He might not want to either. I know you think he's stupid, but he's just old-fashioned really. A lad from Manchester.'

'He doesn't approve of me. But surely, he wouldn't turn me in? Would he?'

Karen did not reply. Tony would turn her in like a shot if someone told him she was associated with the IRA. And to Tony, an Irish Catholic on the run would mean the IRA.

'D'you remember last year?' she said. 'The IRA blew some poor woman's legs off with a bomb? Then they apologised to her, said she wasn't the intended target? Sorry, missus, disregard that one! I thought Tony was going to give himself a fit. He was sick with rage. He'd turn his mother in.'

'Rory's not in the IRA. Rory hates the IRA.'

'Tony reads the *Daily Mail*.'

They had left one pub, in Port St Mary, and were looking for another. Instead, they wandered down the hill towards the water, past the sailing club. They walked out by the fishing boats, moored along the sea wall, with the fishermen looking up at them, probably up their skirts. They sat out on the end, watched the dark green, quiet sea.

'Who do we know in London, though?' asked Jessica, hopelessly. 'It's not my city.'

They had talked this out before. She was being defeatist. There were at least three ex-students who would help.

'Oh stop it. We'll be OK. If Rory can get a boat, you'll be fine. You can see the Welsh mountains from those hills back there on a clear day, it can't be very far. Come on, let's move on. We're not being watched, Jessica, I'm sure of it. Let's make a move, it's not like you, all this. Let's do something positive.'

'Not now,' said Jessica. But she stood up from the mooring bollard, filled her lungs. 'I'm going to ring my Ma and Da tonight. I'm going to tell them we're off to England in the morning, on the plane. That should put the cat among the pigeons.'

She did. She did it from Aunt Jane's, while Aunt Jane pottered with the supper in the kitchen. She spoke first to her mother, then her daddy. Neither of them argued.

'OK,' said Samuel Roberts. 'If you must. You're a free agent, Jessica, don't think otherwise. Ring us when you get there though, all right? We miss you, darling. We worry for you. Come back soon.'

Neither she nor Karen understood what it might mean. But it made them very miserable.

Rosie Kennedy rang Rory's mother, but dialled the business number. Tom Holdfast could transfer her to the bungalow, she knew. She did not dare ring Mrs Collins direct, without advice about her state.

'Mr Holdfast? It's Rosie Kennedy. I've got a message for Mrs Collins. Shall I tell you it? It's for you as well. I'm in a phone box.'

'I'll be brief,' said Holdfast. 'His mother knows about it now. Is he safe and well?'

'He is. He sends his love and tells her not to worry. He would have been in touch, but . . . '

'That's understood. Tell him – if you can – that his mother's fine. She believes in him, she understands.'

'He'll be glad. Should I speak to her?'

'You're better not to. I'll tell her everything. He's in the old place, is that so? Michael's place?'

'He is. He'll be all right. Ach, Mr Holdfast . . . '

Her voice grew choked. Tom Holdfast waited. Then, after a short while, he said: 'You'd better go now, Rosie.

They don't know you at all, I've fathomed that out. Keep it that way, if you can, won't you?'

She snorted, and he said: 'Thank you for the call', and put the phone down. Later, when Martin Parr listened to the tape in Belfast, he picked his thin lips, tinkered with the edges of his smile. Then he made two calls himself.

Next time Tom Holdfast was visited in the night it was at his own home, and the time was two a.m. The men were rougher than they'd been before, and it was not money they demanded. Holdfast, when they left, sat in an armchair in his pyjamas, sipping a glass of the Black Bush. Of necessity, the glass was in both hands. He pondered on the insane two per cent, and realised he'd been wrong. About other things as well. He realised he'd been very wrong indeed.

In fact, Parr was not watching Jessica and Karen on the Isle of Man at all. He had given her his word, and kept to it contentedly because he saw no reason not to. If Jessica came back to Ireland by either plane or ferry, he would know. If she actually left the Isle of Man, he would know. If anybody left it with her, he would also know – and it was other people, one other person, he was most concerned with. Jessica, in short, could do as she pleased. Her job, her role, was to lead him to his target, and for that she needed a long rope, which he was giving her. It was a matter of time, he told her parents, a matter of some short time.

Mrs Roberts, under the sunlamp of Parr's refound confidence, had refound her own. She did not care exactly what the future held for Jessica, so long as it was a future without Rory Collins. She made a little face at the idea of rope – given normally, in metaphor, for somebody to hang themselves – but liked the 'short time' element. A short time before Collins was a captured terrorist, she thought, not a killer on the run. She said this, with a happy lilt, and Martin Parr nodded his agreement. He was amused by the singleness of June Roberts' vision. In his mind the question was more complicated, each complication rather satisfying. A short time before he captured Rory? Killed him? Betrayed their daughter? Married her? The prospects were exciting now, all of them. Fruition would not take very long.

The tapes were being monitored constantly. When he was not in the building in Belfast, he was only ever a phone call or a bleep away. The McCausland car had finally gone back and he was using an official one, a Q-car, with a scrambler and transceiver. It was a family saloon – but modified for speed and handling – with British mainland plates. When he went over the border he would be an English tourist, poodling around the country lanes. If Rosie should happen to even notice.

The call to Rosie at the all-girls house came at ten past six one evening, when Jessica could no longer wait. Parr had given her the rope, and she had reached the end of it. For two clear days, and from a dozen phone boxes, she and Karen had called their friends, told them the clever lies or some of the truth, made their arrangements. They were confident that they could bring it off. If Rory could get to Port Erin in a yacht, they would get to London, via Wales or Lancashire. After that, who knew, who cared? They would get money out of Ireland somehow, Jessica had accounts in England anyway, Europe was like a gigantic honeycomb for them to disappear into. After the next hard stage, the rest was easy.

They made the call from a phone box some miles from Aunt Jane's home. That was superstition, but it gave them both comfort. Nobody could bug the whole Manx public network, even if they'd done a curve around Port Erin's hinterland. It did not occur to either of them that Rosie might be tapped, that the root could be infected. Not that they were specific anyway – the call was brief and cryptic. Jessica, although flooded with a cocktail of emotions, sounded icy cool and businesslike, and got a like response. Rosie, who spent a lot of time these days hovering by the phone, answered herself.

'Hallo, is that Rosie? Can I——?'

'It is Rosie. Is this the message?'

'Yes. Tell him we are waiting, at that place. You remember it?'

'Of course. When?'

'Now. Anytime. As soon as possible. Is he . . . ?'

Rosie almost snapped.

'He'll get the message. He . . . '

She put the phone down.

The call was intercepted. Watchers were in place. Within two minutes Parr was on the road in his Montego, complete with roofrack and a caravan tow-hook. The red Metro — not overlooked in later trawls as it had been at first — was marked for him by other Q-cars, to be picked up among the traffic on the A1 past Dromore. He passed her at the border — waved through on the nod while she was held up for five minutes, deliberately — and dropped back in station behind three lorries after he had waited in the car park of a bar. After Dundalk he had to stay quite close, but there was a fair amount of traffic and he had little fear that she would notice him. She didn't. When she turned off the road into the bushy track, Parr had to work on instinct. He drove past, pulled into a field, and pursued on foot. He could hear a tractor up ahead, its noise swelling and dying irregularly as it worked, and it gave him pause. Then it stopped, the diesel rumbling into silence, and he moved on, still wondering, still assessing what he might find. His relief, when he saw the empty Metro by the lonely ruined house, was considerable. Normally, one would not take such high risks of losing such a quarry, normally one would not work alone. But this was not a normal operation, was it?

Rosie was not inside the house for long, and Parr made no attempt to enter it. When she left she was composed, her face showed no emotion as she got into her car and drove away.

Martin Parr, on the other hand, was smiling as he emerged from the thick greenery. He was going to meet his rival at long last.

TWENTY-SIX

At Port Erin, as the days ground slowly by, Jessica kept her vigil from the cliffs and at the harbour. Karen was always with her, but in attitude they drifted quite rapidly apart. It started within an hour of the phone call, when Jessica insisted that they drive back to take up a position high above the little port. When it occurred to Karen that the lookout had begun, she was uncertain how to respond. Mockery seemed appropriate, but mockery was out. Her friend was tense, unhappy, fragile. Finally, Karen asked her gently if she really believed there was any point in watching the green, empty sea so soon, and Jessica burst into tears. That was the easy part. They could, at least, still talk about it.

Karen led Jessica to the car, and they drove off to a café behind a beach. They were both sick of cafés by now, had laughed at them as a paradigm of life on holiday. All around them on this evening – which was blustery and overcast – the natural desolation of the British seaside resort was in evidence. They were surrounded by grumpy men and tired women, feeding chips and money to bored children and exhorting them to enjoy themselves, try the chocolate fudge cake, go to the arcade, die. Jessica and Karen no longer were amused. They had just tea, and the tea was weak, the waitress frustrated, the prospect grim. It fell in on Karen, looking at the long, unpleasant waves beyond the promenade, that the prospect of them ever bearing Jessica to happiness and safety were equally dismal.

'Look,' she said. 'Love. It'll be a day before he even gets the message, probably. Then he's got to go and find a boat, and set off. If you think it's sensible to go and freeze up on those hills before tomorrow evening at the earliest, you're mad.'

Jessica was fiddling with her teaspoon. A little boy with dried ice-cream on his face stopped at their table, staring at them. Karen forced a smile.

'Go away,' she said. 'We're busy.'

'Alex!' a mother shouted, fortunately. 'Come over here!'

Jessica said: 'I don't feel sensible. I feel terrible. Look at that sea. It's appalling. There'll be gales for days, he won't be able to come. What else do you want me to do? Play bingo? Go to the movies? I want to look.'

'We could get drunk,' Karen replied, lightly. 'We could go to a casino. Look, anything's better than going potty, isn't it? And it's potty, looking out like that, it borders on it. Love, love, he'll come, he knows all about boats, you know he does. But let's not waste our time, let's be positive. Tomorrow night, that's when we should start. Even that's too early, probably.'

This time, it worked. Jessica became more animated, argued it out quite rationally. If Rosie took the message immediately, if Rory had a boat in mind, if it was not too far from Hackballs Cross – at Dundalk, say, or on the Boyne – if there weren't too many hold-ups . . . She conceded, in the end, that there was no hope for today, but she refused to rule the morrow out. He might set sail at night – why not, indeed, the driving to a harbour would be safer after dark – and at least the wind was strong, and in the right direction.

'Dawn,' she said. 'OK, dawn would be the earliest, but—'

'The earliest we could see him,' interrupted Karen. 'And how do we know it's him, by the way? I hope you're not planning to wave to every boat you see in the next five days. People really would think you were cracked!'

'We'll have to move out,' said Jessica, letting the five days go by unchallenged. 'You do realise that, don't you?'

They talked that out as they drove to find a noisy pub. They abandoned the tea and snotty children, who were noisy in the wrong way altogether. Jessica was very rational as she pointed out the reasons for leaving Aunt Jane's place. They were going to be out watching at all hours, then suddenly they were going to disappear, on a moment's notice, just up and bugger off. They would not be able to explain why or where to, either.

'What would we say? We've gone off camping? We've been recruited by white slavers and thought we'd have a bash? It's not just stretching the giddy girls bit, Karen. It would be a disaster. She might even ring my parents.'

'OK,' said Karen. 'Right, you've got a point. But where do you suggest we go? What do you suggest we say? Port Erin's hardly a big city, you know, she'll find out quick enough we're staying down the road.'

'Tell her I can't stand her cooking any more! Tell her the drains smell! Tell her I'm insane! Karen, don't mess about, we've got to go!'

The rationality, thought Karen drily, had begun to slip, even though it was meant to be a joke. But she knew a couple of guest houses up above the town that might do. Luckily her aunt was not a social mixer, she did not have her finger in community pies.

'I suppose we could say we're going for a day or two,' she said. 'You want to see the north part of the island or something and we don't want to drive and drink. At least she knows you've got more money than sense, which helps.'

'And when we disappear, we can ring from England and say we're sorry like good little girls, and she'll forgive us! It'll only be a day or two, you pessimist. Five days! You're horrible.'

'Forgive *us*?' said Karen. 'You think I'm going with

236

you, don't you, in your crummy little boat? You're totally convinced.'

She was pulling into the car park of a bright, brash pub with music pouring out. She drove straight into an empty parking space and stopped the engine.

'Oh come off it,' said Jessica. 'I need you, don't you understand that yet? Of course you do. Don't drop me in it, will you?'

'What will the bridegroom say?' laughed Karen. 'I'll probably throw up over him if the sea's as rough as this. I've never sailed like that before.'

'You can lie down in your bunk like the Queen of bloody Sheba, so you can. I'll bring you tea and toast.'

They moved out in the morning, Karen feeling bad, although Aunt Jane neither commented nor asked awkward questions. They packed the car with far more of Jessica's gear than she had expected, which Jessica explained away by saying that 'you never knew'. Karen, to keep up the appearance, was forced to pack a suitcase also, and told Jane that they might go back to Ireland from the north, Jessica was so impulsive. Aunt Jane seemed neither pleased nor disappointed, nor yet indifferent. There was, in Karen, a growing sense of minor dislocation.

It developed, although the small hotel was normal enough. It was high up, overlooking the harbour entrance and the bay, run by a woman in her forties who was anything but the traditional dragon landlady. She was pleased to see the two young women, was unworried by the fact they had no definitive time scheme for their stay, and told them there were no rules as long as they were quiet after midnight. They booked for bed and breakfast only, but were told the bar was open all day and evening for the guests. In every way, it was a better place to wait than the bungalow.

The trouble was Jessica. The wind still blew hard and cold, the view from their bedroom was excellent, but she would not tear herself away from the high cliff tops that gave unrestricted visibility beyond the headlands. She wanted Karen to be with her, it was insisted on in all practical senses, but her mood deteriorated as the hours crawled by. Each time they saw a sail – infrequent, in the wild Force Six – she became animated, then sank into depression as the close-reefed vessels either went right past Port Erin or proved to be crewed by crowds in oilskins. Even in the car they grew cold, and after her sorties outside, Jessica would return with running nose and blue-tinged extremities. She resisted the idea of going off to eat at lunchtime.

At night, when it was pitch black out to sea and the wind blew what felt like a full gale, Karen had to almost force her to leave the vigil to go to the hotel. When they got there, to get warmed up before they drove off to a restaurant, a quick gin with the landlady became a session, at which Jessica got very drunk and which she ultimately refused to interrupt for anything as mundane as food. The landlady, jolly and unconcerned throughout, fortunately had a cut-off point at twenty past eleven, when she refused to serve more drinks. Jessica began to shout, but Karen hustled her upstairs to bed, drunk herself, but furious. What would they say to Auntie Jane, she burbled, if they got chucked out?

Her worries, over the next two days, turned to fear that Jessica was losing her grip on reality. The chipperness, the jollity, had always had its artificial side, she knew, but as time went by Jessica began to swing from solid depression to moods of wild elation, manic hope. On the morning after her first binge the wind had moderated and the sun was out, and she was utterly convinced that Rory would arrive before lunchtime, was probably somewhere off the harbour entrance at that very moment. She would not wait for breakfast, gave the surprised landlady a blithe Good morning as she surged through the dining room, the shouting match forgotten, and did not mind a bit that Karen would not go with her immediately. She walked up onto the high ground – Karen saw her from the bedroom window, almost running up the steepest parts – and when Karen joined her an hour later was still extremely happy. An hour after that and she was weeping, while Karen – feeling drab and English and destructive – was pointing out to her the difficulties, the wildness of a scheme so fraught with dangers and with problems, wondering herself whether she were trying to kill hope or to bolster it, and which course would really be the best. She had, in fact, never felt so English, nor so miserable about it.

There were times of rationality, as well. Karen suggested, once, that they should ring Rosie. At least, that way, they'd know if the message had got through, however dreadful the answer might be. Jessica weighed it up, decided it was sense, and feasible, then made Karen drive her halfway across the island to make sure their chosen phone box would be 'safe'. After three rings their first call was intercepted, by a woman with a hard voice who said she was the operator. There was a fault on that Belfast number, she told them in a Belfast accent, the engineers were working on it so they should try later. Jessica, gone pale despite her tan, looked at Karen with eyes that actually glittered. They tried an hour later, with the same result, and an hour after that. They went to a pub, where Jessica drank four pints of lager and some whiskies, and tried again. This time, and thereafter, they got only the tone for unobtainable. Karen crashed into despair this time, and Jessica talked her out of it. They went back to the hills above Port Erin with two bottles of wine and drank and talked and cried until the sun sank into the sea, making a broadening pattern, red and silver, down which Rory did not sail. They went back to the hotel when it was dark and went straight up to their beds. The landlady could not make them out at all.

Jessica, after that, achieved an equilibrium that was as

239

breakable as crystal. She no longer wanted reassurance, she maintained that Rory Collins would overcome whatever difficulties should face him, and arrive. Karen, perversely, found herself almost wanting to smash through the surface, make her face the self-delusion. To Karen, it was clear: Rory was not coming, whatever awful reason had prevented him. And Jessica was lying to herself, she could not honestly believe it any more. The two of them still watched together from the hills and cliffs, but there was space between them that added to the pain. The sparkling beauty of the weather, which had become warm and breezy, mocked both of them in different ways. It was perfect to bring a boat from Ireland, and no boat would come. They continued staring out to sea.

Then, as dusk thickened into dark one evening, a yacht appeared not far off the harbour entrance, that Jessica knew was Rory. She had been sitting, resting on a rocky slab, as it had materialised out of the fine haze hanging on the water, and she stood and stared and raised one arm in a mute gesture to make Karen understand. Karen, her throat knotting, also stood, and went to her friend's side.

'It's him,' said Jessica. 'Oh God, it's him.'

Karen tried to say 'it may not be', but could not articulate the words. So cruel and useless, they would be. She went to the car, Jessica following. The yacht was white, with white sails. When they looked very carefully they could see small lights gleaming near the water.

They drove down to the harbour and left the car. The boat was still some way off, fighting the stiff ebb tide, and they could not see it very clearly in the failing light. There was one man in the cockpit, one huddled shape, and after a few minutes he waved, he saluted with one arm, in response to Jessica.

'It's him,' repeated Jessica. 'He doesn't start the engine because he doesn't know the boat. Oh God, oh God.'

It was black by the time the vessel passed their nearest

point, heading for an anchorage in what open water the falling tide had left. All they could see now was the ghostly whiteness of the hull and sail, the red twinkle from a navigation light. After a while they heard the rattle of a chain. Dimly, they sensed the sail growing less, the pale blur diminishing. Then a torch was flashed towards them, towards the shore.

'Rory!' she cried, convulsively. 'Oh Rory!'

Five minutes later, on the hard shingle where small boats were launched between the sheets of mud, they waited as the sound of dipping oars grew louder. It was a rubber dinghy that had been inflated on the yacht. It showed no light.

'There,' breathed Jessica. 'I can see it, Karen. Over there.'

So could Karen, at that instant. But there are two people in it, she thought. Surely, there are two?

But she waited for her friend to say the words.

TWENTY-SEVEN

Parr's interview with Rory Collins was brief and uncivilised. He did not know what he would find inside the house, but it did not bother him. He did not know what he would say, either, and was content to let the situation dictate that. In truth, now that he'd run him down, Parr had no rancour left for Rory Collins. He was the enemy who'd caused him pain, but who had lost the fight. Parr was magnanimous with his defeated enemies, up to a point. He bore no grudges.

After Rosie Kennedy had left, he waited for some minutes before moving. The grim grey eyes of the ruined mansion reflected the scudding clouds, and there was desolation in the soughing of the wind. Now that the Metro was gone, there was little feeling that the scene had ever had a human element, the odd pieces of rusting farm equipment merely emphasising its dereliction. When he moved, it was to skirt the building in a broad sweep, always under cover. He noted the Zetor, poised before an open barn, the tractor he had heard. He noted the one window with a curtain and worked out a route by which to reach the room. Before he entered, he eased the automatic that he carried in a shoulder holster.

Inside the kitchen, it was already dark. Parr studied everything before proceeding, noting hazards that might trip or slow him. In the body of the house he let his eyes grow accustomed at a leisurely pace, registering the ruined glories with great interest. The stairs he treated cautiously – managing, in the process, to reach the top without a creak. Along the passageway he saw the open door but did not make for it until his eyes had covered every aspect, every possibility. There was a light-spill from the door, soft yellow light, that wavered. At the doorway he paused and listened. He heard a tuneless whistling, footsteps. It was not a trap, there was no one sitting waiting with a pistol trained to blast his head off. Parr touched his own once more, then felt another that weighed heavy in his jacket pocket. He drew neither. He was ready.

Rory's back, when Parr stepped forward, was to the door. He was in dirty jeans and a stained tee-shirt, his curly hair dusted with broken stalks of grass. Parr was surprised at how young he looked, how thin, how like a farmer's labourer. The room was like a workman's, too, untidy with a smell of sharp, fresh sweat. Parr's eye, off the quarry for an instant, read the lipstick message on the wall, and he wondered who had written it, and why. Then, as Rory turned, still unaware, he spoke.

'If you've got a gun, don't try to get it, will you? You'd be too late.'

Rory's face, brown and flecked with green grass sap, drained before his eyes. He looked as if he'd buckle at the knees, he put out a hand to the bed end, steadied himself. His mouth opened slightly, emitting a small sound. Parr walked through the door.

'I'm Martin Parr,' he said. 'I am going to marry Jessica. I would have been a relative of Terence Rigby, if you hadn't killed him. What do you say to that?'

Rory could not say anything. His stomach was still clenched with shock, his brain still numbed with horror. Had Rosie betrayed him? She had delivered the message like a ghost, had had to come into the house and sit down before leaving because she had felt sick. She had swallowed two large mouthfuls of John Powers. Then had she betrayed him?

Parr moved further into the room. Rory dropped back. Parr reached into his outer jacket pocket and took out a revolver. Rory made another noise. It was the .38 Webley, the English popgun with which he had killed Terence.

'Yes,' said Parr, 'it's yours. We put the spent cartridge case back with all the others after the tests, it's just as it was found after you'd fired it. The safety catch is on.'

In front of him, between them, was a small round table Rory had cobbled back together. Parr tossed the gun onto it. It slithered to the edge near Rory.

'You could pick it up and shoot me if you wanted. You could try. It's got your prints all over it, you know. It's evidence. Why don't you sit down? You look appalling.'

To Parr's surprise, he sat. He slumped onto a kitchen chair, that squeaked in protest at his weight. Another cobble job. Parr wondered at the furniture, it was all like that. Half in pieces, ill-repaired. Rory's colour still had not come back.

'I'm not a hasty man, nor a vindictive one,' he said. 'But you do realise you've caused a lot of trouble, don't you? A lot of people assume you're a gunman, which is useful, but it's beside the point. The point is you've thrown a spanner in the works. Jessica played by the rules until she met you. A bit of bending here and there, but she fitted in. You nearly destroyed her parents, do you know that? You nearly ruined all our lives.'

Rory's heart was coming back. Slowly, he was recovering. But the handsome, thin-lipped face across the table was horrible to him. You've been with Jessica, he thought, and you think you will again.

'You're talking shite,' he said. He cleared his throat, stabbed by Parr's sardonic smile of pity at his voice. 'You're talking shite. Is that loud enough for you? You're talking racist shite.'

Parr looked around, still smiling. Rory considered, for a split second, trying to get the gun. He rejected it. It would not have a firing pin, or bullets, some damned thing, it would give him an excuse. Parr perched on the bed, sitting sideways, leaning forward.

'Racist,' he said, musingly. 'That's an interesting idea. I don't think so, though. You all strike me as barbarians, over here, whichever tribe you're rooting for. I find the whole sectarian situation brutish in this day and age, it's so far beyond the bounds of reason. My hope for this Province is peace and reconciliation through the law. I'm opposed to terrorists whichever side they're on. Surely you're the racists?'

'So why were you going to marry Jessica? To seal some dirty compact, wasn't it. You're a hypocrite. A liar and a hypocrite.'

'Am, not were. I am going to marry Jessica. You wouldn't understand the reasons.'

It was like a knife, but Rory did not show it.

'She'd never have you,' he replied. 'She'd rather die. She's told me that. She's told me all about you, in some detail.'

This last came as an inspiration. He looked at Parr's thin face, to see if it had struck. But Parr's face did not change.

Soiled goods, thought Rory. I could call her soiled goods. I could tell about the fucking and the sucking and the things we do together. I could not, he thought.

'I love her,' he said, simply. 'She loves me. You'll never change that, Mr Englishman.'

'People forget,' said Martin Parr. 'It doesn't matter, really.'

'However long they lock me up for,' started Rory Collins. There was some curve in the thin lips that stopped him. His stomach swooped away from him, he heard a thundering in his ears. Not in cold blood, surely not? This man would not do that?

'You could try going for the gun,' said Martin Parr. 'That would be ironic.'

His hand went into his jacket, where he touched the

warm butt of the automatic. As he withdrew it, he clicked off the safety catch.

'Come with me,' he said.

Rory did not move.

There were two men in the Avon dinghy, two men from Chesterfield on a sailing holiday, who had come into the harbour under sail alone because the starter of their engine had jammed. One of them had been below attempting to unjam it when Jessica had waved, and the other had waved back because why not? Indeed, they had fantasised happily that this might be the dream come true at last – two lovely young loose women who would come to sea with them for a thousand and one delights. To find them waiting on the shingle was true enchantment.

Karen, as they neared the landing place, was embarrassed and afraid. She watched Jessica's face as the realisation dawned, and hoped that she would not collapse, or scream out, or do some other awful thing. The torch lit up the face, suddenly and blindingly, but Jessica's expression, with her eyes closed, was disconcerting. There was no distress, a kind of eagerness. As Karen made to back away, Jessica held her arm.

'We'll go back,' she said, hardly above a whisper. 'They'll take us back to Ireland.'

The men, at first, were also disconcerted. As they pulled the dinghy out, then prepared to carry her well up the beach for when the tide began to flood again, the girls stood by them, one nervous, one smiling oddly. Face to face, the fantasy was quite difficult to handle. What did one say to start?

Jessica said it.

'Hallo. Have you sailed far? We're going for a drink and we wondered if you'd like to join us, we're on holiday. Jessica. This is Karen.'

246

The yachtsmen found themselves smiling fatuously. It was easy, when you had the knack!

'Hi. Hello. I'm Gary and this is Chris. We're from Chesterfield, in England. Are you both Irish?'

'I'm from Manchester,' said Karen. 'Look — excuse my friend, she's a little . . . '

'Oh don't be boring,' Jessica said. 'Look — are youse coming for a drink or not?'

'You're bloody right we are!' said Chris.

The men tied the rubber dinghy to a ring and left their oilskin jackets jammed underneath the oars. They were both in jeans and sweaters, and both dying for a pint. They were also dying to achieve the dream, which was not surprising, so outrageously did Jessica flirt with them. Karen's reserve, as time went on, became almost icy in response, and the men were intelligent enough to notice it. They were also nice enough, it seemed, to really not care too much how things turned out. After they had had a couple, they suggested a meal and eased off on the chatting up. Karen now relaxed, while Jessica became more moody. At one point in the main course she went off to the ladies and was away ten or fifteen minutes. Chris and Gary asked Karen if anything was wrong, and Karen fenced. But when Jessica returned, her face was set.

'Look,' she said. 'I can't string you boys along like this, I've got a proposition. Will you take us to Ireland in your boat? We're desperate.'

The boys — who were in their early thirties, each married with two children — glanced at each other uneasily. This was getting real.

'We've only got two berths,' said Gary, cautiously. 'Beds, that is. You'd . . . it's not exactly private.'

'We don't exactly care,' said Jessica. 'Listen, it's not illegal or anything, it's something personal. North or South'll suit us, although it's the Republic that we're headed for. You're free agents, aren't you?'

247

It was a challenge, but it was not sexual any more.

'Until the wives find out,' Chris said. 'We could sleep in watches, I suppose.'

'Well, we won't tell them will we, Karen?' said Jessica. 'You don't have to sleep with us, boys, we're not that desperate, you know!'

Joking was all right again, the men were easier now the truth was out. It suited them, no pressure, things could go either way.

It clearly suited Jessica. She was full of smiles once more, and they responded. Karen found it all extraordinary, she was afraid. She listened to the talk of tides, and ports, the best time to set out, and she knew that she had never understood this friend, so animated now with eyes that glowed like coals in her drawn, exhausted face. She had never understood her attitude to men, her willingness to marry Parr, the intensity of her love for Rory Collins. Most of all, this idea of sailing away – into hard reality, but also away from truth, into the impossible dream. She had a feeling, too, weird and inexplicable, that by going with her she might throw off her Englishness at last, learn something that she could not learn in any other way, something wild and dangerous and completely necessary. She would go. She wanted to.

It was nearly midnight when they left the restaurant, and they could not sail till dawn. By then, the men explained, the tide would be full, but moving out again, to speed them on their way if they had not got the engine running. They would return to their boat, get some sleep, clean her up a little, tackle the starter motor – all the joys of sailing, in effect. Merry now, but mellow, they half believed the girls would not be there to meet them on the quayside as arranged for five o'clock, and did not really give a jot.

'We sail the poisoned sea,' they chorused, happily, as they set off for the rubber dinghy. 'Remember, ladies, when we're out there – no turning back, we're on our own!' The ladies, only slightly more sober, blew them kisses and climbed to their hotel, abandoning the car.

'Are we really going?' Karen said, pulling off her shoes. 'Oh Christ, Jessica, it's mad all this. I need my sleep.'

'So sleep,' said Jessica. 'I'm going to have a shower. I'll wake you up, don't worry. Go to sleep.'

'A shower? Why not later, we've got the alarm clock?' She pulled her jeans and pants off, and dragged her duvet back. It was enough. As Jessica moved from her sight, she fell asleep.

Jessica wrote a letter. When Karen was breathing quietly, she quietly opened the large square leather case and took out the antique wedding dress. It was creased, slightly damaged probably, but she did not care. She laid it on her bed, the veil between the shoulder straps, and stared at it.

Rory, she wrote, how can I explain? I screwed other people, I never cared, I thought I'd marry Parr and it would be all right, it seemed OK till I met you. You changed everything, you changed my life. Start again, I sound like some fucking tragedy queen. Dearest Rory, how can I explain? Oh fuck. Look – somehow I've come to realise something. We've failed to realise what it means, in terms of rottenness. I thought it was of no concern to us, just other people's misery and blood. I was wrong, and now they've made me learn my lesson. My dear ma and daddy, among others, and I've been hateful to them, too, and I still love them, too. But you really, Rory, only you. Ireland's (N. Ireland's) corrupt, it's dying, isn't it? Ulster Still Needs Jesus (for fuck's sake!). (Remember?) I was afraid to commit myself before, I was taught not to, it was in my upbringing, don't trust the bastards, any of them (but I'm not blaming anybody else). I commit myself to you, Rory, my darling, and it's too late. I love you. Your dear bent dick. I love you.

She saw herself going to the harbour in the morning wearing the wedding dress. She saw the two men staring at her, horrified, amazed. What were their names? They'd call her Miss Havisham behind their hands, they'd think she was deranged. Maybe she was. Demented. She saw herself in the little rubber boat, being rowed out across the green translucent water of the harbour, a large train of the ancient silk closing and opening like an enormous fan behind them, at every stroke. She could hear the splashing of the oars, the suck and plop as they dipped and pulled, she could see the white fan spread and sink, spread and sink, white within the water. She looked up and met Karen's eyes, watching her silently from the bed.

'I've written him a letter,' she said.

Karen was looking at the wedding dress, two feet from her on the other narrow bed.

'What are you going to do?' she asked. 'You're not going to do it any harm, are you?'

Jessica turned away from the table, staring at the gown.

'Even you think I'm a hard bitch,' she said. 'I was going to put it on. To go and meet my husband. Just a fantasy. Nothing serious.'

Karen saw the tears as they began to roll out of her eyes. Jessica's hand moved slowly across the notepaper, headed with the name of the guest house and the Legs of Man. She crumpled it beneath her fingers as the tears flowed down her cheeks.

'Rory's dead,' she said.

Rory was dead. Tom Holdfast took his mother to the farm at Hackballs Cross because she insisted. He led her to the barn before which the Zetor stood, angled like a pointer on its four large wheels, angled at a great green mound of grass.

'He's under there,' he said. 'He has a bullet wound. You would not want to see it, Margaret.'

'Show me,' she said.

Tom Holdfast moved grass stalks gently with his right hand. Soon he uncovered Rory's hair, then his forehead, then his face. He had closed the eyes already. There was a small blue hole an inch above the eyebrows, in the centre. The face was quite untroubled.

'We will bury him properly,' he said. 'When we're allowed to bring him home.'

Mrs Collins did not weep.

'Thank you,' she said. 'Please cover him for me.'

Then she reached out, caressing the dead cheek for a moment. She turned away as Holdfast spread grass back over Rory's face.

'When will it be?' she said. 'Who killed him, Tom?'

He took her by the arm and walked her back towards his car. They got inside and he started the engine.

'I doubt we'll ever know,' he said. He put it into bottom gear, edged over the first ruts. 'It's not the sort of question we can answer, is it?'

As they moved down the track, a glint of metal caught his eye through the bushes. It was a car, part hidden in a neighbouring field. He did not point it out to Mrs Collins.

And in that car, sitting motionless with an empty, empty smile, sat Martin Parr. Motionless, that is, except for the back part of his head, where large black farm flies crawled among the sticky hair and blood. There were others on the back seat, and down his neck. It was a tourist car, a Montego with a towbar and mainland plates. The driver's window was still open.

Jessica, somewhere on the Irish Sea, moved towards them down the glittering pathway of the sun. There was little wind, and she sat below the billowing genoa, cooled by the down-draught, silent in her bedraggled silk. Astern of her, in the cockpit, her friends from England hardly spoke.

I am going to the land of ancient chaos, thought Jessica, melodramatically. She caught herself at it, despised herself, forgave herself. Her heart was swamped in misery.

I'm going home, she thought.

The Scar
Frank Kippax

The controversial novel that was made into the BBC TV serial

Underbelly

Violent riots and rooftop demonstrations across the country have brought to light the alarming crisis facing Britain's outdated, overcrowded prisons. How long before the fragile fabric of a crumbling system finally gives way . . . ?

In HM Prison Bowscar, there have already been disturbing rumblings of unrest. But when political bungling brings a mass murderer and a crooked financier together under one roof with a group of dangerous men with deadly connections, a plan is hatched to convert the smouldering discontent into explosive insurrection.

As journalists and others struggle to unravel the tangle of official cover-ups and high-level corruption they have unearthed, inside the Scar there is a time-bomb waiting to explode . . .

'A thundering great novel. What's really amazing is how much he seems to know about so many different things . . . a cracking good read.' Tony Parker, *New Statesman & Society*

'So topical . . . Kippax develops a complex, ingenious plot at breakneck speed and has a sharp underdog's eye.'
John McVicar, *Time Out*

'Brilliant. I was grossly entertained and thrilled . . . Frank Kippax is a rare talent.'
Jimmy Boyle

ISBN 0 00 617921 5

Fontana

The Butcher's Bill
Frank Kippax

For fifty years he has kept his silence. Now he must die, and take his secrets to the grave.

In his country's name, Bill Wiley has brought many lives to an end, rarely expecting to understand the reasoning behind his orders. But even he is shocked by the identity of his latest victim. For the man he is to kill is ninety-three years old, the sole inmate of the most heavily guarded prison in the world. They call him Rudolf Hess.

Sensing that the grotesquely simple order hides a deeper mystery, Wiley at first refuses to accept the mission. With the help of Oxford historian Jane Heywood and her uncle – a wartime spy who was involved in the mysterious Hess flights of 1941 – he sets out to unravel truths many men have died for. But Wiley's son, it seems, may soon be added to that number . . .

The Butcher's Bill – a fast-moving and absorbing thriller, and a highly controversial fictional account of the events surrounding Rudolf Hess's flight to Britain and its fifty-year aftermath.

'Kippax unceremoniously kicks Winston Churchill off his pedestal and sniffs out a conspiracy surrounding Rudolf Hess's puzzling flight.' *The Times*

'Calculated to leave ageing colonels twitching and the rest of us open-mouthed . . . seems unlikely to endear him to the secret services.' *Guardian*

ISBN 0 00 617905 3

Fontana

Fontana Fiction

Fontana is a leading paperback publisher of fiction. Below are some recent titles.

- ☐ BLOOD RULES John Trenhaile £4.99
- ☐ PRIDE'S HARVEST Jon Cleary £4.99
- ☐ DUNCTON TALES William Horwood £4.99
- ☐ FORBIDDEN KNOWLEDGE Stephen Donaldson £4.99
- ☐ TIME OF THE ASSASSINS Alastair MacNeill £4.99
- ☐ IMAJICA Clive Barker £5.99
- ☐ THE WINDS OF THE WASTELANDS Antony Swithin £4.99
- ☐ THE HOUSE OF MIRRORS Michael Mullen £4.99
- ☐ TYPHOON Mark Joseph £4.99
- ☐ SEMPER FI W. E. B. Griffin £4.50
- ☐ CALL TO ARMS W. E. B. Griffin £4.50
- ☐ A HIVE OF DEAD MEN Geoffrey Jenkins £4.99

You can buy Fontana Paperbacks at your local bookshops or newsagents. Or you can order them from Fontana, Cash Sales Department, Box 29, Douglas, Isle of Man. Please send a cheque, postal or money order (not currency) worth the price plus 24p per book for postage (maximum postage required is £3.00 for orders within the UK).

NAME (Block letters)_____

ADDRESS_____

_____

While every effort is made to keep prices low, it is sometimes necessary to increase them at short notice. Fontana Paperbacks reserve the right to show new retail prices on covers which may differ from those previously advertised in the text or elsewhere.